THE SHAPE SHIFTER

ALSO BY TONY HILLERMAN

Fiction

Skeleton Man
The Sinister Pig
The Wailing Wind
Hunting Badger
The First Eagle
The Fallen Man
Finding Moon
Sacred Clowns
Coyote Waits
Talking God
A Thief of Time
Skinwalkers
The Ghostway
The Dark Wind
People of Darkness
Listening Woman
Dance Hall of the Dead
The Fly on the Wall
The Blessing Way
The Boy Who Made Dragonfly (for children)
Buster Mesquite's Cowboy Band

Nonfiction

Seldom Disappointed
Hillerman Country (photos by Barney Hillerman)
The Great Taos Bank Robbery
Rio Grande
New Mexico
The Spell of New Mexico
Talking Mysteries (with Ernie Bulow)
Words, Weather and Wolfmen (with Ernie Bulow)
Indian Country (photos by Bela Kalman)
Kilroy Was There (photos by Frank Kessler)
A New Omnibus of Crime (with Rosemary Herbert)

THE SHAPE SHIFTER

TONY HILLERMAN

First published in Great Britain in 2006 by
Allison & Busby Limited
13 Charlotte Mews
London W1T 4EJ
www.allisonandbusby.com

First published in the US in 2006 by
HarperCollins Publishers Inc. New York, New York USA.

A catalogue record for this book is available from
the British Library.

Published by arrangement with
HarperCollins Publishers Inc. New York, New York USA.

10 9 8 7 6 5 4 3 2 1

ISBN 0 7490 8169 4
978-0-7490-8169-0

Printed and bound in Spain by
Liberduplex

This book is dedicated to Anne Margaret, Janet Marie, Anthony Grove, Jr., Steven August, Monica Mary, and Daniel Bernard listed in order of the date they arrived to brighten our lives.

THE SHAPE SHIFTER

1

Lieutenant Joe Leaphorn, retired, stopped his pickup about a hundred yards short of where he had intended to park, turned off the ignition, stared at Sergeant Jim Chee's trailer home, and reconsidered his tactics. The problem was making sure he knew what he could tell them, and what he shouldn't, and how to handle it without offending either Bernie or Jim. First he would hand to whomever opened the door the big woven basket of fruit, flowers, and candies that Professor Louisa Bourbonette had arranged as their wedding gift, and then keep the conversation focused on what they had thought of Hawaii on their honeymoon trip, and apologize for the duties that had forced both Louisa and him to miss the wedding itself. Then he would pound them with questions about their future plans, whether Bernie still intended to return to her job with the Navajo Tribal Police. She would know he already knew the answer to that one, but the longer he could keep them from pressing him with their own questions, the better. Maybe he could avoid that completely. It wasn't likely. His answering machine had been full of calls from one or the other of them. Full of questions. Why hadn't he called them back with the details of that Totter obituary he wanted them to look into? Why was he interested? Hadn't he retired as he'd planned? Was this some old cold case he wanted to clear up as a going away present to the Navajo Tribal Police? And so forth.

Louisa had provided him with a choice of two solutions. Just go ahead and swear them both to secrecy and tell them the whole truth and nothing but the truth. Or just say he simply couldn't talk about it because it was all totally confidential.

"Don't forget, Joe," Louisa had said, "they're both in the awful gossiping circuit you police people operate. They're going to be hearing about the murders, and the shooting, and all the rest of it, and by the time it gets passed along second-, third-, and fourth-hand, it's all going to seem a lot more horrible than what you told me." With that, Louisa had paused, shaken her head, and added: "If that's possible."

Both of Louisa's suggestions were tempting, but neither was practical. Chee and Bernie were both sworn-in officers of the law (or Bernie would be again as soon as the papers were signed) and telling them everything he knew would put them in an awful ethical position. Sort of the same position he had landed in himself, which he really didn't want to think about right now.

Instead he'd think about Chee and Bernie, starting with how Bernie had already seemed to have a civilizing influence on Jim, judging from the nice white curtains

Leaphorn could see in the trailer's windows, and—even more dramatic—the attractive blue-and-white mailbox with a floral design substituted for the rusty old tin box that had always before received Chee's mail. Not, Leaphorn guessed, that many people had been writing to Jim.

Leaphorn restarted his engine and began the slow drive toward the house. Just as he did, the door opened. And there was Bernie, waving to him, and Chee right behind her, big grin on his face. Quit worrying, Leaphorn told himself. I'm going to enjoy this. And he did.

Chee took the basket, looking as if he had no idea what to do with it. Bernie rescued it, declaring it was just what they needed and how thoughtful it was of him and Louisa, and how the basket was beautifully woven, neatly waterproofed with pinyon sap, and would long be treasured. Then came the hand shaking, and the hugs, and inside for coffee and conversation. Leaphorn kept it on the Hawaii trip as long as he could, listening to Bernie's report on her arrangements to rejoin the tribal police and her chances of being assigned to Captain Largo's command and being posted at Teec Nos Pos, which would be convenient, presuming that Chee would still be working out of Shiprock.

And so it went, coffee sipped, cookies nibbled, lots of smiling and laughing, exuberant descriptions of swimming in the cold, cold Pacific surf, a silly scene in which an overenthusiastic Homeland Security man at the Honolulu Airport had been slapped by an elderly woman he was frisking, had seized her, and had been whacked again by her husband, who turned out to be a retired, oft-decorated Marine Corps colonel. This resulted in the Homeland Security supervisor wanting the colonel arrested, and an airport official, who turned out to be an army survivor of the Korean War, apologizing to the colonel's wife and giving the Homeland Security pair a loud public lecture on American history. All happy, easy, and good-natured.

But then Sergeant Jim Chee said: "By the way, Lieutenant, Bernie and I have been wondering what got you interested in the Totter obituary. And why you never called us again. We would have been willing to do some more checking on it for you."

"Well, thanks," Leaphorn said. "I knew you would do it, but I knew of a fellow living right there in Oklahoma City who sort of volunteered for the job. No use bothering you honeymooners again. By the looks of things, you've decided to settle in right here. Right? Great place, here, right on the bank of the San Juan River."

But that effort to change the subject didn't work.

"What did he find out for you?" Bernie asked.

Leaphorn shrugged. Drained his coffee cup, extended it toward Bernie, suggesting the need for a refill. "Didn't amount to anything," he said. "Great coffee you're making, Bernie. I bet you didn't follow Chee's old formula of 'too little grounds, boiled too long.'"

Chee was grinning at Leaphorn, ignoring the jibe.

"Come on, Lieutenant, quit the stalling. What'd you find out? And what got you so interested in the first place?"

"You're a married man now," Leaphorn said, and handed his empty cup to Chee. "Time to learn how to be a good host."

"No more coffee until you quit stalling," Chee said.

Leaphorn sighed, thought a bit. "Well," he said, "it

turned out the obituary was a fake. Mr. Totter hadn't died in that Oklahoma City hospital, and hadn't been buried in that Veterans Administration cemetery." He paused, shrugged.

"Well, go on," Chee said. "Why the obituary? What's the story?"

Bernie took the cup from Leaphorn's hand.

"But don't tell it until I get back with the refill," she said. "I want to hear this."

"Why the fake being dead?" Chee asked. "What happened to Totter?"

Leaphorn pondered. How much of this could he tell? He imagined Chee and Bernie, under oath on the witness stand, the U.S. District Attorney's prosecutor reminding them they were under oath, or the penalty of perjury. "When did you first hear this? Who told you? When did he tell you? After his Navajo Tribal Police retirement, then? But wasn't he still a deputized law enforcement officer for about three Arizona and New Mexico counties?"

"Well?" Chee asked.

"I'm waiting for your wife to get back with the coffee," Leaphorn said. "Being polite. You should learn about that."

"I'm back," Bernie said, and handed him his cup. "I'm curious, too. What happened to Mr. Totter?"

"To tell the truth, we don't really know," Leaphorn said. And paused. "Not for sure, anyway." Another thoughtful pause. "Let me rephrase that. To tell the truth, we think we know what happened to Totter, but we never could have proved it."

Chee, who had been standing, pulled up a chair and sat down. "Hey," he said. "I'll bet this is going to be interesting."

"Let me get some more cookies," Bernie said, hopping out of her chair. "Don't start until I get back."

That gave Leaphorn about two minutes to decide how to handle this.

"Long and complicated story," he said, "and it may cause you both to think I've gone senile. I've got to start it way back by reminding you both of our origin stories, about there being so much meanness, greed, and evil in those first three worlds that the Creator destroyed them, and how our First Man brought all that evil up to this fourth world of ours."

Chee looked puzzled. And impatient. "How can that connect with Totter's obituary?"

Leaphorn chuckled. "You'll probably still be wondering about that when I finish this. But while I'm telling you about it, I want you to think about how our Hero Twins killed the evil monster on the Turquoise Mountain, and how they tried to rid this fourth world of ours of all the other evils and also about that name we sometime use for our worst kind of witches. One version translates into English as *skinwalkers*. Another version comes out as *shape shifters*."

"Fits better sometimes," Chee said. "The last time someone told me about seeing a skinwalker bothering her sheep, she said when she went into the hogan to get her rifle to shoot it, it saw her coming and turned into an owl. Flew away."

"My mother told me about one," Bernie said. "It changed from a wolf into some sort of bird."

"Well, keep that in mind when I tell you about Totter, and so forth," Leaphorn said.

Chee was grinning.

"Okay," he said. "I promise."

"Me, too," said Bernie, who seemed to be taking this a little more seriously. "On with the story."

Leaphorn took a cookie, sampled the fresh coffee.

"For me it started just about the time you two were enjoying yourselves in Hawaii. I had a call telling me I had mail down at the office, so I went down to see what it was. That's what pulled me into it."

He took a bite of cookie, remembering he'd had to park in the visitors' parking lot. It was just starting to rain. "Big lightning bolt just as I parked there," he said. "If I was as well tutored in our Navajo mythology as your husband is, Bernie, I would have recognized right away that the spirit world wasn't happy. I'd have seen that as a bad omen."

Chee had never got quite used to Leaphorn kidding him about his goal of being both a tribal policeman and a certified shaman, conducting Navajo curing ceremonials. Chee was frowning.

"Come on, Lieutenant," he said. "You're saying it was beginning to rain. Lightning flashes. Now tell us what happened next."

"Big lightning bolt just as I got there," he said, smiling at Chee. "And I think when I'm finished with this, with as much as I can tell you anyway, you're going to agree it was a very bad omen."

2

Eleven days earlier . . .

The boom of the lightning bolt caused Lieutenant Joe Leaphorn, retired, to hesitate a moment before he climbed out of his pickup in the visitors' parking lot. He took a serious look at the clouds building up in the western sky as he walked into the Navajo Tribal Police building. End of autumn, he was thinking. Monsoon season pretty much over. Handsome clouds of fog over the Lukachukai range this morning, but nothing promising a really good female rain. Just a noisy male thunderstorm. It would be hunting season soon, he thought, which normally would have meant a lot of work for him. This year he could just kick back, sit by the fire. He'd let younger cops try to keep track of the poachers and go hunting for the city folks who always seemed to be losing themselves in the mountains.

Leaphorn sighed as he walked through the entrance.

He should have been enjoying that sort of thinking, but he wasn't. He felt . . . well . . . retired.

Nobody in the police department hall. Good. He hurried into the reception office. Good again. Nobody there except the pretty young Hopi woman manning the desk, and she was ignoring him, chatting on the telephone.

He took off his hat and waited.

She said: "Just a moment," into the telephone, glanced at him, said: "Yes, sir. Can I help you?"

"I had a message from Captain Pinto. Pinto said I should come in and pick up my mail."

"Mail?" She looked puzzled. "And you are?"

"I'm Joe Leaphorn."

"Leaphorn. Oh, yes," she said. "The captain said you might be in." She fumbled in a desk drawer, pulled out a manila envelope, looked at the address on it. Then at him.

"Lieutenant Joe Leaphorn," she said. "Is that you?"

"That was me," Leaphorn said. "Once." He thanked her, took the envelope back to his truck, and climbed in, feeling even more obsolete than he had as he'd driven by the police-parking-only spaces and stopped in visitors' parking.

The return address looked sort of promising. Why Worry Security, with a Flagstaff, Arizona, street address. The name penned under that was Mel Bork. Bork? Well, at least it wasn't just more of the junk mail he'd been receiving.

"Bork?" Leaphorn said it aloud, suddenly remembering. Smiling. Ah yes. A skinny young man named Bork had been his fellow semi-greenhorn westerner friend from way, way back when both of them were young country-boy cops sent back East to learn some law enforcement rules at the FBI Academy. And his first name, by golly, had been Melvin.

Leaphorn opened his Swiss army knife, slit the envelope, slid out the contents. A page of slick paper from a magazine with a letter clipped to it. He took off the clip and put the letter aside.

The page was from *Luxury Living,* and a color photograph dominated it. It showed a grand high-ceilinged room with a huge fireplace, a trophy-sized rack of elk antlers mounted above it, a tall wall of shelved books on one side, and a sliding-glass door on the other. The glass door offered a view into a walled garden and, above the wall, snow-capped mountains. Leaphorn recognized the mountains. The San Francisco Peaks, with Humphreys Peak lording over them. That told him this *Luxury Living* home was somewhere on the north edge of Flagstaff. The assorted furniture looked plush and expensive. But Leaphorn's attention was drawn away from this by an arrow inked on the photograph. It pointed to a weaving that was hanging beside the fireplace, and under the shank of the arrow were the words:

Hey, Joe, Ain't this that rug you kept telling me about? And if it is, what does that do to that arson case of ours? Remember? The one that the wise men ruled was just a careless smoker. And take a look at those antlers! Folks who know this guy tell me he's a hunting fool.
    See attached letter.

Leaphorn let the letter wait while he stared at the photograph. It did remind him of the rug he had described to Bork—a great rectangle of black, gray, red tones, blues, and yellows all partially encircled by the figure of Rainbow Man. It seemed to be just as his memory told him. He noticed a symbol for Maii'—the Coyote spirit—at his work of turning order into chaos and others representing the weapons that Monster Slayer and Born for Water had stolen from the sun to wage their campaign to make the Dineh safe from the evils that had followed them up from the underworld. But the photograph was printed much too small to show other details that had impressed Leaphorn when he'd seen the original in Totter's trading post gallery before it burned. He remembered seeing faint suggestions of soldiers with rifles, for example, and tiny white dots scattered in clusters here and there, which someone at the gallery had told him the weaver had formed from parts of feathers. They represented big silver peso coins, the currencies in the mountain west in the mid-1860s. And thus they represented greed, the root of all evil in the Navajo value system.

That, of course, was the theme of the famous old rug. And that theme made it a sort of bitter violation of the Navajo tradition. The Dineh taught its people to live in the peace and harmony of *hozho,* they must learn to forgive—a variation of the policy that *belagaana* Christians preached in their Lord's Prayer but all too often didn't seem to practice. And the rug certainly didn't practice forgetting old transgressions. It memorialized the worst cruelty ever imposed on the Navajo. The Long Walk—the captivity, misery, and the terrible death toll imposed on the Navajo by the white culture's fierce hunger for gold and silver—and the final solution they tried to apply to get the Dineh out of the way.

But could this picture torn from the magazine be of that same rug? It looked like it. But it didn't seem likely. Leaphorn remembered standing there examining the rug framed on the gallery wall behind its dusty glass. Remembered someone there telling him of its antiquity and its historical value. If this was a pre-fire photo, then how had it gone from the wall of this lavish house at the edge of Flagstaff to Totter's gallery. The other possibility was that it had been taken from the gallery before the fire. Furniture and other items in the room suggested the photo was recent. So did a distinctly modern painting on another wall.

Leaphorn put the magazine page back on the car seat, and considered another old and unpleasant memory the photo provoked from the day after the fire. The angry face of Grandma Peshlakai glowering at him through the window of his patrol car while he tried to explain why he had to leave—had to drive over to meet Captain Desbah, who had called him from Totter's place.

"It's a federal case," he'd told her. "They had a fire over at Totter's Trading Post Saturday. Burned up a man, and now the FBI thinks the dead man is a murderer they've been after for years. Very dangerous man. The federals are all excited."

"He's dead?"

Leaphorn agreed.

"He can't run then," Grandma said, scowling at him. "This man I want you to catch is running away with my buckets of pinyon sap."

Leaphorn had tried to explain. But Grandma Peshlakai was one of the important old women in her Kin Litsonii (Yellow House) clan. She felt her family was being

slighted. Leaphorn had been young then, and he'd agreed
that the problem of live Navajos should be just as important as learning the name of a dead *belagaana*. Remembering it now, much older, he still agreed with her.

Her case involved the theft of two economy-sized lard
buckets filled with pinyon sap. They had been stolen from
the weaving shed beside her hogan. She'd explained that
the loss was much more significant than it might sound
to a young policeman who had never endured the weary
days of onerous labor collecting that sap.

"And now it's gone, so how do we waterproof our baskets? How do we make them so they hold water and have
that pretty color so tourists will buy them? And now, it is
too late for sap to drip. We can't get more. Not until next
summer."

Grandma had bitten back her anger and listened,
with traditional Navajo courtesy, while he tried to explain
that this dead fellow was probably one of the top people
on the FBI's most wanted list. A very bad and dangerous
man. When he'd finished, rather lamely as he remembered, Grandma nodded.

"But he's dead. Can't hurt nobody now. Our thief is
alive. He has our sap. Two full buckets. Elandra there"—
she nodded to her granddaughter, who was standing
behind her, smiling at Leaphorn—"Elandra saw him driving away. Big blue car. Drove that direction—back toward
the highway. You policemen get paid to catch thieves.
You could find him, I think, and get our sap back. But if
you mess around with the dead man, maybe his *chindi*
will get after you. And if he was as bad as you say, it would
be very, very bad *chindi*."

Leaphorn sighed. Grandma was right, of course.

And the sort of mass murderer that was high on the FBI's Most Wanted list would, based on Leaphorn's memory of his maternal grandfather's hogan stories, be a formidable *chindi*. Since that version of ghost represented all of the unharmonious and evil characteristics that couldn't follow the dead person into his last great adventure, they were the sort any traditional Navajo would prefer to avoid. But, *chindi* or not, duty had called. He drove away, leaving Grandma staring resentfully after him. Remembering, too, the last theory she had offered. When he'd asked Grandma Peshlakai if she had any idea who would want to steal her pinyon sap, she stood silent a long moment, hesitating, looking around, making sure Elandra was out of hearing range.

"They say that sometimes witches need it for something. That sometimes a skinwalker might want it," Grandma had said. That was a version of the witchcraft legend he had never heard before. Leaphorn remembered telling Grandma Peshlakai that he doubted if this very worst tribal version of witchcraft evil would be driving a car. She had frowned at him a moment, shook her head, and said: "Why you think that?"

It was a question he couldn't think of any answer for. And now, all these years later, he still couldn't.

He sighed, picked up the letter:

Dear Joe,

If I remember you correctly, by now you've stared at that picture and examined the rug and you're trying to figure out when the photo was taken. Well, old Jason Delos didn't buy that mansion of his on that mountain slope outside

*of Flagstaff until just a few years ago. As I
remember your story, that famous old "cursed"
rug you told me about was reduced to ashes in
that trading-post fire long before that. Yet there
it is, good as new, posing for the camera. You
remember we agreed there was more going on
in that crime, and that maybe it really was a
crime, and not just a careless drunk accident
and a lot of witchcraft talk.*

*Anyway, I thought you'd be interested in
seeing this. I'm going to look into it myself. See
if I can find out where old man Delos got the
rug, etc. If you're interested, give me a call and
I'll let you know if I learn anything. And if you
ever get as far south and west as Flagstaff, I'll
buy you lunch, and we can tell each other how
we survived that FBI Academy stuff.*

Meanwhile, stay well,

Mel

Below the signature was an address in Flagstaff, and
a telephone number.

Oh, well, Leaphorn thought. Why not?

3

Leaphorn parked in the driveway of his Window Rock house, turned off the ignition, took the cell phone from the glove box, and began punching in Mel Bork's number. Five numbers into that project he stopped, thought a moment, put the cell phone back where he kept it. He had an odd feeling that this call might be important. He'd always tried to avoid making calls of any significance on the little toy telephones, explaining this quirk to his housemate, Professor Louisa Bourbonette, on grounds that cell phones were intended to communicate teen-age chatter and that adults didn't take anything heard on one seriously. Louisa had scoffed at this, bought him one anyway, and insisted he keep it in his truck.

Now he put his old telephone on the kitchen table, poured himself a cup of leftover breakfast coffee, and dialed. The number had a Flagstaff prefix, which by mountain west standards was relatively just down the road from him, but the call would be a long, blind leap into the past. That old case had nagged at him too long. Maybe Bork had hit on something. Maybe learning what happened to the famous old weaving would remove that tickling burr under his saddle, if that figure of speech worked in this case. Maybe it would somehow tie into his hunch that the fire that erased the "Big Handy's Bandit" from the FBI's most-wanted list had been more complicated than anyone had wanted to admit. Bork, he remembered, had thought so, too.

Remembering that, he thought of grouchy old Grandma Peshlakai again and her righteous indignation. If he actually took a little journey down to Flagstaff to talk to Bork and reconnect with his past, it wouldn't take much of a detour to get him into her part of the country. Maybe he'd stop at her hogan to see if she was still alive. Find out if anyone had ever found the thief who ran off with her two big buckets of pinyon sap. See if she was willing to forgive him and the *belagaana* ideas about enforcing the law.

He put Bork's letter and the magazine page on the table beside the telephone and stared at the photo while listening to Bork's phone ring, trying to remember the name of Bork's wife. Grace, he thought it was. Considered the photograph. Most likely his eyes had fooled him. But it certainly resembled the old rug as he recalled it. He shook his head, sighed. Be reasonable, he told himself. Famous as that old weaving had become, someone probably tried to copy it. This would be the photo of an effort to duplicate it. Still, he wanted to find out.

Then, just after Bork's answering machine cut in, a woman's voice took over. She sounded excited. And nervous.

"Yes," she said. "Yes? Mel? Where are you calling . . ."

Leaphorn gave her a moment to complete the question. She didn't.

"This is Joe Leaphorn," he said. "I am calling for Mr. Bork."

Silence. Then: "Mel's not here. I'm Mrs. Bork. What's this about?"

"I have a letter from him," Leaphorn said. "We knew each other years ago when we were in Washington. Both of us were students at the FBI Academy. He sent me a photograph and asked me to call him about it."

"Photograph! Of that damned weaving. Was that it?" she asked. "He said he was going to send that to someone. The picture he cut out of that magazine?"

"Yes," Leaphorn said. "He said he was going to check into it and—"

"You're the policeman," she said. "The Navajo cop. I remember now."

"Well, actually I'm—"

"I need to talk to a policeman," she said. "There's been a threatening telephone call. And, well . . . I don't know what to do."

Leaphorn considered this, sucked in a deep breath. Waited for a question. None came.

"Was the call about the picture?" he asked. "Threatening Mel about that weaving? Who was it? What did he say?"

"I don't know," Grace Bork said. "He didn't say who he was. It was on the answering machine. A man's voice, but I didn't recognize it."

"Don't erase the tape," Leaphorn said.

"I'll let you hear it," she said. "Hold on."

Leaphorn heard the sound of the telephone mouth-
piece bumping against wood, then a sound remembered
from the past: Bork's recorded answering machine voice:
"Can't come to the phone now. Leave a message."

Then a pause, a sigh, and another deeper male voice:
"Mr. Bork, I have some very serious advice for you. You
need to get back to minding your own business. Stop
trying to dig up old bones. Let those old bones rest in
peace. You keep poking at 'em and they'll jump out and
bite you." Silence. Then a chuckle. "You'll be just a set of
new bones." The tape clicked off.

Mrs. Bork said, "What should I do?"

"That call came when?"

"I don't know."

"Has Mel heard it?"

"No. I guess it either came in after he left, or maybe
he didn't notice it on his answering machine. I think he
would have said something about it if he'd heard it. And
now I don't know where he is. He's been gone since the
day before yesterday. I haven't heard from him." Grace
Bork was beginning to sound distraught.

"He didn't say where he was going?"

"Not specifically, he didn't. He just told me he was
going to find out where that rug in that picture came
from. He had made a call to somebody—in an art gallery
or museum, I think. I think he was going to meet the man
he called. Or have lunch with him. I expected him back
in time for dinner, and I've worried ever since. He just
doesn't do things like this. Just rush off and . . . and not
call, or anything." Mrs. Bork added that Mel had explained
that this business with the carpet in that photograph reminded him of what he'd seen in an arson fire in which a

man had been burned, and Leaphorn had talked to him about it when they were both at the FBI Academy.

"He seemed excited about that," she said. "I'm worried. I'm really worried. He has a cell phone. Why doesn't he call me?"

Leaphorn found himself remembering Louisa's plea that he always keep a cell phone in his truck.

"Mrs. Bork," he said, "first, take that tape out of the answering machine and put it somewhere safe. Take care of it. Does Mel always carry that cell phone with him?"

"He keeps one in his car. I've been calling it and calling it, but he doesn't answer."

"I presume your company has some contact with the Flagstaff police, or the sheriff's people. Does Mel have anyone working with him in his investigative service who could help you?"

"Just a woman who keeps his books. She comes in to answer the phone when he's away."

"If you have a friend in law enforcement, I think you should call him and discuss this situation."

"I called Sergeant Garcia last night. He said he didn't think I should worry."

Leaphorn checked his mental inventory of cops in the high, dry, mostly empty Four Corners Country.

"Is that the Garcia with the sheriff's department there? Kelly Garcia, I think it is. Is he a friend?"

"Of Mel's? I think so. Sort of anyway. Sometimes they more or less work together on cases, I think."

"I'd call him back, then. Tell him Mel is still away and doesn't answer his cell phone. Tell him you talked to me. Tell him I thought he should listen to that tape you played for me."

"Yes," Mrs. Bork said.

"And please let me know if you learn anything. Or if I can do anything." He recited his home phone number. Thought a moment, shrugged. "And here's my number, in case I'm not home."

She read back the numbers to him.

"One more thing," Leaphorn said. "Did he mention any names? I mean names of anyone he might be seeing. Or which museum he was going to?"

"Oh, my," she said. "Well, he might have said Tarkington. He's at one of the Indian arts and craft places in Flagstaff. Gerald Tarkington, I think it is."

"I think I know his place," Leaphorn said. "Anyone else?"

"Probably the Heard Museum in Phoenix," she said, hesitantly. "But that's just a guess. He worked for them once, a long time ago. And, Mr. Leaphorn, please let me know."

"I will," Leaphorn said, with a vague feeling that it would be a promise that would find him bringing her bad news. It was a message he'd had to deliver far too often in his career.

4

Leaphorn, being elderly, knew the wisdom of learning all you can about the one you intend to interview before you ask the first question. Thus, before calling Tarkington's gallery in Flagstaff, he dialed a number a few blocks away in Shiprock and talked to Ellen Klah at the Navajo Museum.

"Tarkington? Tarkington," Mrs. Klah said. "Oh, yeah. Well, now. What in the world would you be doing with that man?"

"I need to get some information from him," Leaphorn said. "See if he knows anything about an old rug."

"Something sneaky? Something criminal?"

"I don't know," Leaphorn said, sounding glum. "It's just this rug has turned up. And it looks a lot like one that was supposed to be burned up in a fire at a gallery years ago."

"I bet this involves insurance fraud," Mrs. Klah said.

"I hope not," Leaphorn said. "It was the fire that burned that little gallery at Totter's Trading Post. You remember that?"

"Of course I remember it," Mrs. Klah said. "Wasn't the rug that burned there an old, old tale-teller weaving? The one people called *Woven Sorrow*. Or maybe it was *Sorrow Woven In*? Something like that, anyway." She laughed. "That would fit the story people tell about it, you know. The weaving came out of that Long Walk sorrow, and everywhere it goes it takes troubles with it. I'll bet it's insurance fraud now. Is Tarkington a suspect, or co-conspirator, or what?"

"You're way ahead of me, Ellen," Leaphorn said. "No crime alleged, or anything. I just want to talk to Tarkington about what might have happened to that rug if it didn't actually burn."

"I've been reading in the *Albuquerque Journal* about that grand jury investigation involving Navajo rugs. Three of 'em. Very old. Supposed to be worth about two hundred thousand dollars if you add them all together. Is that what you're into?"

"No, no," Leaphorn said. "Nothing that exciting. I just want to ask you if Tarkington would be the guy to talk to about . . . well, let's say if a famous old rug had been destroyed and you had pictures of it, and wanted to hire a weaver to make you a copy. What would you do? Who could do it? Things like that."

"Well, Tarkington's an old-timer. I'd say he'd be as good as anyone to ask. If ethics are involved, from what I've heard I doubt he'd be worried about them. But are we talking about that *Woven Sorrow* rug? The one that woman wove after she got back from Bosque Redondo, full of things to remind you of all the death and misery that came out of that business. Was that the rug you're talking about?"

"I think that must be the one. That sounds like it."

"The rugs mentioned in that lawsuit all had names," Ellen said, sounding slightly disgruntled.

"I don't know its name. Don't know if it even had one," Leaphorn said. "I just remember a great big, complicated, old rug. I saw it framed behind glass and hanging in Totter's gallery near Tohatchi years ago. And I remember there was a story that went with it. It was supposed to have been cursed by a hand trembler, or some other medicine person."

"Ah," Mrs. Klah said. "Behind glass in a frame, wasn't it? I remember that. That was it. That was *Woven Sorrow*. Wow!"

"Anyway, you think Tarkington could tell me something. Right?"

She laughed. "If you promise him it won't get him in any trouble. Or cost him any money."

So Leaphorn dialed the Tarkington number, got an answering machine that advised him to either leave a message or, if business was involved, call the number at the "downtown gallery."

He called that one. He did the "wait just a moment" duty required by the secretary who took his name, and then: "Joe Leaphorn?" a deep, rusty male voice said. "There used to be a Lieutenant Joe Leaphorn with the Navajo Tribal Police. Is that you?"

"Yes sir," Leaphorn said. "Are you Mr. Tarkington?"

"Right."

"I am trying to get into contact with a Mr. Mel Bork.

His wife said he'd gone to see you on some business we're trying to check into. I thought you might know where I could reach him."

This produced a silence. Then a sigh. "Mel Bork. What was this business of yours about?"

"It concerned a Navajo rug."

"Ah, yes. The magical, mystical rug woven to commemorate the return of the Dineh from captivity at Bosque Redondo. Full of bits and pieces supposed to reflect memories of the miseries, starvation, of the tribe's captivity and that long walk home. It was supposed to be started in the 1860s, finished a lot later. That it?"

"Yes," Leaphorn said, and paused. Noticing that Tarkington's tone had been sarcastic. Waiting for anything Tarkington might add. Deciding how to handle this.

"Well," Tarkington said. "What can I do you for?"

"Can you tell me where Bork was headed when he left you?"

"He didn't say."

Leaphorn waited again. Again, no luck.

"You have no idea?"

"Look, Mr. Leaphorn, I think maybe we do need to talk about this, but not on the phone. Where are you?"

"In Window Rock."

"How about coming to the gallery tomorrow? Could you make it? Maybe have a late lunch?"

Leaphorn thought about what tomorrow held for him. Absolutely nothing.

"I'll be there," he said.

5

Leaphorn was on the road early, driving with a gaudy sunrise in his rearview mirror. He took Navajo Route 12, joined Interstate 40, set his speed at a modest (but legal) seventy-five miles per hour, and let the flood of westbound speeders race by him. He would reach Flagstaff with time to find Tarkington's gallery, and the drive would give him a chance to consider what he was getting into.

The first step was reexamining his memory of the tape Mrs. Bork had played for him and what little else he'd learned from her in that short conversation. That didn't take long.

She'd remembered that seeing the picture had excited Bork. She'd said Mel had told her about the old crime, and about having talked to Leaphorn about it in Washington years ago. Then Mel had made two, maybe three telephone calls. She hadn't heard who he was calling. After the last one he had shouted something to her about the Tarkington gallery, and maybe coming home late, and to tell anyone who called he'd be back in his office tomorrow. Then he had driven away. Nothing in that helped much.

By the time he reached the Sanders, Arizona, exit, Leaphorn decided it was coffee time and pulled off the interstate at a diner to see what he could learn. The old Burnham trading post here had been known for its Navajo weavers. The Navajo Nation had bought territory along the Santa Fe Railway mainline here and used it as relocation places for the five hundred Navajo families forced out of the old Navajo-Hopi Joint Use reservation. The weavers among the refugees had developed some new patterns that came to be called the New Lands rugs, and a Sanders trader had been sort of an authority on them, and on rugs in general. If he could find this fellow, Leaphorn planned to show him the photo of the old carpet to see what he knew about it.

The waitress who brought him his coffee was about eighteen and had never heard of any of this. The man behind the cash register had heard of him, and he recommended Leaphorn find Austin Sam, who had been a candidate for the Tribal Council and seemed to know just about everybody in the New Lands Chapter House territory. But the cashier didn't know where Mr. Sam could be found. Neither did Leaphorn.

Thus Leaphorn reentered the roaring river of Interstate 40 traffic no wiser than before. He rolled into Flagstaff and found the Tarkington Museum Gallery parking lot about ten minutes before noon. A tall man, gray-bearded, wearing an off-white linen jacket, was standing at the door, smiling, waiting for him.

"Lieutenant Leaphorn," he said. "You look just like the pictures I've seen of you. You drove all the way from Window Rock this morning?"

"I did," Leaphorn said, as Tarkington ushered him into the gallery.

"Then freshen up if you wish," Tarkington said, pointing toward the restroom, "and then let's have some lunch and talk."

When Leaphorn emerged refreshed, he found lunch was being served in an alcove just off the gallery. A girl, who Leaphorn identified as probably a Hopi, was pouring ice water into glasses on a neatly set table. Tarkington was already seated with a copy of *Luxury Living* in front of him, opened to the photograph.

"Unless you want something special, we could get lunch here," he said. "Just sandwiches and fruit. Would that satisfy you?"

"Sure," Leaphorn said, and seated himself, weighing what this development might mean. Obviously it meant Tarkington must consider this talk important. Why else would he be taking the trouble to put Leaphorn in the role of guest, with the psychological disadvantage that went with that. But it did save time. Not that Leaphorn didn't have plenty of that.

The girl passed Leaphorn an attractive plate of neatly trimmed sandwiches in a variety of types. He took one offering ham, cheese, and lettuce. She asked if he'd like coffee. He would. She poured it for him from a silver urn. Tarkington watched all this in silence. Now he served himself a sandwich and toasted Leaphorn with his water glass.

"Down to business now?" he said, making it a question. "Or just make chat while we eat?"

"Well, I am here trying to find an old friend, but I am also hungry."

"You are looking for Melvin Bork, right? The private investigator?"

Leaphorn nodded. He sipped his coffee. Excellent. He looked at his sandwich, took a small bite. Also fine.

"Why look here?"

"Because his wife thought he would be coming here to ask you about a rug. Is that correct?"

"Oh, yes. He was here." Tarkington was smiling, looking amused. "Three days ago. He had a copy of one of those expensive upscale real estate magazines with a picture of it. This magazine." He tapped the picture, smiling at Leaphorn.

Leaphorn nodded.

"He asked if I had seen a rug that looked like that, and I said yes, I had. One much like that got burned up in a fire way back. A real shame. It was a famous tale-teller rug. Famous among the bunch who love the really old weavings, and especially among the odd ones who dote on the artifacts that have scary stories attached. And this one does. Dandy stories. Full of death, starvation, all that."

He smiled at Leaphorn again, picked up his glass, rattled the ice in it.

"And it was also a wonderful example of the weavers' art. A real beauty. Bork asked me to take a close look at the magazine photo and tell him what I could about it."

Tarkington paused to take a sip of his water. And, Leaphorn presumed, to decide just how much he wanted to say about this.

"I told him the picture resembled a very old, very valuable antique. Rug people called such weavings tale tellers because they usually represent someone, or something, memorable. And the tale in this one was of all the dying, humiliation, and misery you Navajos went through when the army put you in that concentration camp over on the Pecos back about a hundred and fifty years ago."

Tarkington extracted a reading-sized magnifying glass from his jacket pocket and held it close to the photograph, studying places here and there. "Yes, it does look something like that old rug Totter had at his trading post years ago."

"Something like?" Leaphorn asked. "Can you be a little more specific than that?"

Tarkington put down the glass, studied Leaphorn. "That brings up an interesting question, doesn't it? That one was burned—let's see—back in the very late 1960s or early 1970s I think. So the question I want to ask you is, when was this photograph taken?"

"I don't know," Leaphorn said.

Tarkington considered that, shrugged.

"Well, Bork asked me if I thought it could be a photograph of a copy of the rug Totter had, and I said I guessed anything is possible, but it didn't make much sense. Even if you had real good detailed photos of the original to work from, the weavers would still be dealing with trying to match yarns, and vegetable dyes, and using different people with different weaving techniques. And with this particular rug, they would even be trying to work in the same kind of bird feathers, petals from cactus blossoms, stems and such. For example . . ." Tarkington paused, tapped a place on the photo with a finger. "For example, this deep color of red right here—presuming this is a good color reproduction—is pretty rare. The old weavers

got it from the egg sac of one of the big desert spiders."
He smiled at Leaphorn. "Sounds weird, I guess, but that's
what the experts say. And it gives you an idea how tough
it would be to make a copy."

Tarkington sipped his water again, eyes on Leaphorn,
waiting for a reaction.

"I guess you're telling me that Bork asked you for an
opinion about whether the photograph was of a copy of
the original."

"Yep. He did. And I told him it was probably a photograph of somebody's effort at making a copy. Pretty
damned good one, too. I suggested he might call the
fellow who has it on his wall. See if he'd let him take a
look at it. And then Mr. Bork said he thought he would
do that, but he wanted to find out what I thought about
it first. And I said those superrich folks who collect artifacts like that are going to be very careful about who they
let into their house unless they know you. Bork said he
thought about that and he wanted me to sort of introduce
him so the man would let him in. And I had to tell him I
didn't actually know the man myself. Just by reputation."
Tarkington picked up his cup, noticed it was empty, put
it down.

"Bork thought a man named Jason Delos had bought
that house. I guess I could call information to get his telephone number. If it's listed," Leaphorn said. "Is that the
right name? I think I'll need to go talk to him."

"You're right about the number being unlisted," Tarkington said. "And Jason Delos is the name. I guess he
must be out of a Greek family."

Leaphorn nodded. "Am I right in guessing you know
his number?"

"Carrie," Tarkington shouted. "Bring Mr. Leaphorn some more coffee and me some more ice water."

"You know him just by reputation? Who is he?"

Tarkington laughed. "I know him just as a potential future customer. It's obvious he has a lot of money. Collects expensive stuff. Moved in here a while back, either from Southern California because the sun was bad for his wife's skin condition, or Oregon, because the fog and humidity depressed his wife." Tarkington gave Leaphorn a wry smile. "You know how reliable gossip is out here where we don't have a lot of people to gossip about. Frankly, I wouldn't be surprised to hear he doesn't have a wife. Nobody seems ever to have met her. He has a middle-aged Asian man living out there with him. Sort of a butler, I think. And he uses a maid/laundry service, and so forth. And that butler leads into another story."

With that Tarkington shook his head and laughed, signaling to Leaphorn that this story did not carry his certification.

"This one makes Mr. Delos some sort of CIA agent, did a lot of work in the Vietnam War, retired after that and went into some sort of investment business. Then another version is that he got kicked out of the CIA because a bunch of the money our government was using to pay off South Vietnam government types when they were arranging that coup to get rid of President Diem—you remember that business?"

"I've read about it," Leaphorn said. "As I remember, it blew up into a big battle in Saigon with paratroopers attacking Diem's bunch in the Presidential Palace."

"Yeah. It brought in a new president more popular with President Kennedy. Well, anyway, the way the gossip goes, the CIA, or whatever they were calling it then, had been handing out bags of money to help arrange that, and some of the generals who were getting it thought they were shorted. One of those quiet investigations got started, and it was concluded that some of those money bags got lighter when in the custody of Mr. Delos."

"Oh," Leaphorn said, and nodded.

Tarkington shrugged. "Well, you could probably find a couple of other versions of the Delos biography if you wanted to ask around in Flagstaff. He just sits up there all alone on his mountain and gives us somebody interesting to talk about. Take your pick, whichever version you prefer. Like a lot of rich folks, he's into protecting his family's privacy, so our gossiping fraternity has to be creative."

The Hopi girl returned, smiled at Leaphorn, refilled his coffee cup, refilled Tarkington's glass, and left.

"What I really want to know, I guess, is how he got that rug. Then I track it back, find out who made it, and that's the end of it," Leaphorn said. "So I need to know his telephone number so I can go ask him."

Tarkington was grinning. "So you can be done with this case, and go back to your usual police duties?"

"So I can go back to being a bored-stiff-by-retirement former policeman."

"Well," Tarkington said, staring at Leaphorn. "If you do learn anything interesting—for example, who copied it if anyone actually did, and why, and so forth—I'd sure appreciate hearing all about it."

Leaphorn considered that. "All right," he said.

Now Tarkington took a moment to think. He sipped his water again, while Leaphorn sipped coffee.

"You may have noticed I love to talk," Tarkington said, emphasizing the statement with a wry smile. "That would give me something new to talk about."

Leaphorn nodded. "But you haven't told me his number."

"You had the name right," Tarkington said. "Jason Delos."

Leaphorn picked up a second sandwich, took a bite. Judged it as very good.

"Of course I collect stuff myself," Tarkington said, and gestured into the gallery to demonstrate. "And I collect stories. Love 'em. And that damned *Woven Sorrow* tale-teller rug collected them like dogs collect fleas. And I want to know what you find out from Delos, if anything, and how this all turns out. Will you promise me that?"

"If it's possible," Leaphorn said.

Tarkington leaned forward, pointed at an odd-looking pot on a desk by the wall. "See that image of the snake on that ceramic there? That's a Supai pot. But why is that snake pink? It's a rattler, and they're not that color. Well, I guess they are in one deep part of the Grand Canyon. There's a very rare and officially endangered species down there in Havasupai territory, and they have a great story in their mythology about how it came to be pink. And that's going to make that pot a lot more valuable to the fellow who collects it."

He stared at Leaphorn, looking for some sign of agreement.

"I know that's true," Leaphorn said. "But I'm not sure I understand why."

"Because the collector gets the story along with the pot. People say why is that snake pink. He explains. That makes him an authority." Tarkington laughed. "You Navajos don't practice that one-upmanship game like we do. You fellows who stay in that harmony philosophy."

Leaphorn grinned. "Be more accurate to say a lot of Navajos try, but remember we have a curing ceremony to heal us when we start getting vengeful, or greedy, or— what do you call it—'getting ahead of the Joneses.'"

"Yeah," Tarkington said. "I could tell you a tale about trying to get a Navajo businessman to buy a really fancy saddle. Lots of silver decorations, beautiful stitching, even turquoise worked in. He was interested. Then I told him it would make him look like the richest man on the big reservation. And he took a step back and said it would make him look like a witch."

Leaphorn nodded. "Yes," he said. "At least it would make the traditional Dineh suspicious. Unless he didn't have any poor kinfolks whom he should have been helping. And all of us have poor kinfolks."

Tarkington shrugged. "Prestige," he said. "You Navajos aren't so hungry for that. I'll ask a Navajo about something that I know he's downright expert about. He won't just tell me. He'll precede telling me by saying, 'They say.' Not wanting me to think he is claiming the credit."

"I guess I've heard that preamble a million times," Leaphorn said. "In fact, I do it myself sometimes." He was thinking that at his age, already retired, left on the shelf like the pink snake, he should understand that white cultural values were different from those of the Dineh, remembering how Navajo kids were conditioned by their elders to be part of the community, not to stand out, not to be the authority; remembering how poorly that attitude had served his generation, the age group that had been bused away to Bureau of Indian Affairs boarding schools to be melded into the *belagaana* culture.

"Who discovered America?" the teacher would ask. Every student in the class knew the *belagaana* answer was Christopher Columbus, but only the Hopi and Zuni kids would hold up their hands. And if the teacher pointed to a Navajo kid, that kid would inevitably precede his answer with the "they say" disclaimer. And the teacher, instead of crediting the Navajo with being politely modest, would presume he was taking a politically correct Native American attitude and implying that he was refusing to agree with what textbook and teacher had been telling him. Remembering all that, and the confusion it sometimes produced, caused Leaphorn to smile.

The smile puzzled Tarkington. He looked slightly disappointed.

"Anyway, I'd like to hear more about the stories you've collected about this tale-teller rug," Leaphorn said. "I'll tell you what I hear if it's anything new."

Tarkington took another sandwich. He passed the tray to Leaphorn, his expression genial again.

"First one I'll tell you is pretty well documented, I think. Probably mostly true. Seems the rug was started by a young woman named Cries a Lot, a woman in the Streams Come Together clan. It was in the final days of the stay in the Bosque Redondo concentration camp. She was one of the nine thousand of your people the army rounded up and marched way over to the Pecos River Valley to get them out of the way."

Tarkington paused, raised his eyebrows. "But I guess

I don't need to refresh your memory about the Long Walk."

"No," Leaphorn said, smiling. "My maternal grandfather used to tell us about freezing to death out there in his winter hogan stories when I was a boy. And then my paternal great-grandfather had his own stories about the bunch who escaped that roundup, and spent those years hiding out in the mountains."

Tarkington chuckled "And the government then makes sure you don't forget it. Calls a big piece of your space out here the Kit Carson National Forest, in memory of the colonel in charge of rounding you up, and burning down your hogans, and chopping down your peach orchards."

"We don't blame Kit Carson much," Leaphorn said. "He comes out pretty decent in the hogan stories, and the history books, too. It was General George Carlton who issued that General Order 15 and gave the shoot-to-kill and scorched-earth orders."

"Most Americans never heard of that, I'm afraid," Tarkington said. "We don't teach our kids our version of how we tried Hitler's final solution on you folks. Round you all up, kill anyone who tries to escape, drive off the cattle, let the Indians starve. We ought to have a chapter in all our history books describing that."

Tarkington took the final bite of his sandwich, considering this, seeming to Leaphorn to be more troubled by the failing of historians than by the deed itself.

"There'll never be a chapter on that," Leaphorn said. "And I'm glad there isn't. Why keep that kind of hatred alive? We have our curing ceremonials to get people back in harmony. Get rid of the anger. Get happy again."

"I know," Tarkington said. "But according to the stories I hear, a lot of memories of that brutality live on in that *Woven Sorrow* rug. They say that when the Navajo headmen signed that treaty with General Sherman in 1866 and the survivors started their long walk home, that young woman and her sister brought the beginnings of the rug with them and kept working on it, working in little reminders of their treatment. Little bit of a root woven in here, and rat hair there, and so forth, as reminders of what they were eating to keep from starving. Anyway, so the story goes, the weaving went on when the families began getting their flocks reestablished for some good wool. And other people heard about it, and more weavers got a hand in it and added another bitter memory of misery and murder and dying children. And then, finally, one of the clan headmen, some say it was either Barboncito or Manuelito, told the weavers it violated the Navajo way to preserve evil. He wanted all the weavers to arrange an Enemy Way sing to cure themselves of all those hateful memories and restore themselves to harmony."

Tarkington took a sip of water. "What do you think of that?"

"Interesting," Leaphorn said. "My mother's mother told us something like that one winter when I was about ten or so. She didn't approve of what those weavers were doing either. She told us about three of the shamans in her clan getting together and putting a special sort of curse on that rug."

"I heard something like that, too," Tarkington said. "They said it had too many *chindi* associated with it. Too many ghosts of dead Navajos, starved and frozen and killed by the soldiers. The rug would make people sick, bring down evil on people involved with it."

"Well, that's the way it's supposed to work. You keep your bad memories, grudges, hatreds, and all that alive with you, and it makes you sick." Leaphorn chuckled. "Not bad reasoning for people who never enrolled in introduction to psychology."

"Christians have that thought in their Lord's Prayer," Tarkington said. "You know: 'Forgive us our sins as we forgive those who sin against us.' Too bad a lot of 'em don't practice what they're preaching."

Leaphorn let that pass.

Tarkington stared at him. "I'm thinking about people crying when the judge gives the guy who killed their kid just life in prison instead of the death penalty they were praying for."

Leaphorn nodded.

Tarkington sighed. "But back to the rug. I've heard bad luck stories about people who owned it down through the years." He shrugged. "You know. Murders, suicides, bad luck."

"We Dineh don't believe much in luck," Leaphorn said. "More in a sort of inevitable chain of causes producing naturally inevitable effects."

And when he said that, he was thinking of Grace Bork's fear, and of what sort of cosmic cause-and-effect chain might involve that *Woven Sorrow* rug, the photo of it, the fire at Totter's Trading Post, the wanted murderer burned in there, Mel Bork's being sucked into it, and the death threat taped on his answering machine. Then, suddenly, he was thinking of himself being sucked in as well. By being at Grandma Peshlakai's hogan and having his hunt for her pinyon sap bandit being interrupted by the fire because it destroyed the FBI's most wanted murderer. He shook his head, produced a rueful smile. No. That seemed to be stretching the Navajo cosmic natural connection philosophy a little too far.

6

Luxury Living magazine protected the privacy of those who allowed its photographers access to their mansions. It published neither names nor addresses. Leaphorn had concluded, by studying the view through the window beside the *Woven Sorrow* rug, that the house was in the high slopes outside Flagstaff—one of the handsome residences built as summer homes for those who enjoyed the long views and the cool mountain air and could afford a second home. After some stalling, Tarkington checked his address file and read all the information off it that he considered pertinent to Leaphorn. But the telephone number? It's unlisted, Tarkington said. But you'd certainly know it, Leaphorn had insisted. Well, yes, Tarkington had admitted. But don't let anyone know you got it from me.

And thus Leaphorn left the Tarkington Museum Gallery with nothing much more than he arrived with—except for an expert's vague opinion that the rug in the photo might or might not be a copy of the original *Woven Sorrow*, and that making such a copy would be very difficult and, besides, who would want to do it? Beyond that, he had enjoyed two cups of excellent coffee, two tasty but not filling sandwiches, and an interesting version of the story of how that rug had come to be woven, and its history of spreading the misery, brutality, and misfortune it was designed to recall. The only thing he'd received that might help him was the telephone number of Jason Delos.

Leaphorn pulled into a Burger King, ordered a burger, found the pay phone, picked up the receiver, then decided not to call Delos. Not yet. First he would call the Coconino Sheriff's Department and find Sergeant Kelly Garcia.

If Garcia was in, he might know something useful about Mel Bork. And if Grace Bork had played that telephone tape for him as she said she would, maybe Garcia would have some ideas about that. Anyway, it was a reasonable way of postponing the call to Delos. He had a sad feeling that the call would lead him to a dead end. But if he just called Grace Bork saying he had nothing helpful to tell her, and then made the long drive back to Shiprock, he would be welcomed there by the loneliness of an empty house and the smell of an almost-full half gallon of milk, thoroughly soured by now, which he had forgotten to put back in the fridge.

He dialed the sheriff's office. Yes, Sergeant Garcia was in.

"This is Garcia," the next voice said.

"Joe Leaphorn," Leaphorn said. "I used to be with—"

"Hey, Lieutenant Leaphorn," Garcia said, sounding pleased. "Haven't heard your voice since we worked on that Ute Mountain burglary thing. Somebody told me you were going to retire," Garcia continued. "I said, no way. Old Leaphorn ain't the kind of man you'll see out there chasing those golf balls around the grass. Just couldn't quite imagine that."

"Well, I am retired," Leaphorn admitted. "You're right about the golf thing. And now I'm trying to act like a detective again. Trying to find a friend from way back. A fellow named Mel Bork. Runs a private-eye business."

"Yeah," Garcia said. "Mrs. Bork called me. Said she had talked to you. Had me listen to her answering machine tape." Garcia made a clicking sound with his tongue.

"What did you think?"

"Makes you wonder what Mel's got himself into, doesn't it?"

"It made me wonder. And if you have any time, I'd like to talk to you about it. Could we get together for a cup of coffee?"

"I can't handle it today," Garcia said.

Leaphorn overheard him shouting at someone, then a little bit of one end of a conversation, then Garcia came back on the phone.

"Okay," he said. "Maybe I can. You remember the Havacup Café there by the courthouse? How about meeting me there. Thirty minutes or so."

"I'll be there," Leaphorn said. "By the way, do you know anything about a man named Jason Delos?"

A moment of silence. "Delos? Not much. Understand he's rich. Not one of the old families, or anything like that, but I guess he's sort of prominent." He chuckled. "Guy I know in the game and fish department said he thought he had him once for spotlighting deer, but he moved too quick. No shots fired. Didn't have enough to file a charge. Otherwise, he's not the sort of citizen we'd be having much dealings with, I guess, but—"

The sound of someone yelling, "Hey, Kelly," interrupted. "Got to go, Joe. I'll see you at the Havacup in thirty minutes."

7

The changes Leaphorn noticed in Garcia as the Coconino sheriff's sergeant walked up to the booth were mostly in hair style. Leaphorn remembered him with bushy black hair, a bushy black mustache, and prominent black eyebrows. All still there, but all neatly trimmed now, and the black was modified into various shades of gray. Otherwise he was medium sized, trim and neat, and his eyes had retained their bright brown glint.

"How time flies," Garcia said, after shaking Leaphorn's hand and slipping into the booth. "But I see you still drink coffee."

"I guess I'm an addict. And I asked the young lady to bring a cup for you, but she didn't."

"Good thing," Garcia said. "I swore off the stuff. Switched to drinking tea."

"Oh," Leaphorn said.

"Kept me awake."

Leaphorn nodded.

"Why you hunting Melvin Bork?"

Leaphorn considered that a moment. "Well, he's sort of a friend. Used to be, way back. Haven't seen him for years. We sort of got together in our rookie days, when I went to the FBI school back east. We met there. But maybe it's partly just curiosity."

Garcia was studying him. "Curious? Yeah, me, too."

Leaphorn let that hang.

"So you're saying you really are retired now, right? How long?"

"Just getting started at it. This is the first month."

"How you like it?"

Leaphorn shrugged. "Not much. I think it takes some getting used to."

Garcia sighed. "I'm up for it end of this year."

"You don't look old enough."

Garcia made a wry face. "Getting tired though. Tired of doing all the damned paperwork. Messing with the federal regulations, dealing with drunks, and women beating up on their husbands, and vice versa, all that, and working with some of those young city boys the Federal Bureau of Ineptitude sends out here to our waterless desert."

Leaphorn sipped his coffee.

"How about you, Joe. You miss being a cop?"

"I still am one, sort of. I carry a Coconino deputy sheriff's badge, and ones from San Juan and McKinley counties in New Mexico."

Garcia raised his eyebrows. "I think you're supposed to turn those in, aren't you? After all, you're just a—ah, just a civilian now."

"Hadn't thought about it," Leaphorn said, and smiled. "Are you going to report me to the sheriff?"

Garcia laughed.

The waiter arrived. Garcia ordered iced tea and two doughnuts.

"Now you're going to ask me about Bork," he said. "Well, I like him. We worked with him on some stuff. He's smart. Former deputy himself. Seemed honorable."

He sipped his tea, looked at Leaphorn. "But I didn't like the sound of that telephone call."

"No," Leaphorn said.

"The missus said you'd told her to let me hear that tape. What's he into? Any ideas about that?"

"Here's all I know," Leaphorn said. He handed Garcia Bork's letter and the magazine photo of the tale-teller rug. Then he told Garcia about remembering how it had been burned to ashes in the Totter's Trading Post fire— along with one of the FBI's most wanted bad men.

Garcia studied the photo, looking thoughtful.

"I never saw the original," he said. "Is this it?"

"I saw it just once in Totter's gallery," Leaphorn said. "Not long before the fire. Stood and stared at it a long time. I'd heard some of the old stories about it from my grandmother. The photo looks like the rug I remember looking at. But it doesn't seem possible. I talked to Mr. Tarkington at his gallery here. He thought it might be a copy. But he wasn't ready to make any bets."

Garcia looked up from the photo. "Pretty flossy house it's hanging in," he said. "Judging from the view through the window, that might be old John Raskins's house."

"That's what Tarkington told me. He told me this Delos fella lives there now."

"I take it you haven't talked to Delos yet? Asked him where he got the rug?"

"I intend to do that tomorrow. Thought I'd call him and see if he'll let me in. Let me look at the rug."

Garcia smiled. "Good luck," he said. "He's pretty high society for Flagstaff. He's probably going to refer you to his Asian housekeeper. What are you going to tell him? Going to just show him your Coconino deputy sheriff's badge and tell him you're investigating a crime?"

Leaphorn shook his head. "I see your point. What's the crime?"

"Exactly." Garcia tested his tea again, looking thoughtful.

Leaphorn waited.

"So you're curious, too?" Garcia asked.

"Afraid so," Leaphorn said. "After all these years."

Garcia drained his iced tea, picked up the ticket, put on his hat.

"Joe," he said. "Let's drive out to that old Totter place and look around and have a talk. I'll explain why I'm still curious, and then you tell me what's bothering you."

"It's a long drive," Leaphorn said. "All the way up there past Lukachukai."

"Well, it's a long story, too," Garcia said. "And a real sad one. Goes all the way back to that crime that put Ray Shewnack on the FBI's Most Wanted list. And I wouldn't think you'd be too busy. Being retired."

"I'm afraid you're right," Leaphorn said, with a rueful chuckle.

"We'll burn Coconino County sheriff gasoline," Garcia said, as they got into his patrol car. "And re-member, you've got to tell me more about what pulled you into this. As I recall, all you were doing up there at Totter's that day was sort of taking orders from the federals."

"My story isn't all that long," Leaphorn said. "To tell you the truth, I don't really understand it myself."

8

Garcia swerved off the interstate at Holbrook and roared up Highway 71 past Bidahochi, took 191 to Chinli, and thence along the north rim of Canyon de Chelly to Lukachukai and onward past Round Rock onto the gravel road that wandered between Los Gigante buttes into the empty rough country. Here the Carrizo Mountains ended and became the Lukachukai stem of the Chuska range. That represented a three-hour drive, but Garcia made it in less than that. Talking all the way, and sometimes listening to Leaphorn.

Leaphorn had been doing some listening, too, but mostly he was enjoying his role as passenger—a position that policemen almost never hold. He had wasted a few moments trying to remember the last time he had rolled down a highway without being the driver. Then he concentrated on enjoying the experience, savoring the beauty of the landscape, the pattern of cloud shadows on the hills—all those details you miss when you're navigating through traffic—happy to surrender the job of staring at the center stripe, reading road signs, and so forth, to Sergeant Garcia.

Anyway a lot of what Garcia was telling him was already stored in his memory. It dealt with the old double murder of an elderly couple named Handy at their place of business. It had been so ruthlessly coldhearted that it had put Ray Shewnack right up among the FBI's blue ribbon Most Wanted felons, advertised in post offices across the nation. But most of what Leaphorn had learned had been just hearsay filtered through police coffee talks. With Garcia he was hearing it right from the horse's mouth. Or almost. Garcia had been too green to be at the middle of the first chase. But he'd been deeply involved in the cleanup work.

"Funny thing, Joe. Naturally it seemed downright too evil to believe for me back then. I was just a rookie. Hadn't seen a lot of violent crime." Garcia shook his head, laughed. "But here I am now. Seen just about everything from incest murders to just-for-fun killings, and it still shocks me when I think about it."

"You don't mean the robbery itself," Leaphorn said. "You mean . . ."

"Well, not exactly. I mean the coldhearted and clever way Shewnack set it up. The way he used his partners and then betrayed them. Planning things so he could use his friends sort of as bait while he was driving away with all the loot. And that's why I've always thought we should have taken a harder look at the Totter fire. Some people really, really, really hated Shewnack. And I have to admit he did give 'em a damn good reason to want to burn him to death." He laughed. "Burn him now. Sort of get a jump on the devil."

Although Leaphorn's Navajo culture hardly allowed even good reasons for hatred, he had to admit Shewnack had given Benny Begay, Tomas Delonie, and Ellie McFee some unusually strong causes for resentment. Ellie, as Garcia explained it, had been the clerk and cashier at the Big Handy's service station/grocery store/trading post at the Chinli junction.

She had been, so she had told police, Shewnack's girlfriend and soon to be his bride. But that would be after the robbery. Leading up to that she was the way Shewnack knew that Mr. Handy kept his accumulated sales collections in a backroom safe and made his deposits in a Gallup bank just once a month. So Shewnack had assigned Ellie her job in the robbery and told her that when it was over she should wait at a roadside turnout for him to pick her up and take her away to be married. She stayed there with her suitcase and waited until two Coconino County deputies came looking for her.

"She seemed like a nice young woman," Garcia said. "Not a real good looker, and too chunky for the taste of some, but nice eyes, nice smile." He shook his head. "Not that she was doing much smiling when I was talking to her. She told me it had taken her a long time to believe that Shewnack was the one who had tipped off the cops about where to find her. And she still didn't seem to really believe he'd done that to her."

"I guess it was quite a contrast to the honeymoon trip he'd had her expecting," Leaphorn said.

"How about that for a reason for some hatred?" Garcia asked. "Hell hath no fury like a woman scorned, they say."

He glanced at Leaphorn. "Scorned and betrayed. And she was out and about when Shewnack got burned up. She'd gone to prison, done her years, earned some time off for good behavior, and then got a quick parole."

"So she's your suspect?" Leaphorn asked, and grinned. "I mean if the feds hadn't taken over and ruled it was an accidental death."

"Well, maybe," Garcia said. "Delonie was still in stir when it happened. Benny Begay was just out on parole, but Benny didn't seem like a killer to me. Or to anyone else. The judge agreed. He gave him just five to seven and he got that shortened with nothing but good conduct reports. Besides, he hadn't had much to do with the crime."

Begay, Garcia explained, had been sort of a stock boy, cleanup man, and gasoline pumper at Handy's place. His role in the crime was disconnecting the telephone to delay the call for police help. Tomas Delonie was the outside man—assigned to be there, armed with pistol and shotgun to make sure no one came along and interrupted the action. After that, Shewnack had instructed him to collect Benny and drive them both down that unimproved road that leads from Chinli down through Beautiful Valley. There they waited on a trail down into Bis-E ah Wash for Shewnack, to come by and deliver their half of the loot. They did exactly what he'd told them to do. The story he told them to give to the police was that they hadn't actually seen the robbery. They were to say they saw Shewnack drive away, suspected something bad had happened, tried to follow him in Delonie's pickup, but had lost him. They were to wait by the road about three hours, then return to the store and report what happened to the police who, Shewnack explained to them, would surely be there by then.

"Of course it didn't work that way," Garcia said. "Here's the way it actually went. Shewnack drove up to Handy's place in his pickup truck, walked in, pointed his pistol at Mr. Handy, and demanded all the cash. Handy started to argue. Shewnack shot him three times. Then Mrs. Handy came running in to see who was shooting, and Shewnack shot her twice. Ellie told me that she had started screaming then because Shewnack had promised her nobody would get hurt. So he hustled her into the back room, filled the sacks Ellie had kept there for him with money from the safe. The safe was standing open because Ellie had signaled him to come in just when Handy was starting his daily job of adding the day's revenue to the stash."

"Signaled?" Leaphorn said. "How?"

Garcia laughed. "Nothing very high tech. She went to the window and pulled down the blind. Just as Shewnack had instructed her. She said the plan was for Shewnack to tie up her and Handy, have Benny and Tomas take off pretending to chase him, then wait for him at a pickup place in the Bis-E ah Wash. He'd come there and they'd divide up the loot. He told her he'd have a bottle of chloroform to put Handy to sleep and he'd pretend to do the same with her. She was supposed to wait ten minutes after hearing him drive off and then reconnect the telephone and call the law."

Garcia shook his head, chuckled.

"She told the highway patrol Shewnack had told her to sound totally hysterical. He even had her practice screaming and sobbing into the telephone."

"Sounds like he would have made a pretty efficient professional criminal," Leaphorn said. "Guess he did. Didn't the federals have him as a top suspect in a couple of other robberies after that?"

"Yeah," Garcia agreed. "A whole bunch of them. Jobs with a sort of similar MO. But maybe some other bad guys had heard about it and were copying the system. Anyway, Ellie said that practicing hysteria wasn't necessary. Once she saw Shewnack shooting Handy, and then killing Mrs. Handy when the old lady came rushing in, the hysteria was genuine. Came naturally."

Leaphorn found himself feeling sympathy for Ellie.

Before the long evening was over, Garcia continued, police had received another excited call, telling them that two suspicious-looking young men, one armed with a pistol, were parked down in Bis-E ah Wash. The caller said the two ran up to his truck when he drove down the track there, looked at him, and then waved him on. Who was he? Well, the call was from an old-fashioned short-wave radio; the caller said he was Horse Hauler Mike, and a word or two later the radio shorted out—as was usual those days. When the state police showed up at Tomas Delonie's pickup in the wash, Delonie said no such truck driver, or anyone else, had come by since they got there. They insisted they knew nothing of the robbery, but since Shewnack had handed them one of the sacks Ellie had left with a little bit of the loot in it, that didn't seem credible to the policemen.

"I guess that does sort of establish a new level in ratting out your partners," Leaphorn said. "I mean, setting it up before the crime happens so you don't have to split the loot and arranging for the police to get them quick so they're not chasing you. I'd say any of those three would have motive for burning Shewnack."

Garcia shook his head. "Of course only Ellie was free when Shewnack was cremated, but maybe the others could have arranged something. Communicated with friends on the outside. But how would they have known where to find Shewnack? You have any ideas to offer on that?"

"Not offhand," Leaphorn said. "I'd have to know their families. And their friends. But it sounds pretty near impossible to me."

"Yeah," Garcia said. "I did a little casual asking around and got nothing. Well, anyway they're all out now. Like I said, Ellie got part of her five-year sentence whacked off for good behavior. She was living at Gallup last I heard. Delonie got a twenty-five-year rap, and Begay's was a lot shorter. But I've heard that Begay's dead. When he got out, he got married and he and his wife lived up near Teec Nos Pos. Worked as a sheep shearer, handy man, so forth. Supposed to have learned a lot about working with tools and fixing things in the penitentiary, and for a while he worked for a sporting goods store in Farmington. Mostly from what I heard repairing outboard motors, sporting equipment, things like that. I remember the first time I saw him after he was paroled he was helping out at one of those booths at the Four Corners Monument parking place. Very cool about it. Said he'd had an enemy way cure. Got himself restored to harmony. He sounded like he was very much occupied with forgetting his old mistakes. And all those bad years."

"You say Begay's dead now. How'd that happen?"

"Shot himself," Garcia said.

"You mean suicide?"

"No. Not Benny. I guess he wasn't as good at fixing as he thought he was. He had taken some stuff home from the Fish and Hunt Shop over the weekend to repair it. Had himself a workbench in his garage, and when his wife got home from whatever she was doing, he was there on the floor. And one of those old German World War II pistols on the floor beside him. A Walther. The one they called the P-38. The magazine was out of it on the table, but the empty shell casing was still in the chamber." Garcia looked at Leaphorn, shrugged.

"That's how it can happen," Leaphorn said. "Working with an unfamiliar weapon. You think you unloaded it and you didn't. No sign of foul play?"

"That was over here in New Mexico," Garcia said. "Not my case, but I doubt it. Probably handled by the San Juan County sheriff. Wouldn't be any reason to be suspicious. Who'd want to kill Benny Begay?"

"Good question," Leaphorn said. He found himself trying to visualize how Begay, a gunsmith then by practice, had managed to point that pistol at his head and pull the trigger. He'd extracted the magazine. What was he doing. Peering into the pistol barrel. That would make no sense.

Garcia studied Leaphorn. "You know, you Navajos have a lot of damn fine ideas in your culture."

"Yes," Leaphorn said. "And we have a lot of trouble these days sticking to them. Begay managed it, I guess. But how about Delonie. Was he that forgiving?"

Garcia laughed "Delonie's no Navajo. I think he is part Pottawatomie, or maybe it's Seminole. He wasn't quite like Ellie and Begay, who were clean as a whistle.

Delonie had already accumulated himself a little rap sheet. He'd done a little time in the Oklahoma reformatory as a juvenile, and then got himself arrested as an adult for stealing cars out of parking lots. The cops who worked Handy's case from the beginning told me Delonie might have been the reason it happened."

Leaphorn considered that, raised his eyebrows, provoking Garcia to explain what he meant.

"You know how it sometimes works. A professional robbery type looking for a way to make some money asks around among the proper level of citizens for some locals who might have spotted a likely job, and so forth. He hears about Delonie. Checks with him. Delonie says Handy's looks ripe for a robbery. Shewnack offers to buy in. Something like that. You know what I mean?"

"Sure," Leaphorn said. "I remember the double murder years ago on old Route 66 near the Laguna Reservation. At Budville. Bud Rice and someone else shot. Turned out a bandit type from Alabama or somewhere shopped around in Albuquerque for someone to rob, paid the locals a fee, they provided him a car, all the information, he did the job and got away."

"Killed himself in prison," Garcia said.

"But doing time for another crime," Leaphorn said. "He decided to confess to the Budville murders before he died. But you're saying the thinking was that Shewnack had contacted Delonie, offered to organize the crime for him?"

"The thinking is Shewnack showed up in Albuquerque, hanging around in the bars where the hard guys do their socializing, let it be known he was ready for some action, heard about Delonie. Having a hard-guy reputation, so forth."

"Sounds reasonable," Leaphorn said.

"Anyway, whether or not robbing Handy's was Delonie's original idea, I don't think he gets the blame for the way Shewnack set them all up. He told his parole officer that Ellie was his girlfriend. He was going to marry her, or so he thought, before Shewnack showed up and wooed her away from him and then wrecked her life. Apparently he talked about that a lot in prison. Anyway, his parole was passed over the first time because the board heard he'd been telling other cons he was going to hunt down the son of a bitch who'd ratted on him and kill him. He didn't get out until early this year."

"How's he doing since then?" Leaphorn asked.

Garcia shrugged. "Okay, I guess. His parole officer told me he's been checking in and behaving himself. Turns out Delonie was sort of like Begay in prison. Turned himself into a skilled laborer. Got to be an electrician, plumber, that sort of thing. Good with fixing things—from your refrigerator to your truck. He married a Navajo woman over near Torrejón, and I think he does maintenance and general handyman stuff over at the chapter house out there."

Leaphorn considered that. "Wonder how he managed that?"

"What I heard, he's married to a woman who's involved with that Christian mission place out there, and she's one of the people working at the chapter house. Keeps the records or something," Garcia said. "I've heard some gossip that the marriage didn't last long. But he didn't have Delonie on his 'watch out for trouble' list."

Leaphorn sighed.

Garcia chuckled. "You sound disappointed."

"Well, I'm just beginning to wonder what we think

we're looking for out here. Where we are now with what we know, all we could take to the district attorney's office is a funny feeling. Not a hint of evidence about anything." He laughed. "I guess we could tell him we just don't feel right about that Shewnack death, and that fire either, and that maybe somebody stole an antique rug, and so forth, and if it was a murder, the one with the best motive would be Delonie. And then he reminds us that Delonie was in custody when Totter's place burned and that he could call in a whole crowd of prison guards to back up his alibi, and about then the D.A. would recommend that we make an appointment to see a shrink."

Garcia laughed. "I'm beginning to think that might not be a bad idea."

"Well," Leaphorn said, "I have to admit that all I have is that funny feeling I started with. The arson experts said there was no evidence of any kerosene or gasoline, or any of those fire spreaders arsonists use. Totter's insurance company lawyers must have worked that over very thoroughly."

"You think so?"

"Well, from what I've heard, Totter collected on a lot of valuable stuff burned with his store. So they would have done some looking."

"Which brings us back to that damned rug," Garcia said. "Bork didn't seem to think it burned after he saw that picture. So we have us a clever insurance fraud arson with Shewnack burned up by accident. Or maybe burned on purpose to provide the careless drunk starting it with a cigarette."

Garcia paused, waiting a Leaphorn reaction. Got none, and went on.

"Or maybe Totter killed him for some reason or other, and needed to dispose of the body, and then added in a little insurance fraud as a by-product."

Leaphorn didn't comment.

"I'll bet you'd already thought about that," Garcia said.

"Well, yes," Leaphorn said. "And I admit I'd like to know more about the fire. But nobody's likely to help us reopen that case. Just think about it. The FBI was just delighted to get Shewnack's name off its list after all those years. They won't be eager to prove they missed the fact somebody murdered him."

"And who's around these days who cares?" Garcia asked.

"There's me," Leaphorn said. "And then there's the man who made that call to Mel Bork. That caller seemed to care. He didn't want Mel messing with Shewnack's old ashes."

Garcia nodded.

"You have any idea who made that call?" Leaphorn said.

"I wish I did. And I've got a puzzle you could solve for me. How did you get involved in this business? What's your interest?"

"I showed you Bork's letter."

"I meant what got you into it in the first place."

"I wasn't really into it," Leaphorn said. "I was out here looking into a sort of funny burglary of an old woman's hogan. She and her daughter weave baskets out of willow, or reeds, then waterproof them with sap from pinyon trees and sell them to tourists. Anyway, somebody drove up while the old lady was away, broke into the shed where they do their work, and stole about ten gallons of that sap. Captain Skeet—you remember him? I was a rookie then, and he sent me out to investigate and then had me drop that and go over to see what the federals were so excited about at Totter's place."

"Day or so after the fire then?"

"Yeah, when they went through all the victim's stuff and found out he was Shewnack."

Garcia was looking thoughtful. "Who stole that pinyon sap?"

Leaphorn laughed. "I guess you'd have to add that to your list of cold cases. The granddaughter said she saw a blue sedan roaring away. It looked to her like it might be almost new. Didn't get a look at the driver and didn't get a license number. She said there wasn't a license plate on the bumper, but maybe one of those paper dealer's permits was on the back window. Said it looked shiny new."

"What else was stolen?"

"That was it, so they said. Just two big old lard buckets filled with pinyon sap."

Garcia shook his head, shrugged. "Maybe they needed the buckets."

"Or, let's try this idea. Maybe Shewnack had taken that job with Totter intending to rob him. Sort of a repeat of the Handy affair. Let's say Totter resisted, killed Shewnack, decided to dispose of the body, and he knew that pinyon sap would get things hot enough to turn Shewnack into ashes. How about that idea?"

"Yes, indeed," Garcia said. "And since everybody around here burns pinyon as firewood, it wouldn't look suspicious to arson inspectors. Totter could get a profit out of it."

They drove in silence then until Garcia pointed to the slope ahead, to what was left of the old Totter's Trading Post. The soot-blackened adobe walls still stood. The old grocery store was mostly intact, as was an adjoining stone structure that had been Totter's residence. But its doors were missing and its window frames were also empty.

"Scene of the crime," Garcia said. "Except officially it wasn't a crime. Just another fire caused by lighting up that last cigarette when you're too drunk to know what you're doing."

"Look's like someone has done a little pilfering anyway," Leaphorn said.

Garcia laughed. "You could probably find those doors and window frames built into some sheep herder's place," he said. "But Totter sold the place after he collected his insurance loot. And the buyer never did anything with it. Don't think you could get the D.A. to file any charges."

As they neared the junction of the eroded trail that had been the access road to Totter's parking lot, Leaphorn noticed Garcia was slowing, and he saw why. That road seemed to have had some fairly recent traffic.

"See that?" Garcia said, pointing to the tire tracks through the weeds. "I'll bet I can tell you who did that. Ever since Delonie got his parole, I've had this old case on my mind. And when I heard that telephone threat to Mel Bork, and you told me about that rug, I've had a yen to come up here and look around."

Leaphorn nodded. "So you wanted to see if Delonie would return to the scene of his crime?"

"Not exactly that, because it couldn't be his crime.

If it was a crime. I just thought he'd be, ah, well, let's say, curious."

"Seems logical, since Delonie just got out," Leaphorn said. "But here's the way my mind works. Delonie knows Shewnack got away from that Handy robbery with a bagful of cash. Delonie probably knows no large sums were found with the body. Shewnack wouldn't have kept a big bundle in his pockets while he was working here. He probably intended to rob Totter's too, when he could set it up properly. So there's a good chance that Shewnack found himself a place right here, or near enough to be handy, to stash away his funds."

"Exactly," Garcia said. "And Delonie would come looking for it." He was grinning. "I guess us cops all get into the habit of thinking the same way," he said. "I'll bet we find some places where somebody's been digging."

They were bumping up the access road now toward what fire, weather, and inattention had left of Totter's Trading Post.

"Or maybe still digging," Leaphorn said. He pointed past the wall of the main structure to a vehicle protruding from behind it. "Dark green. Looks like a Cherokee."

As he spoke, a man stepped through the empty doorway of the building. He stood staring at them. A tall man in a plaid shirt, much-faded blue jeans, long billed cap, and sunglasses. His hair needed trimming, and so did a short but scraggly beard.

"I do believe I recognize Mr. Tomas Delonie," Kelly Garcia said. "Which means this is going to save me the trouble of driving all over looking for him."

9

Tomas Delonie's reaction to the arrival of a police car and a deputy sheriff was just what Leaphorn had learned to expect from ex-cons out on parole. He was a big man, a little stooped, looking tense, slightly defensive, and generally unfriendly. Not moving, hands by his sides. Just waiting for whatever fate had in store for him.

Leaphorn sat watching. Garcia got out, shut the door behind him, said: "Mr. Delonie? You remember me?"

The man nodded. "Yes."

"Deputy Sheriff Kelly Garcia," Garcia said. "Glad to see you again. I was hoping to get a chance to talk to you."

"Talk?" Delonie said. "About what?"

"About this place here," Garcia said with a sweeping gesture. "About what happened here?"

"I don't know a damn thing about that," Delonie said. "I was up there in the New Mexico State Prison.

Near Santa Fe. Long way from here when that was happening."

Leaphorn got out of the car, nodded to Delonie.

"This is Mr. Joe Leaphorn," Garcia said. "He's interested in what happened here too."

"Oh?" Delonie said, looking slightly surprised. "I wonder why that would be? Is he an insurance man? Or a cop? Or what?"

"Just curious, I guess, about what could be found. And so are you," Garcia said. "Or you wouldn't be here. So we have something in common to talk about."

Delonie nodded. Looking at Leaphorn.

Leaphorn smiled. "Have you found anything yet?"

Delonie's expression abruptly changed from his stolid neutral pose. His mouth twisted, his eyes pinched shut, his head bowed. "What do you mean by that?" Delonie said, his voice strangled.

"I meant, maybe you might have been looking for something Ray Shewnack might have left behind for you."

"That dirty son of a bitch," Delonie said, the words pronounced with heavy, well-spaced emphasis. "He wouldn't leave anything for me."

"You mean Raymond Shewnack?" Leaphorn said.

"That bastard." Delonie wiped the back of his hand across his eyes, looked up at Leaphorn. "No, I didn't find a damned thing."

Garcia cleared his throat. "What are you looking for?"

"This is the place where the federals claim he got burned up, isn't it? I was looking for just a tiny little bit of what that bastard owed me," Delonie said.

"You mean like part of the money out of old man Handy's safe?" Garcia asked.

"That'd be just fine," Delonie said, wiping his eyes again. "If I found all of it, it wouldn't cover what he owes me."

"I don't think there'd be enough money in the whole world to cover what he did to you," Leaphorn said. "Not for the way he treated all of you at Handy's."

"Well . . ." Delonie said, staring at Leaphorn. He nodded.

"You know, if you do find a bunch of money," Garcia said, "or anything valuable, you'd have to—"

"Sure, sure," Delonie said. "I know the law. I'd turn it all in. I know that. I was just curious."

"Any place in the store there where we can sit down and talk?" Garcia asked.

Totter's store had been pretty thoroughly stripped of furniture, but a table with bench seating had been shoved against a wall amid a jumble of fallen shelving. Delonie sat on the table bench. Garcia stood looking at him. Leaphorn wandered to the back door, noticing how lines of dust blown in through the vacant windows had formed across the floor, observing the piles of leaves in the corners, thinking how quickly nature moved to restore the damage done by man. He looked out at the burned remains of the gallery section, remembering how a typical torrential rain of the monsoon season had arrived in time to save this part of the Handy's establishment. But not much left of the adjoining Indian artifacts gallery or its storage room where Shewnack had his sleeping space. Where Shewnack's cigarette had ignited the fire. Where Shewnack was too drunk to awaken. Where Shewnack had burned to bones and ashes. Behind him Garcia was asking Delonie what he had been doing lately, where he was working.

Leaphorn walked out into the yard, around the building, toward Delonie's vehicle. It was a dirty Jeep Cherokee, middle-aged, with the dents and crunches of hard use. A brown woolen blanket was folded on the front seat. Through the driver's-side window he could see nothing interesting. Scanning through the rear side windows revealed only Delonie's habit of tossing old hamburger wrappers and beer cans there instead of into garbage cans. He lifted the rear door, checked around, found nothing. On the passenger's side, he opened the front door, felt under the seat, extracted an old New Mexico road map, put it back. Checked the glove box and found it locked. Checked the door pockets. Another New Mexico road map, newer version. Stared at the folded blanket, detecting the shape of something under it. He reached in and lifted the end of it. It was covering a rifle.

Leaphorn folded the blanket back. The rifle was an old model Savage 30-30, a fairly typical type of deer rifle that had been popular when he was young. What was less typical was the telescopic sight mounted on it. That looked new. Leaphorn pulled the blanket back over the rifle, restored its folds, and walked back into the building.

Delonie was shaking his head, looking grim.

"So you didn't just get out here today?" Garcia asked.

"Yesterday," Delonie said. "I'm about ready to give up."

"You just came looking for anything useful Shewnack might have had that didn't get burned up with him?"

"Like I said, I figured if he had any money with him,

if he was planning to stay with Totter as a hired hand, he might have tucked it away someplace safe. Maybe buried it. Hid it under something."

"But you didn't find anything?"

"Not yet."

"You think you will?"

Delonie thought a while. "I guess not. I think I'm ready to quit looking." He sighed, took a deep breath, looked down. "Don't know," he said. "I guess maybe I found what I really wanted. I wanted to just see for myself that the bastard was really dead." He looked up at Garcia, then at Leaphorn. Forced a smile. "Get closure. Isn't that what the shrinks are calling it now? Put it behind you.

"Mr. Leaphorn here, if he's a Navajo like he looks, then he'd know about that. They have that curing ceremony to help them forgive and forget when they get screwed. Bennie Begay, he had one of those. An enemy way ceremony, he said it was."

"You look like you might be Indian," Leaphorn said. "Not Navajo?"

"Part Pottawatomie, part Seminole," Delonie said. "Probably part French, too. We never had such a ceremony. Neither tribe. But maybe just seeing where the bastard burned up will work for me. Anyway, it gave me a little satisfaction. Maybe it wasn't as hot as the hell he's enjoying now but it must have been next to it. People who knew this place said Totter stored his firewood in that gallery back room where Shewnack was sleeping. That wood burns hot."

That provoked a brief, thoughtful silence.

Leaphorn cleared his throat. "This Shewnack must have been quite a man," he said. "I'm thinking about the

the way he sucked all of you into that plot he was working up. Sounds like he was awful damn persuasive. A genuine, bona fide charmer."

Delonie produced a bitter-sounding laugh. "You bet. I remember Ellie saying he was the prettiest man she ever saw." He laughed again. "Anyway, a lot prettier than me."

"I don't think there's anything in the records about where he came from. Was he a local man? Family? Anything like that? If he had any criminal record, it must have been under some other name."

"He told us he was from California, or somewhere out on the West Coast," Delonie said. "But after Ellie got to know him, she said he was actually from San Francisco. Great talker, though. Always smiling, always cheerful. Never said anything bad about anybody or anything. Seemed to know just about everything." Delonie stopped, shook his head, gave Leaphorn a wry smile. "For example, how to unlock a locked car, or jump-start it; how to avoid leaving fingerprints. He even showed me and Bennie Begay how to get out of those plastic cuffs highway patrolmen carry."

"You think he had a record?" Leaphorn asked.

"I think maybe he used to be a policeman," Delonie said. "He seemed to know so much about cops and law enforcement. But I don't know. Then I thought maybe he had worked in a machine shop or something like that. He seemed to know a lot about construction and machinery. But with him, I think most of what he was saying was just sort of talk intended to give you a phony idea of who he was. Or had been." He shook his head and chuckled. "I remember a preacher we used to listen to when I was a boy. He'd have called Shewnack the 'Father of Liars.'"

"Like the devil himself," Garcia said.

"Yep," Delonie said, "exactly."

"Did he ever talk about what he'd done for a living?" he asked. "Any mention at all?"

Delonie shook his head. "Not really. Anytime anyone got serious about things like that he'd say something about there being lots of easy ways to get money. Once he made a crack about how coyotes know you don't have to raise chickens to eat them."

"Quite a guy," Garcia said. "Well, look, Mr. Delonie, if you do decide to look some more, and you find anything, I want you to give me a call." He handed Delonie his card. "And don't forget to keep checking in with your parole officer."

"Yeah," Leaphorn said, "and you should—" But he stopped. Why inject himself into this until he knew a lot more than he did. Delonie would know that parolees were not allowed to possess firearms.

10

It was quiet in the patrol car until it had rolled down the last hump of the old Totter's Trading Post access track and was reaching the junction of the gravel road.

"If you do a left here, we could take a three-or-so-mile detour and get to Grandma Peshlakai's place," Leaphorn said. "Wouldn't take long. Unless you have something else to do."

Garcia glanced at him, looking surprised. "You want to do that?"

"I'd like to see if she ever got her pinyon sap back. Or found out who stole it. Or anything."

"Well, why not? That would probably be as useful as anything we learned here."

They came to a culvert bridging the borrow ditch beside the county road. Up the hillside beyond it was an old-fashioned dirt-topped hogan; a zinc water tank sat atop a platform beside it. Behind it was a slab-sided outhouse, a rusty-looking camping trailer, and a sheep pen with a loading ramp. Garcia slowed.

"That it?"

"Yep," Leaphorn said.

"Probably nobody home," Garcia said. "I don't see any vehicles."

"There's that old tire hanging on the gate post though," Leaphorn said, pointing. "Most people out here, they take that off when they leave the hogan."

"Yeah. Some of 'em still do," Garcia said. "But that old custom is sort of dying out. Tells the neighbors it's safe to come in and see what they can steal."

Leaphorn frowned, and Garcia noticed it.

"Didn't mean that as an insult," Garcia said.

"Trouble is, it's true."

"Well, times change," Garcia said, looking apologetic. "It ain't like it used to be."

But it was at the Peshlakai place. As they drove up the track and stopped east of the hogan, a woman pulled back the carpet hanging across the doorway and stepped out.

Leaphorn got out of the car, nodded to her, said, *"Ya eeh teh."*

She acknowledged that, nodded, looked surprised, and laughed. "Hey," she said. "Are you that policeman that made Grandma so mad years and years ago?"

Leaphorn grinned. "I guess so, and I came to apologize. Is she here?"

"No, no," the girl said. "She's gone off to Austin Sam's place. He's one of her grandsons, and she's taking care of one of her great-grandchildren. She does that for him some when Austin is off doing political campaigning. Running for the Tribal Council seat in his district."

Leaphorn considered that a moment, wondering how old Grandma Peshlakai would be now. In her nineties at least, he was thinking, and still working.

"I'm sorry I missed her. Please tell her I said, *Ya eeh teh*."

This very mature woman, he was thinking, must be Elandra, who had been a lot younger when he'd first met her.

"Elandra, this man here is Sergeant Garcia, a deputy with the sheriff's office down in Flagstaff."

The glad-to-meet-yous were exchanged, and Elandra, looking puzzled, held back the doorway carpet and invited them in. "I don't have anything ready to offer you," she said, "but I could make some coffee."

Leaphorn was shaking his head. "Oh, no," he said. "I just came by to see your grandmother." He paused, looking embarrassed. "And I was wondering if anything new had come up in that burglary you had."

Elandra's eyes widened. "Lots of years gone by since then. Lot of things happened."

"Long ago as it was, I always felt sorry that I couldn't stay on that case. I got called away by my boss because the federals wanted help on that fire at the Totter store."

Elandra's expression made it clear that she remembered. She laughed.

"I'll tell her you told her 'ya eeh teh,' but telling Grandma to 'be cool' isn't going to do it. She's still mad at you for running off without finding that pinyon sap." Then she had another sudden memory. "In fact, long time ago when she was going off to help with Austin's kids, she said you had told her you would come back sometime to deal with that stolen sap problem, and she left something for me to give you if you did. Just a minute. I'll see if I can find it."

It was closer to five minutes later when Elandra emerged from the bedroom. She was carrying a sheet of notebook paper folded together and clasped with two hairpins. She grinned at Leaphorn and handed it to him. On it was printed in pencil: TO THAT BOY POLICEMAN.

"That wasn't my idea," Elandra said. "She was mad at you. What she wanted to write was worse than that."

"I guess I should read it?" Leaphorn said.

Elandra nodded.

Inside was the neatly penciled message:

Young policeman.

Get my sap back here before it spoils. If not, get back $10 for each bucketful, and $5 for each bucket. Rather have sap. Otherwise $30.

Garcia had been watching all this, his expression amused.

"What does it say?" he asked. "That is, if it's not secret."

Leaphorn read it to him.

Garcia nodded. "You know how much time and labor goes into collecting that damned pinyon sap," he said. "Did you ever try to get sticky stuff off of you? I'd say that thirty dollars would be a very fair price."

Leaphorn put the note in his shirt pocket.

Elandra looked slightly abashed. "Grandma is usually very polite. But she thought you were practicing racial discrimination against us Indians. Remember? Or maybe she just wanted somebody to blame."

"Well, I could see her point."

"You want to know if we got our pinyon sap back?"

"Anything at all you can tell me about that."

Elandra laughed. "We didn't recover any sap, but Grandma Peshlakai did get our buckets back. So I guess you should cut ten dollars off that bill."

Garcia's eyebrows rose. "Got the buckets back? Well, now," he said.

Leaphorn drew in a breath. "She recovered the buckets?" he said. "Tell me how she managed to do that."

"Well, after that fire at Totter's place, Grandma had been asking around everywhere. Right from the start she had the notion that Totter might have gotten that sap." She laughed. "She thought he was going to start making his own baskets. Compete with us. Anyway, she noticed people were going over there after Mr. Totter moved with what was left of his stuff. And they were picking up things. Walking away with it. Just taking things away." She paused.

"Like stealing stuff?" Garcia said.

Elandra nodded. "So Grandma rode over there and looked around, and she came back with our buckets."

Leaphorn leaned forward. "Where were they?"

"I don't know exactly. She said they were laying out by the porch. Or maybe out by the back door. I don't really remember."

"Empty buckets?" Leaphorn said.

Elandra nodded. "And dented up some, too," she said. "But they still hold water."

Leaphorn noticed that Garcia was grinning. That turned into a chuckle.

"I guess we could make a burglary-theft case against Totter now, Joe. If we knew where he moved to when he left here. You want to try?"

Leaphorn was embarrassed. In no mood to be joshed.

"I think it would be a good idea to find out where he went," he said. "Remember, one of his hired hands burned to death in that fire."

"Okay, okay," Garcia said. "I didn't mean that to sound like I was joking."

"Well, then—" Leaphorn began, but Elandra violated the "never interrupt" rule of her tribe.

"You don't know where he is?" she said. She shook her head. "You don't know about Mr. Totter? You don't know he's dead?"

"Dead?" Garcia said.

"How do you know that?" Leaphorn asked.

"It was in the newspaper," she said. "After Grandma found the buckets, and knew for sure Mr. Totter had stolen our pinyon sap, she had a real angry spell. Really mad about it. So everywhere she went she would tell people about what he'd done and ask about him. And quite a while later somebody in a store where she was buying something told her Totter had died. He told her he'd seen it in the newspaper. That's how we knew."

"What newspaper?" Leaphorn asked.

"She was in Gallup, I think. I guess it was the Gallup paper."

"The *Gallup Independent*," Garcia said.

"Was it a news story about his being killed? Shot? Or in an accident?"

"I don't know," Elandra said. "But I don't think so. I

think the man said it was one of those little pieces where they tell where you're going to be buried, and who your relatives are, for sending flowers, all that."

"An obituary item, I guess," Garcia said.

"Well, since we know within a year or two when that was printed, I guess we can track that down," Leaphorn said.

As he said it, he was wishing that Sergeant Jim Chee and Officer Bernadette Manuelito were not off somewhere on their honeymoon. Otherwise, retired or not, he could talk Chee into going down to Gallup and digging through their microfiche files of back copies until he found it. Or maybe Chee could talk Bernie into doing it for him. She'd get it done quicker, and not come back with the wrong obituary.

11

Back in Flagstaff, back in his own car, with farewells said to Sergeant Garcia, an agreement reached that they had pretty well wasted a tiresome day and a lot of the sheriff's department's gasoline budget, Leaphorn again pulled into the Burger King parking lot. He sat. Organized his thoughts.

Was he too tired to drive all the way back to Shiprock tonight? Probably. But the alternative was renting a cold and uncomfortable motel room, making futile and frustrating efforts to adjust the air conditioner, and generally feeling disgusted. Then he'd have to awaken in the morning, stiff from a night on a strange mattress, and do the long drive anyway. He went in, got a cup of coffee and a hamburger for dinner. Halfway through that meal, and halfway through the list of things he had to do before he went back and told Mrs. Bork that he had absolutely no good news for her about her missing husband, he got up and went back out to his pickup. He extracted the cell phone from the glove box, returned with it to his waiting hamburger, and carefully punched in Jim Chee's home number. Maybe Chee and Bernie would be back from their honeymoon. Maybe not.

They were.

"Hello," Chee said, sounding sort of grumpy.

"Chee. This is Joe Leaphorn. How busy are you?"

"Ah. Um. Lieutenant Leaphorn? Well, um. Well, we just got back and . . ."

This statement trailed off unfinished, was followed by a moment of silence and then a sigh and the clearing of a throat.

"What do you want me to do?" Chee asked.

"Ah, um. Is there any chance you'd be going down to Gallup pretty soon?"

"Like when?"

"Well, maybe tomorrow?"

Chee laughed. "You know, Lieutenant, this reminds me of old times."

"Too busy, I guess," Leaphorn said, sadly.

"What do you want me to do?"

"I know you and Bernie are newlyweds," Leaphorn said. "So why don't you take her along."

"I probably would," Chee said. "But to do what?"

"It takes a while to explain," Leaphorn said, and explained it, Navajo style, starting at the beginning. And when he finished he waited for a reaction.

"That's it?" Chee asked, after waiting a polite moment to be sure he wasn't interrupting.

"Yes."

"You want me to prowl through back issues of the

Gallup Independent looking for that Totter obituary, find it, get them to make a copy of it for you, and then find someone old enough to remember when they received it and how, and who brought it in, and—"

"Or mailed it in. Or called it in," Leaphorn said. "But I'll bet Miss Manuelito would be good at all that."

"Probably better than me, because she's organized and patient. Yes. But Lieutenant, she's not Miss Manuelito now, she's Mrs. Bernadette Chee."

"Sorry," Leaphorn said.

"And it was probably published years ago after that fire at Totter's Trading Post. There'd be a story about finding the burned man who was a star figure on the FBI bad boy list, I guess. I could look for that story, and then skip ahead a few months to make sure I didn't miss it, and then keep looking for a couple of years. Right?"

"Well, I think they have it on microfiche. You know. You just push the button and it gives you the next page, and skip the full-page ads, and the sports pages."

"How soon do you need it?" Chee asked. "And can you explain why again? It sounded sort of vague."

"I guess it is sort of vague. I just have a general feeling that something is very peculiar about this whole business." He paused, thinking. "Tell you what, Jim, I want to think about this some more. Maybe I'm just wasting everybody's time. Just put it on hold until I call you back."

"You mean the fire was peculiar?"

Leaphorn sighed. "That and everything else."

"Well," Chee said, " I guess . . . Wait a second, here's Bernie."

And the next voice Leaphorn heard was that of Mrs. Bernadette Chee, sounding happy, exuberant, asking about his health, about Professor Louisa Bourbonette, about what he was doing, had he actually retired and, finally, wondering what he and Chee were talking about.

Leaphorn told her.

"Tomorrow?" Bernie asked. "Sure. We'd be happy to take care of that. Have you explained to Jim what you need?"

"Well, yes," Leaphorn said. Then thought a second. "Just sort of explained," he added, and went through it all again.

"Okay, Lieutenant," Bernie said. "How soon do you need it and what's your cell phone number?"

Leaphorn gave it to her. "But hold off until I understand what in the world I'm doing," he said. "And welcome home, Bernie."

"It's Mrs. Chee, now," she said.

12

Joe Leaphorn awakened unusually late the next morning. Just as he had expected, his back was stiff, his head
was stuffy from a night of breathing air-conditioned motel
air, and his mood was glum. Exactly what he had anticipated. The foreboding that had caused him to decide to
drive back to Shiprock last night instead of enduring the
motel was justified. But talking with Chee and Bernie,
two youngsters, had made him face the fact that he was
old and too weary to be a safe nighttime driver when the
drunks were on the highways. So now he was still in Flagstaff, and the long drive still confronted him.

But the sleeplessness provoked by the lumpy motel
mattress had caused him to do a lot of thinking, each toss
and turn changing the subject of his speculation. First,
he had covered what he would say to Mrs. Bork. Since he
was, alas, still here in Flagstaff, he should call her right
now, not leave her biting her nails with worry. Telling her

he hadn't learned anything useful wouldn't help much,
but courtesy demanded it. Next, he decided he had to
quit stalling and set up a meeting with this Jason Delos
fellow, who seemed to have that damned rug, or at least
a copy of it, and find out where he had obtained it. With
that out of the way, he would just start doing some old-
fashioned police work, going to Bork's office, hunting
down his friends and associates, collecting some clues
as to what might have happened to him, and trying to
learn who had made that ominous-sounding telephone
call.

He took advantage of the motel's much-advertised
free breakfast for two slices of French toast, a bowl of
raisin bran, and two cups of coffee. Then he called Mrs.
Bork. Her joy at first hearing his voice quickly faded. The
forlorn sound of her sorrow was exactly what he needed
to propel him into the next call.

The number with which Tarkington had finally provided him produced a young-sounding and accented male
voice: "Delos residence. Whom shall I say is calling?"

"This is Joe Leaphorn," Leaphorn said. "I need to
talk to Mr. Delos about a very old Navajo tale-teller's rug.
The curator of the Navajo Tribal Gallery at Window Rock
suggested he might have information to determine if a
copy might have been made of it. Whether it might be
available."

This produced a long moment of silence. Then: "From
where are you calling, sir?"

"I am here in Flagstaff," Leaphorn said. "I was hoping
to make an appointment to meet with Mr. Delos. That rug
has accumulated some very colorful history down through
the years. I thought he might be interested."

Another pause. "Please hold, sir. I will see if he is available."

Leaphorn held. He thought about the staleness of the motel coffee, about whether his car was overdue for an oil change. He glanced at his watch, considered the listings waiting for his attention back in Shiprock, wondered how long it would be before Louisa returned from her research project and helped him keep his house clean and reduce its loneliness, glanced at his watch again, changed the telephone from left ear to right.

"Mr. Leaphorn," the voice said, "Mr. Delos say he can see you. He ask you to be here at eleven."

"Eleven A.M." Leaphorn said, with another glance at his watch. "Tell me how to get there from the downtown Flagstaff interstate exit."

The young man gave him the directions, very precisely. As Leaphorn had suspected, from the view he'd noticed through the window in the *Luxury Living* photo, the route led him into the foothills rising beyond Flagstaff's northern limits. Expensive landscape, rising far above Flagstaff's seventy-two hundred feet above sea level, and offering views extending approximately forever.

"I'll be there," Leaphorn said.

The residence of Jason Delos was a little less monumental than Leaphorn had expected. It was a structure of stone and timber built on two levels, rising above an under-the-house triple garage and conforming with the wooded slope of its setting. The asphalt of this mountain road had reverted to gravel three miles back, but here, through the bars on a fancy cast-iron gate, the driveway that curved toward the garage had been paved. Built as a summer home, Leaphorn deduced, probably in the high

end of the half-million-dollar range when it was built—
and that probably had been back in the 1960s. Now the
price would be much more than that.

Leaphorn parked beside an entry post equipped with
a sign which read:

PLEASE PUSH BUTTON
IDENTIFY YOURSELF

He checked his watch. Six minutes early. He wasted
a few of those enjoying this close view of the San Francisco Peaks. If Jason Delos collected Indian antiquities,
he probably knew their role in mythology. Not terribly
crucial for his Dineh people as he remembered the
winter hogan stories from his boyhood. He had heard
them mentioned mostly because of Great Bear spirit
and his misadventures. But they were sacred indeed for
the Hopis. They recognized Humphreys Peak (at 12,600
feet, the tallest of the San Francisco chain) as the gate-
way to the other world, the route their spirits used to
visit during ceremonials when Hopi priests called them.
For the Zunis, as Leaphorn understood what he'd been
told by Zuni friends, it was one of the roads taken by spirits of Hopi dead to reach the wonderful dance grounds
where the good among them would celebrate their eternal rewards. He interrupted that thought to glance at his
watch again. It was time. He reached out and punched
the button.

The response was immediate.

"Mr. Leaphorn," it said. "Come in, sir. And please park
at the paved place to the south of the entrance porch."

"Right," Leaphorn said, uneasily aware as he said it

that whoever owned the voice had been looking out at him, probably wondering why he was waiting. It was the same voice he had heard on the Delos telephone.

The gate swung open. Leaphorn drove through it, admiring the house. A handsome place with its landscaping left to nature. No flat country lawn grass. Just the vegetation that flourished in the high-dry mountain country. As he pulled into the parking area, a man stepped from a side door and stood, waiting for him. A small man, straight and slender, in his early forties, with short black hair and a very smooth, flawless complexion. Possibly a Hopi or Zuni, Leaphorn thought. But at second glance, Leaphorn switched that to probably Vietnamese or Laotian. As he turned off the ignition, the man was opening the door for him.

"I am Tommy Vang," he said, smiling. "Mr. Delos say thank you for being so prompt. He say to give you some time to visit the restroom if you wish to do so, and then bring you to the office."

Tommy Vang was waiting again when Leaphorn emerged from the restroom. The man escorted Leaphorn down a hallway and through the same large and lavish living room he remembered from the *Luxury Living* photograph. No framed rug was hanging by the fireplace now. The massive elk antlers trophy was still mounted on one side of the glass door, along with several deer antlers. A pronghorn antelope head stared at him from the opposing wall, with a huge bear head, teeth bared, beside it. A big-game hunter, perhaps, or perhaps they had come with the house when Delos bought it. Leaphorn took a second look at the bear.

"That's the only bear I ever shot."

The man who spoke was emerging from a hallway, walking toward them. A tall man, handsome, well over six feet, tanned, trim, white-haired, wearing gray slacks and a red shirt, looking like a healthy, active seventy-year-old. He was smiling and holding out his hand.

"Come on in the office," he said, taking Leaphorn's hand. "I'm Jason Delos, and I'm glad to meet you. I'm looking forward to hearing what you have to tell me about this old rug of mine."

"Judging from all those trophy heads, I'd guess you are quite a hunter," Leaphorn said. "Really good at it."

Delos produced a deprecatory smile.

"That, and collecting cultural antiques, are about my only hobbies," he said. "I'm told practice makes perfect."

"I'd say you picked a good place to live then. Good hunting for big game all through this Four Corners country," Leaphorn said. "When I was a youngster there was even a season on bighorn sheep in the San Juan Mountains."

"I never had a chance at one of those," Delos said. "They're pretty much all gone now. But old people say they used to hunt them in the foothills and even in the high end of the Rio Grande Gorge, about where the river comes out of Colorado into New Mexico, where it cut that deep canyon through the old lava flow."

"I've heard that, too," Leaphorn said. "An old fellow who runs the J. D. Ranch up there told me he used to see them on the cliffs when he was a boy."

"That's a ranch I've hunted on," Delos said. "I get elk permits from the foreman. A fellow named Arlen Roper. In fact, I'm going up there this week." He laughed, made an expansive gesture. "Going to try to get me an absolute record-breaking set of antlers before I get too old for it."

"I think I already am," Leaphorn said.

"Well, I can't climb up the cliffs, and down into the canyons like I used to, but Roper has some blinds set up in the trees on a hillside up there. One of them lets you look right down on the Brazos. Elk come in, morning and evening, to get themselves a drink out of the stream. I've got that one reserved for next week."

Leaphorn nodded, without comment. Ranchers who allowed deer, elk, and antelope herds to share grazing with their cattle were granted hunting permits as a recompense. They could either harvest their winter meat supply themselves or sell the permits to others. It was not a practice Leaphorn endorsed. Not much sportsmanship in it, he thought, but perfectly pragmatic and legal. Traditional Navajos hunted only for food, not for sport. He remembered his maternal uncle explaining to him that to make hunting deer a sport, you would have to give the deer rifles and teach them how to shoot back. His first deer hunt, and all that followed, had been preceded by the prescribed ceremony with his uncles and nephews, with the prayer calling to the deer to join in the venture, to assure the animal that cosmic eternal law would return him to his next existence in the infinite circle of life. A lot of time and work was involved in the Navajo way—the treatment of the deer hide, the pains taken to waste nothing, and, finally, the prayers that led to that first delicious meal of venison. Leaphorn had known many *belagaana* hunters who shared the "waste no venison" attitude, but none who bought into the ceremonial partnership between man and animal. And this was not the place nor the time to discuss it. Instead, he said he'd heard hunting was expected to be unusually good in the Brazos country this season.

Delos smiled. "I've always liked to claim that the skill of the hunter determined how good the season turns out."

"Probably true," Leaphorn said. "But if one comes home empty, he likes something else to blame."

The only trophy head on the wall of the Delos office was that of a large male bobcat snarling above an antique-looking rolltop desk. But a rifle rack against a wall revealed the nature of the Delos hobby. Behind its glass door four rifles and two shotguns were lined up in their racks. Delos motioned Leaphorn into a chair and seated himself beside his desk.

"Is the time right for a drink? A Scotch or something? But I bet you'd prefer coffee?"

"Coffee, if it's no trouble," Leaphorn said, seating himself and processing his impressions. The trophy heads, the gun collection, how Delos had presumed Leaphorn would want coffee, the sense of serene and confident dignity the man presented.

"Coffee," Delos told Tommy Vang, "for both of us." Then he leaned back in his chair, folded his hands across his belly, and smiled at Leaphorn.

"Down to business," he said. "I asked around, and I understand from my friends that you are a Navajo Tribal Policeman. I gather you have no jurisdiction here. Therefore, I am curious about why you came. I would like to think that you had learned that I obtained the tale-teller's rug shown in that magazine and you simply, and very generously, wanted to reward me with some of the colorful tales of its past." Delos smiled, raised his eyebrows, gave Leaphorn a few seconds to respond.

Leaphorn nodded.

Delos sighed. "But being well into my seventh decade, I have learned that it usually takes more than a generous spirit to send one on such a long trip. Normally some trade-off is involved. Some sort of tit-for-tat exchange. Am I right about that?"

"You are," Leaphorn said. "I have a whole list of things I hope to get from you, Mr. Delos." He held up a finger. "Most important, I hope you can provide some information that will help me find out what happened to a friend of mine. Mel Bork. He seems to have disappeared. Second, I hope you'll let me take a look at that tale-teller rug shown in that magazine. I admired that rug many years ago, and I haven't seen it for years. Finally, I hope you will let me know where you obtained it."

Delos sat a moment, looking at his hands, apparently thinking. He shook his head, looked up. "That's all?"

Leaphorn nodded.

"And what do you deliver to me in return?"

Leaphorn shrugged. "Not a lot, I'm afraid. About all I can do is tell you what I remember of the hogan stories as a boy. Some of them were about the 'rug woven from sorrows.' And I could tell you how to get in touch with some of the old weavers who could tell you more." He produced a wry smile. "But I expect you could do that with your own resources."

"Perhaps I could," Delos said. "Some of it anyway. But only you can tell me why you thought I could help you find this friend of yours. This Mel Bork."

Leaphorn noticed Delos had put his hope of help in finding Bork in the past tense.

"I still hope you can help me with that," he said. "I

hope you will tell me where he said he was going when he left here. And everything he said. Some of that might give me at least a hint of where he was going."

Delos threw up his hands, laughed. "I can tell you but if it's helpful then it means you are indeed what my friends have told me about you. That you are a very shrewd detective." Delos was smiling.

Leaphorn, registering that Delos hadn't denied that Bork had been here, returned the smile.

"That causes me to ask another question: What prompted you to ask your friends about me? And which friends advised you?"

The Delos smile faded.

"I exaggerated. It was only Mr. Bork."

"Another question then. Why did Mr. Bork get me into his conversation with you?"

Delos didn't answer that. He shook his head. "I've led us off into a digression," he said. "Let me start at the beginning. Mr. Bork called, asked for an appointment. He said, or perhaps just implied, that he was working in an insurance fraud investigation involving my tale-teller rug. He asked if he could see it. I said yes. He came out. I showed him the rug. He compared it to the photograph from the magazine. He said something like the photo and the rug looking identical." Delos paused, awaiting reaction.

"What did you say to that?"

"I agree they looked very similar."

A tap at the office portal interrupted the answer. Tommy Vang stood there, a tray cart in front of him, smiling and waiting.

Delos waved him in. Vang deposited a tray on a serving table beside Delos's desk, slid it into reachable position between the two men, poured coffee into two saucered cups, removed the lids from a silver sugar bowl and a container of cream. Then, with a flourish and a broad smile, he whipped away a white cloth that had been covering a plate of cake slices and a bowl of nuts.

"He makes that cake himself," Delos said. "Fruitcake. It's downright delicious."

"It looks very good," Leaphorn said, admiring the cherry on top. He reached for his coffee cup.

"But back to your question," Delos said. "I told Bork that old rugs look a lot alike to me, so he showed me a white spot in the rug. Said it was a bird feather woven in. And a rough place. He said that was from some sort of bush that grows out at the Bosque Redondo camp where the Navajos were held captive. And he showed me the same spots on the photograph. I couldn't argue with that. Then he asked me if I knew the rug was supposedly burned in a trading post fire. I said I'd heard about that, but figured it must have been another rug. And he said it looked to him like a hard rug to copy, and asked me where I had gotten it. He said the man who owned the trading post had collected insurance on it, and it looked like an insurance fraud case."

Leaphorn nodded. "What did you tell him?"

"I told him I had bought it at the Indian market, or whatever they call it, in Santa Fe several years ago. Anyway, I got it from an Indian under that sidewalk sales area on the plaza."

"Not in a gallery? That sidewalk at the Palace of the Governors?"

"Right," Delos said.

"Who sold it to you?" Leaphorn asked, thinking he was wasting his breath. He was.

Delos frowned, looked thoughtful. "It was an Indian name," he said. "Spanish-sounding, but I'm almost sure he was from one of the pueblos. Two of the women sitting just up from him against the wall were from San Felipe Pueblo, I remember that."

"Did the salesman tell you where he got it?"

"Said it was an old Navajo rug. His mother had bought it years ago. Either at a tribal fair on the Navajo Reservation, or maybe at that rug auction the weavers have at the Crownpoint Elementary School gymnasium. He said when she died, she left it to him."

"No names then."

Delos shook his head. "Afraid it's not much help."

"Oh, well," Leaphorn said, and sipped his coffee. Excellent. He sipped again. "At least it tells me that this isn't the rug destroyed in that fire." But as he said it, he was thinking he hadn't phrased that well. He should have said it proved that the tale-teller rug hadn't been burned. But actually, it hadn't really proved anything.

"Try that fruitcake," Delos said. "Tommy's a damn fine cook, and that cake is his pride and joy. Everything's in it. Apricots, apple, cherries, six kinds of nuts, just the right spices, all measured out just right. World's best fruitcake."

"It sure looks good," Leaphorn said. "Trouble is, I never did learn to like fruitcake." He dipped into the nut dish. "I'll eat more than my share of those walnuts and pecans instead."

Delos shrugged. "Well, I'll guarantee you that you'd

like Tommy's version of it. I'll have him make you a little snack package to take with you. If you don't like it, toss it out for the birds. Now, let's go see what you think of this famous rug."

The rug was displayed on the wall in a little sitting room adjoining the office, mounted on a hardwood frame. Leaphorn stared at it, trying to remember the time before the fatal fire when he examined it in Totter's little gallery. It looked the same. He found the brilliant red spots formed by the liquid taken from the spider's egg sacs, the little white spots formed by the dove's feathers, other feathers from birds of different colors, and places where fibers from cactus, snakeweed, and other flora of eastern New Mexico grew. He found the sign of the trickster coyote, and of witchcraft, of the silver dollar, and of other assorted symbols of greed, the ultimate evil in the Dineh value system. And, sickening to Leaphorn, all of that evidence of sorrow and disharmony was surrounded by the enfolding symbol of Rainbow Man, the guardian spirit of Dineh harmony. That made it all an ultimate irony. The weaving, as his grandmother had always told them, was the work of an artist. But it was easy to understand why the shamans who saw it condemned it and put their curse on it.

Delos was staring at it, too.

"I always thought it was an interesting work," he said. "After that picture got published in the magazine, a lawyer I know told me old man Totter had put in an insurance claim on it for forty thousand dollars. Said he finally settled for twelve thousand on the rug. About half of what he got for all the other stuff that he claimed was destroyed in that fire."

"You think this could be a copy of the original?" Leap-horn asked.

Delos weighed that, staring at the rug. He shook his head. "I have no idea. No way for me to judge."

"Well, if my opinion was recognized as expert, I'd tell the insurance company that here it is, the original, right off old man Totter's wall, that they were swindled. But the statute of limitations on that's run out long ago, I guess. And anyway, old man Totter's dead."

Delos's eyebrows rose. "Dead?"

"His obituary was published in the *Gallup Independent*," Leaphorn said.

"Really?" Delos said. "When did that happen?"

"I don't know exactly," Leaphorn said. "I heard they had an obituary item in the paper some years ago."

"I never met the man," Delos said. "But I guess he'd make another case for that rug bringing bad luck with it."

"Yeah," Leaphorn said. "Why don't you get rid of it?"

"You know," Delos said, looking thoughtful, "I hadn't heard about Totter dying. I think I'll see what I can get for it."

"I would," Leaphorn said. "I'm not really what you'd call superstitious, but I wouldn't want it hanging on my wall."

Delos laughed, a wry sound. "Think I'll advertise it in the antique collectors' journals. List all those semigeno-cidal horrors that inspired those women to weave it, and all the bad luck that has gone with it. That kind of leg-endary stuff makes artifacts more precious to some." He laughed again. "Like the pistol that killed President Lin-coln. Or the dagger that stabbed Julius Caesar."

"I know," Leaphorn said. "We've had people contact us about trying to get genuine suicide notes. Or trying to get us to make copies for them."

"No accounting for taste, I guess," Delos said, smiling at Leaphorn. "For example, just like your saying you don't like fruitcake."

13

Halfway down the slope from the Delos mansion a sharp "ting-a-ling" sound from the seat beside Leaphorn startled him and interrupted his troubled thoughts. It came, he realized, from the cell phone he'd forgotten in the pocket of his jacket. He pulled to the side of the road, parked, fished it out, pushed the Talk button, identified himself, heard Bernadette Manuelito's voice.

"Lieutenant Leaphorn," Bernie was saying, "this is the former Officer Bernadette Manuelito, who is now Mrs. Bernadette Chee. We decided not to wait for your callback. Got that obituary information you needed. Or at least some of it."

"I'm not used to this Mrs. Chee title yet," Leaphorn said. "I'll just call you Bernie."

"I'm going to be Officer Manuelito again pretty soon," she said, sounding happy about it. "Captain Largo said they kept that job open for me. Isn't that great?"

"Great for us," Leaphorn said, realizing as he said it that he wasn't part of that "us" anymore. "Great for the Navajo Tribal Police Department. How is your husband behaving?"

"He's wonderful," Bernie said. "I should have captured him long ago. And you should come to visit us. I want you to see how we're fixing up Jim's trailer house. It's going to be very nice."

"Well, I'm happy you got him, Bernie. And I will accept that invitation as soon as I can get there." He found himself trying to imagine Chee's rusty trailer with curtains in the windows, throw rugs here and there. Maybe even some colorful wallpaper pasted to those aluminum walls.

"Here's the stuff on the Totter obituary," Bernie said, reverting to her role as a policewoman. "You want me to read it to you?"

"Sure."

"Erwin James Totter, operator of Totter's Trading Post and Art Gallery north of Gallup for many years, died last week in Saint Anthony's Hospital in Oklahoma City. He was admitted there earlier this month with complications following a heart attack.

"Mr. Totter was born in Ada, Oklahoma, April 3, 1939. A bachelor, he left no known dependents. A navy veteran who had served in the Vietnam War, he was interred in the Veterans Administration cemetery at Oklahoma City. He had asked that, in lieu of flowers, any memorial contributions be made to the Red Cross in an account at the Wells Fargo Bank of Oklahoma City."

Bernie paused. "It wasn't very long," she said, sounding regretful.

"That was it?" Leaphorn asked. "No mention of any family. Nothing about any survivors?"

"Just what I read to you," Bernie said. "The woman at the desk, the one who helped me find it, she said she thought it came in a letter, with some cash with it to pay the publication fee. She couldn't remember who sent it. She said maybe Mr. Totter had written it himself when he knew he was dying and just got the hospital to mail it. Does that sound reasonable?"

"Not very," Leaphorn said. He chuckled. "But then nothing much about this whole business seems very reasonable. For example, I'm not sure what the devil I'm doing out here."

"You want me to check on it?" Bernie's tone carried a sort of plaintive sound.

"Golly, Bernie," Leaphorn said. "I hope it didn't sound like I was complaining. You did exactly what I asked you to do. Tell the truth, I think I'm just floundering around feeling frustrated."

"Maybe I could find out from the bank if any contributions had come in. And who made them. Would that help?"

Leaphorn laughed. "Bernie, the trouble is, I don't really know what I'm looking for. I guess the bank would cooperate on that. We don't seem to have any reason for asking. If we did, I guess someone could check for people named Totter in Ada. Find out something about him. It sounds like a small town."

"No crime involved though? Is that right? Wasn't there a fire involved?"

"A fire, yes. But no evidence of arson. A man who worked for Totter was burned up, but the arson folks blamed a drunk smoking in bed and no sign of crime beyond carelessness," he said. "Anyway, thanks. And now can I ask you another favor?"

This produced a pause.

After all, Leaphorn thought, she's a new bride, busy with all sorts of things. "Never mind. I don't want to impose on—"

"Sure," Bernie said. "Doing what?"

Leaphorn struggled briefly with his conscience and won. "If you are still formally, officially a policewoman— you are, aren't you? Just on a leave?"

"That's right."

"Then maybe you could ask that hospital in Oklahoma City to give you the date and details of Totter's death, mortuary arrangements, all that."

"I'll do it," Bernie said, "and if Captain Largo suspends me because I can't explain what I am doing that for, I will refer him to Lieutenant Joe Leaphorn."

"Fair enough," Leaphorn said, "and I'll have to tell him I don't know myself."

Leaphorn spent a few moments digesting the information, or lack of it, that Bernie Manuelito's call had provided. Its effect was to add one more oddity to the pile of oddities that seemed to cluster around this damned taleteller's rug. For him, at least, it had started with an oddity. Why would anyone, especially anyone driving a fairly new, fairly expensive vehicle, get into the work shed behind Grandma Peshlakai's hogan and steal two lard buckets full of the pinyon sap she had collected? Maybe he shouldn't link that with the rug. It was a separate case. A wee little larceny memorable to him only because Grandma's resentment of the way he had abandoned her problem to deal with the case of a deceased white man still seemed morally justified. But now it seemed vaguely possible there was a link. Grandma had found the purloined lard buckets at Totter's gallery, which would make him the most likely suspect in that theft. And he had owned the rug. And now he was buried in a Veterans Administration cemetery at Oklahoma City. Or seemed to be.

Leaphorn groaned. To hell with this. He was going home. He would make a fire in the fireplace. He was going to spread his old Triple A Indian Country map out on the kitchen table, put a calendar down beside it, and try to make some sense out of all of this. Then he would call Mrs. Bork and tell her to let him know if anything turned up, if there was anything he could help her with. Better to make such unpleasant calls when one was at home and comfortable.

He opened the glove box, pushed the cell phone back into its place there, and encountered the neatly folded sack lunch Tommy Vang had handed him as he escorted him back to his truck.

"For your drive home," Tommy had said, smiling at him. "Mr. Delos says people get hungry when they are driving. It be good to eat."

True enough, Leaphorn thought, but this lunch would be better to eat if he took the time and trouble to put in the cooler box he kept behind the seat for such hunger and thirst moments. He leaned over the seat, opened the lid, and slid the sack in between his thermos jug and a shoe box that usually held a candy bar or two, and on which Louisa had lettered "Emergency Rations." That reminded him of home, and he suddenly wanted to be there.

And he was, finally. But only after about five hours of

driving eastward on Interstate 40 through Winslow, then northward on Arizona 87 past Chimney Butte to the turn east on U.S. 15 through Dilkon through Bidahochi, Lower Greasewood, and Cornfield to the Ganado junction, then north again on U.S. 64 past Two Story and St. Michael's to Window Rock and home. On that last stretch Leaphorn was watching the big harvest moon rising over the Defiance Plateau. By the time he had parked, unloaded his suitcase from the car, and got the fireplace going and the coffeepot perking, he was almost too exhausted to take the time to eat the late supper he'd planned. But he poured himself a cup anyway, got two slices of salami from the refrigerator, and a loaf from the breadbox. Doing that reminded him of the lunch sack Tommy had handed him when he was bidding good-bye to Jason Delos. It was still in his pickup, still protected from his appetite by his aversion to whatever it was in fruitcake that gave him indigestion. Well, it would keep until tomorrow. He sat down with a sigh and switched on the TV.

It was time, he noticed, for the ten o'clock news. He ate his first sandwich, thinking his thoughts to the background sound of a car dealer touting the benefits of a Dodge Ram pickup. His thoughts were not particularly cheerful. The fireplace was helping, but the house still had that cold lonely feeling that greets one coming home to a vacant place. He spent a moment remembering how pleasant it had been when Emma was alive. Glad to see him, interested in hearing what the day had done for him, sympathetic when fate had dealt him nothing but disappointments and frustrations, often able to gently and obliquely make him aware of something helpful he'd overlooked, something he'd failed to check. In an odd way

Louisa Bourbonette was helpful, too. She wasn't Emma. No one could ever replace Emma. But it would be pleasant if Bourbonette were here tonight. She'd be reporting what she had added to her oral history archives—telling him another version of an oft-told southern Ute myth, or maybe happily reporting she found a new tale that extended the old ones. But Bourbonette wasn't Emma. If Emma were here now, she would be reminding him that he should close that chain mail screen in front of the fireplace better because the pinyon logs he was burning would be popping as the sap heated and begin spraying sparks and ashes out onto the floor. Leaphorn leaned forward, adjusted the screen properly, and dusted back the ash that had already escaped. Louisa probably wouldn't have noticed that problem.

And while he was considering their differences and sipping his second cup of coffee, the newscaster's voice was intruding on his thoughts. Someone named Elrod was being quoted about finding a fatal accident.

"While state police wouldn't confirm the victim's identity until next of kin had been notified, sources at the scene said the body that Mr. Elrod found in the vehicle was believed to be that of a former Arizona lawman and a well-known Flagstaff businessman. His vehicle had apparently swerved on a sharp curve where the county road intersects with the access road to Forest Service fire watch stations in the San Francisco Peaks. Police reported the vehicle skidded in the roadside gravel and then rolled down the embankment and plunged into the canyon. Officers said the car wasn't seen by passing traffic until Mr. Elrod noticed the slanting afternoon sunlight reflecting off the vehicle's windshield. Elrod told police he then pulled off the road, climbed down, saw the victim's body in the front seat, and called the police on his cell phone. The police spokesman said the accident had apparently happened about two days ago and the view of the vehicle was obscured by trees and brush.

"In another tragic accident here in Phoenix, police report a local teenager was killed when the all-terrain vehicle he was driving along an irrigation drain flipped over and rolled. Police said . . ."

But Leaphorn was no longer listening. He considered the "apparently happened about two days ago" statement. He put down his coffee cup, reached for the telephone, and dialed Sergeant Garcia's home number. He considered the timing and the circumstances while the phone rang and the answering machine told him to leave a message.

"Sergeant, this is Joe Leaphorn. Call me as soon as you can about that wreck. If it was two days ago, it sure sounds like it might have been Mel Bork. And if it was Bork, then I think we might want to go for an autopsy." He paused. "Even if it looks just like another traffic accident."

The rest of the evening news flickered past on the screen without distracting Leaphorn from his thoughts. He pulled open the drawer in the table under the telephone, fumbled through it for a notepad and pen stockpiled there, opened it to a blank page, thought a moment, and printed SHEWNACK near the top. He underlined that, skipped down two inches, wrote TOTTER, stared at the auto dealer offering cash back to purchasers of Dodge Ram trucks, and tapped the pen against the pad. A bit lower, he wrote MEL BORK. Then he stopped. He reached out and

switched off the TV, considered the flames working about the pinyon logs, shook his head, and started writing.
Under Shewnack's name he wrote:

FBI Most Wanted. Two homicides at Handy's. FBI thinks probably others.

Handy's killing, summer 1961. Shewnack probably in his thirties then, been around for several months. Came from either California or Midwest, or who knows where. Disappeared. Shows up at Totter's Trading Post/Gallery in 1965. Was he intending to rob Totter? What happened to the loot he took from Handy's? Had Shewnack tried to kill Totter as he'd killed Handy, gotten killed by Totter instead, and then Totter decides to burn the body erasing evidence of the crime, leaving it so he could keep any loot Shewnack had with him from the Handy's crime, and add to the profits by pulling off a fire insurance fraud?

He stared at the last line a moment, shook his head and crossed it out. It just didn't seem quite logical.
Under Totter's name he wrote:

Born 1939, Ada, Okla. Came to Four-Corners Country when? Opened trading-post gallery when? Place burned autumn 1965. Totter dies in Okla City in 1967. Leaves no kith nor kin, no survivors. So why did he go back to Oklahoma?

Leaphorn finished his coffee. Printed JASON DELOS on

the sheet, got up to refill his cup in the kitchen, and then stood staring into the fire, thinking of the two empty five-gallon lard cans Grandma Peshlakai had found at Totter's gallery. Navajos used lots of lard and usually got it in those cans because the cans themselves were so useful.

His own fire was burning hot now, and the room was filled with the wonderful perfume that only pinyon fires can produce. The aroma of the forest, of quiet places, of peace, tranquility. He sat again, picked up the pen and wrote:

> Few days before Totter fire, Totter apparently stole pinyon sap from Grandma Peshlakai's work shed. Why? As fire accelerant? To get fire hot enough to destroy Shewnack's body beyond identification? Why would he do that? The burned man was apparently not a local. Nobody seemed to come forward to ask about him. Garcia guessed he was a transient coming through who had noticed Totter's HELP WANTED sign. But coming through from where?

He looked at that, produced a wry smile, and added: "Or for waterproofing some of his own baskets for sale to tourists?"

He started to scratch that out. Stopped. Shook his head. Instead wrote: Joe Leaphorn LOSING IT!!

Skipped some space on the page. Wrote:

"An'n ti'." Frowned. Lined that out and wrote *"an' t I'."* Studied that sort of generic Navajo word for witchcraft in general, said it aloud, approved it, underlined it. Then he wrote *an't'zi*, the Navajo word for the specie of witchcraft employing corpse powder poisons to cause fatal illnesses.

Under that he wrote "*ye-na-L o si,*" underlined it, thought a moment and slashed an X over the entire list. The *ye-na-L o si* expression described what the *belagaana* scholars preferred to call skinwalkers, relating them to their European witchcraft stories of werewolves.

At the bottom of the page, he underlined Leaphorn LOSING IT!! And added: SEEMS LIKE I HAVE ALREADY LOST IT.

He wadded the paper. Tossed it into the fire. Leaphorn didn't believe in witchcraft. He believed in evil, firmly believed in it, saw it practiced all around him in its various forms—greed, ambition, malice—and a variety of others. But he didn't believe in supernatural witches. Or did he? And he was dead tired and, to hell with it all, he was going to bed to get some sleep.

Easier said than done. He found himself thinking of Emma, missing her, yearning for her. Telling her about the carpet, about Delos, about Totter's fire, about Shewnack, about the Handy case, about people who didn't seem to have beginnings anywhere and who faded away into ashes and odd mailed-in obituary notices. And Emma smiling at him, understanding him all too well, telling him that she guessed he already had this all figured out and his problem was he just didn't like his solution because he didn't like the idea of "shape shifters," of his suspects turning into owls and flying away. Which seemed painfully close to true.

He drifted from that into wishing that he could have been in the hogan all those winters when his elderly maternal relatives were telling their winter stories—explaining the reasons behind the curing ceremonials, the basis for Dineh values. He'd missed too much of that.

Emma hadn't. Neither had Jim Chee. Chee, for example, had once passed along to him how Hosteen Adowe Claw, one of Chee's shaman kinsmen, had clarified the meaning of the incident in the story of the Dineh emergence from the flooded third world into this glittering world, in which First Man realizes he had left his medicine bundle behind, with all of humanity's greed, malice, and assorted other evils. And then sent a heron back into the flood waters of that world destroyed by God because of those evils and told that diving bird to find the bundle and bring it to him. And tell the heron not to tell anyone that it contained evil, to just tell them it was "the way to make money."

14

It proved to be another uneasy sleep, broken by trouble-some dreams, by long thoughts about whether the dead man found in the car was Mel Bork, and if not him, who, and what then had happened to Bork? When Leaphorn finally came fully awake, it was because he thought he had heard a door opening. He sat up, totally alert, tensed, listening. Now came the sound of the door closing. It would have been the garage/kitchen door. Now the sound of footsteps. Light footsteps. Someone trying not to disturb him. Probably Louisa, he thought. Probably she had cut off her southern Ute research a little early. Some of the tension went away. But not much. He slid across over the bed toward the nightstand, pulled open the drawer, feeling for the little .32-caliber pistol he kept there, finding it, clutching it, remembering that once, when someone with children was visiting, Louisa had persuaded him to leave it unloaded.

The sound of another door opening. At Louisa's adjoining bedroom just down the hall. More steps. Sounds of bathroom water running. Sounds of the shower. Then assorted sounds that Leaphorn identified as connected with unpacking a suitcase, hanging things in the closet, putting things in drawers. Then the sneaky sound of slipper-clad feet. The sound of his doorknob turning, of the door to his bedroom opening just a little. Light from the hall streaming in.

He could see the outline of Louisa's head, peering in at him.

"Joe," Louisa's said, very softly, "you asleep?"

Leaphorn exhaled a huge breath.

"I was," he said.

"Sorry I woke you," Louisa said.

"Don't be," Leaphorn said. "I am delighted it's you."

She laughed. "Just who were you expecting?"

Leaphorn didn't know how to answer that. He said, "Did you find any good Southern Ute sources?"

"I did! A really great old lady. Full of stories about all their troubles with the Comanches when they were being pushed west into Utah. But go back to sleep. I'll give you a complete report at breakfast. And how about you? All quiet on the home front?"

"Relatively," Leaphorn said. "But if you just drove in, you must be tired. It can wait. Get some sleep."

Leaphorn's next awakening was much less stressful. He was lured out of his sleep by the sound of perking coffee and the aroma of bacon in the frying pan. Louisa was at the kitchen table, reading something in her notebook, sipping coffee. Leaphorn poured himself a cup and joined her. She told him about what her very, very elderly

Ute source had told her of the clever tactics her tribesmen had used to confuse the Comanches, about horses
stolen and enemies tricked. She was heading back to her
office at Northern Arizona University after breakfast, but
first she needed an account of what Leaphorn had been
doing, and his copy of last month's utility bills so she could
pay her share. While she served the bacon and eggs,
Leaphorn dug out the paperwork and decided what, and
how much, he wanted to tell her. He wouldn't tell her that
he was afraid that Mel Bork was dead, not until that was
confirmed. And even if it was, he didn't think he'd report
his suspicions about Tommy Vang's fruitcake. That all
seemed sort of silly to him, even though he'd been offered
the stuff himself. He was pretty sure it would sound even
sillier to the professor.

He started his account with the letter from Mel Bork.
He skipped through all that happened next rapidly, skip-
ping a lot of it, and being stopped several times by her
questions about the rug. By the time he'd finished his rec-
itation, he found himself forced back to his conclusion of
the previous night—that he had wasted a lot of time and
accomplished nothing useful.

But Louisa's interest, naturally, was in the cultur-
ally significant rug. The history of that weaving fit precisely into her professional preoccupation with tribal
cultures. What did Leaphorn think had happened to
it? That led up and down the list of questions that
Leaphorn had been asking himself, and he couldn't
answer a single one of them with anything better than
guesses. Louisa's curiosity eventually, over the second
cup of coffee, settled on Jason Delos. One of her graduate students at NAU had done some landscape work at

his place, had become an acquaintance of Tommy Vang, and had regaled one of her graduate student sessions with Vang's stories of life among his fellow tribesmen in the mountains along the Vietnam/Cambodia/Laos borders.

"It all seemed totally authentic," she said, "and interesting. But what we were hearing, of course, was second-hand. So I sent Mr. Vang an invitation to come in and talk to our little seminar. But he didn't come."

"Did he say why?" Leaphorn asked. "I'd love to know how he got connected with Mr. Delos."

"He just said he couldn't do it," Louisa said. "Our landscaping grad student said he had the impression that Tommy's family had been some of the tribesmen who worked with the CIA in the latter phases of the Vietnam War, about the time we were poking into Cambodia. This student of mine was sort of edgy about it. He told me, more or less privately, that he thought Tommy's family had been sort of wiped out during all that back-and-forth fighting, that Delos had been with the CIA and had sort of rescued him as a boy and brought him back to the States."

"Well, now," Leaphorn said.

"Does that sound sensible? Based on what you know?"

"It sounds as sensible as anything else I know about Delos. Which is damned near nothing," Leaphorn said. "About all I know for almost certain is that he is a dedicated big-game hunter, likes to collect antiques; and if you'd like to have that old tale-teller rug, he says he's thinking about getting rid of it."

"I've heard he's fairly new to Flagstaff," Louisa said.

"Certainly not old family. And I gather he doesn't mix much socially."

Leaphorn nodded. "That fits," he said.

Louisa had been studying him during this conversation.

"Joe," she said, "you seem sort of down. Depressed. Tired. Is this business of being retired getting to you? From what you said, this rug affair sort of ties in with one of your old cases. So it doesn't sound like being retired has stopped you from acting like a detective."

Leaphorn laughed. He reached into his shirt pocket, pulled out the utility bills, and handed them to her.

"Perfect time for this. Here what it's costing you for this unorthodox, possibly even un-American arrangement we've been having. But I'll let you do the figuring of the percentages."

She took the slips, glanced at them.

"I was just going to remind you about that," she said, smiling at him. "I will turn them over to my accountant at the university to make sure you're not cheating. I will also remind you that I am behind on our room rental deal. Remember, I stayed up here about three times during the summer."

During all this Leaphorn had been studying her, remembering Emma.

"You know, Louisa, we could save this paperwork, this sort of thing, if you would just go ahead and marry me."

She smiled at him. "You have probably just established a *Ripley's Believe It or Not* record for the most unromantic proposal ever made."

"It wasn't intended to be romantic," Leaphorn said. "It was intended to be just downright practical."

She looked down at her coffee cup, picked it up, held it, replaced it in the saucer, smiled at him ruefully.

"Do you remember what I said the first time you came up with this idea? Let's see. About nineteen—"

"Several years ago," Leaphorn said, interrupting her. "I remember exactly every word of it. You said. 'Joe, I tried being married once. I didn't care for it.'"

"Yep," she said, looking at him fondly. "That's exactly the way I put it."

"Have you since changed your mind? Found me more attractive?"

That brought a thoughtful silence. A sigh. Another picking up and putting down of the coffee cup. Then: "Joe, I'll bet you remember that adage—I'm sure you do because I think you are the very first person I heard using it. It's about how hard it is for old dogs to learn new tricks. Or something like that. Anyway, how do I say it? I guess I'll use something an old lady once told me in one of my oral history interviews. She said, 'Don't marry a really good friend 'cause they're a lot better than a husband.'"

Leaphorn let that hang there. He was noticing that his reaction to her reaction was a sort of relief.

She was watching him, looking sort of penitent. "Or maybe I got that wrong. Maybe she said it would spoil the friendship."

"However she worded it," Leaphorn said, "I damn sure don't want that to happen to us."

"Nor me either," Louisa said, and got up and carried her plate, cup, saucer, and cutlery to the sink. "And just to make sure you don't think I might be willing to revert to full-time housekeeper, I will leave this in the sink for you to wash, while I collect my stuff and head south toward my great stack of midterm papers waiting to be graded." She started to add his plate to her load, but stopped. Instead, she smiled at him.

"Good friends are too hard to collect," she said.

15

The good mood Louisa's attitude had left with Joe Leaphorn lasted only about half an hour. While he was watching the professor drive away, with a mixture of sadness and relief, he heard his telephone ringing. It would be Grace Bork, he thought, calling to tell him that Mel Bork was, just as he suspected, the man found dead in the wreck. It would lead to a conversation he'd expected, something he dreaded. What could he tell her? Only that he had wasted his time. But the voice on the telephone was Sergeant Kelly Garcia's.

"Lieutenant Leaphorn," Garcia said. "I want you to tell me how you knew that body would be Mel Bork?"

"I was just guessing," Leaphorn said. "That's all I've been doing lately. So it was him? What was the cause of death?"

Garcia snorted. "Wasn't it obvious? You're not satisfied with tumbling your car down into a canyon, landing upside down in what's left of it, broken bones, multiple concussions and contusions, general bodily trauma? That's what we have. And you still want an autopsy."

"Don't you?"

That produced a moment of silence.

"Well, I guess I have to admit it would relieve my mind," Garcia said. "I'd like to know what caused him to be so damned careless on that curve."

"Have you asked about an autopsy?"

"Yeah, sort of suggested to Saunders that I'd like one. And he said, What for? And I said an old retired Navajo cop I used to know is sort of vaguely suspicious about it and asked me to check on the cause of death. And Saunders said the only problem about that is deciding which of his nineteen or so auto crash trauma injuries actually did the job. He offered to take me in there to look at the body and let me take my pick."

"Is the pathologist still Roger Saunders?" Leaphorn asked. "I've always heard tales of how testy he was. Did he say you'd have to get a court order, or what?"

Garcia chuckled. "You know about Roger then, don't you? He told me he is backed up with work on actual homicide cases. But when I whined a little, he said that if we can arouse his curiosity, he'll do it."

"Tell him we think Bork might have been poisoned by a slice of fruitcake. That should get him interested."

Garcia laughed. "I don't think so. I think he'd refer me to a psychiatrist. I'm dead certain he'd ask me why we think that. Why do we?"

Leaphorn described the urging he'd received to eat the special cake made by Mr. Delos's cook and helpmate, a man named Tommy Vang, and how Bork had been given a slice of same as a snack just before he drove away from the Delos place, and how the timing made it just about right for Bork to be feeling its effects and losing control of his car about where he did. Leaphorn added a few details to his explanation and awaited a response.

It was a skeptical-sounding snort.

"You're not happy with that?"

"Well, it explains what you mean when you said you were guessing," Garcia said. "About a dozen guesses to reach that conclusion. You guess that Bork ate the cake, and when he ate it, it took however long for whatever poison to work, that Mr. Delos has a motive, and so forth."

"I plead guilty to that."

"Well, I'll go anyway. You have anything else we could tell Saunders to get him interested?"

"That's it," Leaphorn said.

"That's it then. Come on," Garcia said, his tone somewhere between scornful and incredulous. "But you still want me to push for the autopsy?"

"Well, there's also the fact that Bork, a longtime law officer, is a very experienced driver in our mountainous country. He is extremely unlikely to have that sort of accident. Don't you agree? And we can also argue that Delos probably thought Bork was poking into some sort of insurance fraud involving that tale-teller rug. Maybe that would satisfy the need for a motive. And then maybe you could get him to listen to that threatening telephone tape."

More silence from Garcia. Then a sigh.

"Well, it might appeal to Dr. Saunders. He always

seems to get a kick out of discovering different kinds of homicide weapons anyway. Breaks the monotony. Maybe that notion of a fruitcake as the murder weapon would appeal to him."

"And Sergeant, would you please let me know what he finds out? Delos gave me a slice of that fruitcake, too. I have it in a sack in my truck cooler box."

Garcia laughed. "Playing it safe, are you? Well, keep it there a while, and remind me of your cell phone number."

Leaphorn provided the number. "And one more thing," he said. "Do you remember the names of the FBI people who were there at Totter's Trading Post? Working on it after the fire."

"Well, let me think about that a minute," Garcia said. "That was a long time ago."

"Yeah," Leaphorn said, and waited.

"Well, let's see." He chuckled. "One of them was Special Agent John O'Malley. I'll bet you remember him."

"Unfortunately," Leaphorn said. "I had some trouble with him down through the years."

"Me, too," Garcia said. "And I remember Ted Rostic was there, too. Out of the Gallup office then, I think. Nice guy, he was. And then Sharkey. Remember him? Don't recall his first name."

"Jay, I think it was. Or Jason. Another hard man to work with. Anyone else?"

"Probably. They sort of swarmed in when it turned out the burned man was Shewnack. But I don't remember who."

"All retired by now, I guess."

"Probably. I heard O'Malley had died back in Washington. Don't know about Sharkey. I know Rostic is re-tired. I heard he lives in Gallup."

"Good," Leaphorn said.

"For what?" Garcia said. "What are you after?"

"I can't seem to let this thing go," Leaphorn said. "I mean that Totter fire. The whole thing. If I can get hold of Rostic, I'll see what he remembers about it."

The information operator found no number for Ted Rostic in the Gallup directory.

"But, there's a Ted in Crownpoint. Could that be him?"

"I'll bet it is."

"Want me to ring him for you? For seventy-five cents?"

"I'm on Social Security," Leaphorn said. "I'll dial it myself." He did, and Rostic answered on the fourth ring.

"Leaphorn. Leaphorn," Rostic said. "That sounds familiar. Sounds like a young fellow I knew once with the Navajo Tribal Police."

"Yeah," Leaphorn said. "We met on that Ashie Pinto business. When one of our officers got burned up in his car."

"Uh-huh," Rostic said. "That was a sad piece of business."

"I'm interested in another fire now. The one years ago at Totter's Trading Post with an FBI Most-Wanted felon burned up in it. Do you remember that one?"

"Oh, boy," Rostic said. "I sure do. Ray Shewnack was the victim's name. I think that was my first real excitement as a police officer. Real big deal. Finding one of our top targets. A real genuine villain, that Shewnack was."

"Any reason you can't talk about it now?"

"I'm retired," Rostic said. "But it's hard for me to believe anyone would still be interested. What are you doing? You wouldn't be writing one of those serial killer celebrity books, would you?"

"No. Just trying to satisfy one of those old nagging questions."

"Where you calling from?"

"Home in Shiprock. I'm retired, too."

"And probably just as bored with it as I am," said Rostic. "If you want to drive on over, I'll meet you at that little place across from the Crownpoint High School. How about for lunch? Now you've reminded me of that business, I'd like to talk about it, too. Could you make it for noon?"

"Easily. Plenty of time," Leaphorn said. "I'll see you there."

Plenty of time, indeed. Just about seventy miles from Leaphorn's garage to the fried-chicken place across the street from Crownpoint High, and it was now just a little after sunrise. He would just cruise along, maybe stop here and there to see if he could find an old friend at the Yah-Ta-Hay store, and look in at the chapter houses at Twin Lakes, Coyote Canyon, and Standing Rock. In his days as Officer Leaphorn, patrolling that part of the Rez, he had learned the chapter house almost always had a pot of coffee on the stove and maybe a muffin or something to go with it while he updated information about current affairs involving cattle theft, booze bootlegging, or other disruptions of harmony. He would use this unhurried trip to see if he could get himself into the proper mood that the retirement world seems to demand, if one was going to survive in it.

The stop at Ya-Ta-Hay was a disappointment. Those working at the place seemed to be universally of the much-younger generation. No one he knew. At Twin Lakes, the parking lot was empty except for an old Ford Pinto, whose owner was an elderly lady whom he had known for about forty years but who was the grumpy sort. He was not in a mood today to be the audience for her inexhaustible armory of complaints about the ineptitude of the Tribal Council, nor to provide explanations for why the Navajo Tribal Police could not stamp out the reservation's plague of drunk drivers.

His luck got better after he made the turn toward the east onto Navajo Route 9. The morning sunlight was glittering off the early snowpack on the high slopes of Soodzil, Mount Taylor on *belagaana* road maps, or *dootl'izhiidziil* to traditional Navajo shaman; it was Joe Leaphorn's favorite view. Locally it was called Turquoise Mountain, and known as the sacred mountain of the South, built by First Man of materials brought up from the dark, flooded third world, and pinned to the earth with a magic flint knife by that powerful *yei* when it tried to float away. As Leaphorn had learned in the hogan stories of his childhood winters, it had been magically decorated with turquoise, fog, and female rain, and had been made home of *dootl'altsoil 'at'eed* and *anaa'ji at'eed*, whose names translated to Yellow Corn Girl and Turquoise Boy, both friendly *yei*. The holy people had also made the mountain home for all sorts of animals, including the first flocks of wild turkey Leaphorn had seen.

But most important in Navajo mythology, it was where Monster Slayer and his thoughtful twin, Born for Water, had confronted Ye'iitsoh, the chief of the enemy gods.

They had killed him on the mountain after a terrible battle, thus beginning their campaign to clear this glittering world from the evils of greed and malice, the nasty conduct that had caused God to destroy the third world and which, alas, had followed the Dineh up from below.

And, Leaphorn was thinking, it was still on the prowl in this part of the glittering world, or why would all these things that were puzzling him—and killing people—be happening?

As he pulled into the parking lot at the Coyote Canyon Chapter House and saw old Eugene Bydonie standing at the door, holding his big black reservation hat in his hand and saying good-bye to an even more elderly lady, Leaphorn climbed out of his car and waved. "*Ya teeh albini*, Eugene," he shouted. "Is the coffeepot on?"

Bydonie peered, recognized him, shouted, "And good morning to you, Lieutenant. It's been a long time, Joe. What crime have we committed now to warrant some police attention again?"

"Well, you gave me stale coffee last time I was here. How is it today?"

"Come on in," Bydonie said, laughing and holding the door. "I just made a fresh supply."

While drinking it, they discussed old times, mutual friends—many of whom seemed to be dying off—and the bad conditions of grazing, the price of sheep, and the higher and higher fees the shearers were trying to charge. They concluded with a rundown of which weaver had been selling what at last month's Crownpoint rug auction. And finally Leaphorn asked him if he knew Ted Rostic.

"Rostic? There at Crownpoint? I think I've met him.

They say he's married to Mary Ann Kayete. Daughter of Old Lady Notah. Streams Comes Together people, and I think her daddy was a Towering House man."

"Oh," Leaphorn said. "What else do you know about him?"

"Well, they say he's a retired FBI special agent. Guess he lives on his pension. Drives a Dodge Ram King Cab pickup. They say his wife used to teach at Crownpoint High School, and they tell me Rostic is sometimes called in to talk to students about the law."

Bydonie's face, which was narrow, weathered, and decorated with a dry, gray ragged mustache, produced a wry smile. "These kids we're raising today, they could use a lot of that kind of talk. Somebody telling them about getting locked up in jail."

"Pretty mean around here?" Leaphorn asked.

"Pretty mean everywhere," Bydonie said. "Nobody's got any respect for anything anymore."

"I've got to go see him to ask him about an old, old case he worked on. Anything else you could tell me about him that might be useful to know?"

"I don't think so," Bydonie said.

Though that proved to be correct, it didn't prevent him from talking through a second cup of coffee. Thus, Leaphorn arrived at his luncheon meeting with Rostic almost seven minutes late.

He saw Rostic sitting at a table next to the window, menu in front of him, short, stocky, wire-rimmed glasses, looking exactly like an older version of the FBI special agent Leaphorn remembered.

"Sorry I'm late," Leaphorn said. "Good of you to have some time for this."

Ted Rostic slid back his chair, stood, held out his hand, grinning.

"Lieutenant Leaphorn," he said. "It's been many a year since I've seen you. By the way, you don't need to worry yourself any about my having time. As I said, I'm retired."

Leaphorn was grinning, too, thinking how long and boring this retirement scheme could be if you took it seriously. "I've just started this retirement thing. I hope you're going to tell me it gets to be fun once you get the hang of it."

"Not for me, it isn't," Rostic said. He reseated himself, handed Leaphorn a menu. "I'd recommend either the hamburger or the hot dog," Rostic said. "I'd steer clear of the pizza or the meat loaf dinner."

"I'm thinking about maybe just a cup of coffee and a doughnut. Something sweet."

"I presume from that you didn't drive all the way out here just for a fancy Crownpoint luncheon then," Rostic said. "And I am very eager to learn what aroused your interest, after all these years, into the cremation of ole Ray Shewnack."

A waiter had arrived, a Navajo boy in his teens, who brought them each a glass of water, and took Rostic's hamburger order. "Hamburger for me, too," Leaphorn said. "And a doughnut."

"Doughnut for me, too. What kind?"

"The fattest one," Leaphorn said, "with frosting on it."

"What aroused our interest in that fire, as I remember, was a call from the New Mexico State Police, who had a call from the McKinley County sheriff's office, that someone had called from Totter's Trading Post, said they had a man burned to death out there, and that this dead fellow might be someone on our Most-Wanted list. So I, being the newest man in the New Mexico side of our Gallup office, got sent out to look into it."

Leaphorn sipped his water, waiting for Rostic to add to that. But Rostic was awaiting a Leaphorn question. He occupied himself staring at Leaphorn.

"Well," Leaphorn said. "Did the caller explain why he thought the dead man was a noted fugitive?"

"It was a woman. The first caller, I mean. Time it got to me the story was thirdhand. Actually fourth. Woman told sheriff's office, who called state police, who called Gallup FBI office, from which I get the message. But apparently this burned man had a bunch of those Wanted posters in a folder on the seat of his car, or somewhere. Collected from here and there."

Leaphorn nodded, considering this. "Just Shewnack posters, I presume?"

Rostic laughed. "I know what you're thinking. Some creepy people might just collect Wanted posters. But who, who but Shewnack himself, would just collect Shewnack posters? They didn't even have the usual photograph on them."

"Oh?"

"Because we never got a photograph of the slippery bastard. He was never arrested, at least not under that name. As a matter of fact, I don't know anybody in the bureau who ever actually identified the bastard. Always seemed to pick places without surveillance video or many people around to do his robbing. Crime scene people would collect all sorts of fingerprints. Most of them would be people who worked there, others would be unidentifiable. Maybe Shewnack, maybe a customer. After it began looking like this guy was a genuine serial bandit, the lab went back and tried to do comparisons on the various crime scene sets." Rostic laughed, made a dismissing gesture.

"In fact," he said, "got to be sort of a hobby for some of the old timers who had time on their hands. Comparing crime scene stuff. Huge job, and finally they came up with one set that showed up in four places."

Rostic was grinning as he recounted the details of this. "Then they finally nailed the guy with the fingerprints. Turned out he was a salesman who took orders at all those places. I sort of made a hobby of it myself, since this Shewnack business was my first really weird one. I finally found an old-timer retired from CIA special operations who thought he knew this bird's real name. Or at least one that went all the way back before our famous Handy's affair."

Their hamburgers arrived, plus the doughnuts and refills of their coffee cups. Leaphorn took a careful bite, waiting. Not wanting to break Rostic's chain of thought, anxious to hear Rostic's statement concluded. The pastry was good. Not quite up to Dunkin' Donuts' high standards, but very tasty. Coffee was good, too. He sipped.

"Another name? Another identity?"

"Just bureau gossip, of course. You know. The bureau knocking the agency. FBI finding ways to offset the CIA's looking down its lofty secretive noses at the bureau."

Leaphorn smiled. Nodded. "Yeah. The word was this Shewnack was CIA?"

Rostic depreciated his gossip with a shrug. "Had been, anyway. The way it went he was a guy in the early stages of those special operations deals in Vietnam. Back when the Kennedy group had decided that President Diem wasn't cutting it and that little bunch of South Viet generals were being lined up for the coup. Remember that?"

"Sure," Leaphorn said. "Diem was ousted, but it didn't seem to be a very slick operation. Or very secret either."

"Far from it. Lots of CIA careers dented. Lots of bad political fallout. Little bits of bad stuff started leaking out of cracks later, when people were quitting. And one of the bad-news items was about a special ops guy running something in the mountains, in Laos, I think it was. Anyway, the story was that the ARVN generals he was delivering the money bags to, they started claiming that they'd been shorted in their share of the payoff. Amounted to a lot of money. The guy who was telling me said it amounted to better than eight hundred thousand dollars."

"Wow," Leaphorn said. "I picked up that gossip before, but the tale I heard didn't have the dollar amount with it."

"Probably exaggerated," Rostic said. Anyway, the bird supposed to have the sticky fingers was, was . . . let me put it this way. He was George Perkins then, but he was showing that shrewdness that made Shewnack our Most-Wanted hero. He rigged it up so he left the proper memos, notes, etc., in all the right files so he could present the CIA brass with an unpleasant choice. They could lock him up and watch him try to demonstrate to all who would listen that all he did was heroically deliver the taxpayers' money to a bunch of corrupt ARVN generals. Generals who, it seemed to Perkins, must be splitting the loot back with the CIA accountants. And yes indeed, he would be perfectly willing to testify and help the taxpayers recover their money from these villains."

"Let me guess," Leaphorn said. "So they said, 'Oh, well, boys will be boys. You resign, and we'll put such little things behind us.'"

Rostic laughed. "Leaphorn," he said, "you have been there in the J. Edgar Hoover building, and you understand how federal law enforcement bureaucracy works."

"But I don't understand how this connects with Shewnack. Or any of the rest of this."

"Well, nobody could ever prove there is any connection," Rostic said. "But the shrewd way he made the money sort of disappear reminded me of the way he planned things. And then, according to my gossip, this guy shows up in Northern California, under some different name, no longer George Perkins. The FBI wouldn't have minded seeing the CIA get its feathers burned, so it tried to keep a sort of halfway eye on him. Of course, the ex-Mr. Perkins, being an old, old hand at that game, seems to have caught on in a hurry. Maybe he was already calling himself Ray Shewnack. Anyway, the bureau lost track of him."

Rostic shrugged, considered what he'd been saying, then went on. "But the timing was right. I mean, the sort of slick Shewnack-type jobs happened a time or two. And then when I think the agency was catching on and checking, Perkins seems to have sensed he was being looked at by the FBI. He just disappeared. Next thing you know, a couple of crimes turned up in New Mexico that reminded the bureau of Shewnack jobs in California. And then the double murder of the Handy couple, with the slick setup that left fall guys behind, and absolutely no witnesses or fingerprints. By then that Shewnack MO was familiar."

"But no actual physical evidence?"

"No, nary a trace that I've heard about."

"You're an old hand in this business. What do you think?"

"I would imagine that Shewnack might have previously been George Perkins, or who knows who else. But I would also bet nobody is ever going to know for sure. My trouble is I had the bad luck of getting sent over to check on that Totter fire, and there the bastard was, all burned up, and I got stuck with him. And he's such a spectacularly evil son of a bitch that he's hard to forget."

"What I'd like you to do," said Leaphorn, "is sort of give me a picture of what happened when you got to Totter's place."

Rostic thought. Nodded. "Two cops already there. A sheriff's deputy and a state policeman. My only business, as a federal, would be if the burned man was wanted for a federal crime. So I looked at the corpse. They'd moved it out of that burned-up gallery place and laid it out on the trading post floor." He grimaced. "I guess you guys see a lot of violent scenes, but we're more into the white-collar crimes. I can still see that bunch of baked meat and scorched bones in my dreams. So then they showed me the folder full of posters. Eleven of them, with a note on the bottom of each naming where it came from. There was Farmington, New Mexico, Seattle, Salt Lake City, Tulsa, Tucson, Los Angeles, and so forth. Eleven different places. But all of them from western states."

"Enough to make you suspicious."

"More than that," Rostic said. "I call in the list of

places. Gallup checked the files on Shewnack. Six of the eleven had the sort of out-of-the-way robberies that fit our idea of Shewnack's mode of operations. When they checked later, the other seven looked like they fit, too."

"You mean the same MO?" Leaphorn asked. "Carefully planned. No fingerprints left behind. Places with no security cameras. Relatively small communities? And how about leaving accomplices behind to take the rap?"

"That, too, in some of them."

"Were there any live witnesses left in any of those?"

Rostic laughed. "How come you waited so long to ask about leaving witnesses behind? Of course he didn't."

Leaphorn sighed, feeling sort of sick. "I guess I didn't want to hear it."

"I can't blame you. In most cases it worked pretty much like the Handy robbery. If they got a good look at him, he shot 'em."

Leaphorn nodded.

"Usually twice. The dead tell no tales."

"A very careful man from what little I know about him," Leaphorn said. "Did it make you wonder why he'd left those Wanted posters out on the front seat of his car?"

Rostic looked thoughtful. "No, not then, but now that you mention it, you'd think he'd have tucked them away out of sight. Most likely packed in with his stuff locked up in the car trunk."

"That was going to be one of my questions. Had Totter, or the fire department boys, or the other cops gotten all that out by the time you got there?"

"No. They'd broken one of those wing windows to reach in and get that folder with the posters in it, but the car was still locked. When we got the call, Delbert James was in charge, and he told the sheriff that if the victim was Shewnack, it was very important, and he should make damn sure everything was secure and not messed with until we could take over."

Leaphorn nodded.

"I see you grinning," Rostic said, and laughed. "I know how you local cops feel about that. To tell the truth, I can't say I blame you. The feds come in, take over, screw everything up because they don't know the territory. They take the credit if a bust gets made, and if it doesn't they write up reports on how the locals made all the mistakes."

"Yep," Leaphorn said. "But we don't blame it on you guys doing the work. We blame it on the Washington politicians looking over your shoulders."

"As you should," Rostic said. "They're the ones we blame."

"And sometimes we notice we'll be dealing with a special agent who just got in from Miami, or from Portland, Maine, and he's giving our people directions when—"

Leaphorn cut that complaint short, noticing that even now just thinking of the couple of horrible examples he was about to use was causing him to lose his temper.

"I can finish that for you," Rostic said. "We're giving your people directions when this is the first time we've set foot on the reservations, and if we wanted to get to Window Rock we'd have to ask what road to take."

"Something like that," Leaphorn said.

"Or as Captain Largo often told me, 'It ain't that we think you federals are plain stupid. It's just that you don't know nothing yet. It's the total absolute invincible ignorance that trips you up.'"

"That's about it," Leaphorn said, chuckling at Rostic's imitation of Largo's emphatic way of expressing himself. "But right now I am very glad you did take over and made sure nobody got into whatever Shewnack had locked safely away in his car trunk."

"He had some things locked in the glove compartment, too. One particularly useful item. An almost empty pint bottle of cognac. Very expensive stuff." Rostic was smiling as he related this. "And being glass, a gold mine of the very first fingerprints we ever had of the murderous bastard."

"Wonderful," Leaphorn said. "This is just exactly what I hoped you could tell me. And how did they match with the prints the bureau must have collected from all those other places where you had noticed his MO."

"Also got prints off his stuff in the car trunk. And other evidence, too. For example, a fancy little gold-trimmed paper weight that had been part of the loot in a convenience story robbery in Tulsa. And an expensive little leather zipper bag that still had the Salt Lake City victim's name and address stitched in the lining. Couple of other things, too. A pair of those fancy soft-soled shoes good for sneaking up on people with, and which leave that soft rubber streak on hard floors if you're not careful. The rubber matches what the crime scene boys had scraped up from the floor at the Tucson killing."

"Sort of like he kept souvenirs of his crimes," Leaphorn said. "How about money? Sergeant Garcia went out to the Totter fire site and found that Delonie there."

"The assistant bandit at Handy's?"

"Yeah. He was out on parole. He told us he'd heard Shewnack had burned up there, and he figured, slick as Shewnack was, he would have hidden the loot from his latest robbery somewhere. And Delonie was digging around, looking for it. He said he hadn't found anything."

"Neither did we," Rostic said. "We had the same idea. He wasn't the kind of man who would trust Mr. Totter, or anyone else, not to steal his money."

Rostic finished his hamburger. Shook his head. "I guess we could credit him pretty positively with most of those suspicious cases. That would get him up close to the record for a serial killer."

Leaphorn drained his cup. Put it down without comment.

"You have any more questions? About the fire or anything?" Rostic asked.

"Well, you didn't answer my question about the prints on that cognac bottle. Did they match?"

"Of course not," Rostic said. "Any more questions?"

"How about you? You satisfied?"

Rostic peered at him. Sighed. "Well, hell," he said. "I don't know what it is, exactly, but when a guy is as slick as Shewnack seemed to be . . . Well, you always feel sort of uneasy about it. Not quite as confident as you'd like to be."

"That's my problem, too," Leaphorn said. "You have time for another cup?"

"I'm retired," Rostic said. "I can either sit here and exchange war-against-crime stories with you or go on home and play Free Cell games on my computer. And by the way, you never told me what got you interested in this old case."

Leaphorn waved at the waiter, ordered coffee refills. "Then I'll tell you about Grandma Peshlakai, the theft of two five-gallon lard cans full of pinyon sap from the work shed behind her hogan, how she came to recover the empty cans at Totter's Trading Post, and how she discovered that Totter had died before he could be brought to justice and—"

"Wait at minute," Rostic said. He stopped sugaring his coffee and was looking very interested. "Back up. You're telling me Totter stole the old woman's pinyon sap? What the devil for? And he's dead? I want to hear more of this."

And so Leaphorn told him, and before the tale was finished so was a third cup of coffee and two more doughnuts. When it was finished, Rostic considered what he'd heard for a long silent moment.

"Couple of questions," he said. "Tell me why Totter stole the pinyon sap. And tell me why you're so interested in him now if he's dead and gone."

"If he stole the sap, and the only real evidence supporting that is empty buckets at the trading post, then it might have been something like this," Leaphorn said, "and I warn you, it is based on guesswork." With that, Leaphorn recounted the discussion he and Garcia had had speculating that Shewnack had planned to rob Totter, had tried it, had been killed by Totter, and Totter had decided that instead of dealing with a homicide trial he would use the sap to rush the fire along, convert both body and gallery to ashes, thereby disposing of homicide evidence and cashing in on his fire insurance without leaving behind the sort of evidence arson investigators look for.

"You mean the sap?" Rostic said, looking quizzical.

Leaphorn nodded. "Everybody burns pinyon. And that sap burns very, very hot."

"So how about the profit from the fire. You think Totter took the valuable stuff out first?"

"Now we come to this damned rug, the photograph of which sucked me into this business. Somebody seems to have taken that rug out. I'll bet it was the most valuable item Totter had. I saw it in Totter's gallery before the fire, and there it was on the wall of a mansion outside of Flagstaff after the fire. Unless somebody made a copy of it. Which seems to be very doubtful."

Rostic was chewing on his lower lip, face full of thought, frowning at Leaphorn, then producing a rueful grin. "That would make the bureau look sort of foolish, wouldn't it? But maybe it's right. It seems to make a certain amount of sense." He shook his head. "But now I want you to tell me how you'd like it if you had to go to a judge and try to get him to sign an arrest warrant for Totter. Of course you don't have to worry about that now, with him dead. But think about what you have. If you could get a judge to go even that far, how about trying to get him indicted? You think you could?"

Leaphorn laughed. "Not unless he was willing to confess."

"Tell me about Totter being dead," Rostic said. "How did that happen?"

"All I know is the *Gallup Independent* printed a little obituary notice, just saying he died of complications after a heart attack. Brief illness, I think it said. Died in an Oklahoma City hospital. Said he was buried in the VA cemetery at Oklahoma City, born in Ada, Oklahoma, never married, no survivors listed, any contributions for flowers should go to some charity."

Rostic looked skeptical.

"Who brought it in?"

"U.S. mail, with some money attached to pay the publication fee."

"Sent by whom?"

"Come on," Leaphorn said, sounding defensive, remembering how he had felt as a rookie cop being grilled by his boss. "All I know is what a secretary at the paper remembered about it. Bernie Manuelito went in there to get me a copy of it. I have the obit at home, and I remember it ran just two years or so after the fire."

"Okay, then," Rostic said. "I am getting more and more interested. The obit mentioned burial in the Veterans Administration cemetery in Oklahoma City. You sure they have one there?"

"No," Leaphorn said.

Rostic thought. "You know," he said. "I think I'll check on this."

"It would be easy for you," Leaphorn said. "Just call the FBI official there."

"Hah!" Rostic said. "First they'd refer me to the agent in charge, and he'd want to know my name, identification details, whether I was still in the bureau, and was this my case, and the violation of which federal law was involved, and what was the bureau's interest in it. Then, after about fifteen minutes of that, he'd tell me to send him a written report specifying the crime being investigated, and—" Rostic noticed Leaphorn's expression and stopped.

"You see what I mean? I used to work out of that Oklahoma City office. It always went strictly by the book. I'll bet it still does."

"I can understand that," Leaphorn said. "I was thinking I might go back there myself. Or maybe get Bernie to go."

"Investigating a crime in Navajo jurisdiction? How do you explain that?"

"To tell the truth, Bernie's sort of on administrative leave now, and she's now Mrs. Jim Chee."

"Sergeant Chee? Your assistant in the criminal investigation office?"

"Yes. They just got married. I'd ask her to do it sort of semi-unofficially, as a favor. Pay her travel expenses, and so forth."

"I've got a better idea," Rostic said. "I have an old friend back there, a longtime reporter. Guy named Carter Bradley. He was manager of United Press operations in Oklahoma when I was with the bureau there. Sort of famous for knowing everybody who knew anything. Not just knowing who knew. That's usually easy for reporters. But Carter knew who would be willing to talk about it. I think he'd do it for me."

"But if you knew him way back then, he's probably retired by now."

Rostic laughed. "Exactly. Just like us. Retired. Bored stiff. Wanting something interesting to do. Give me that obituary and I'll call him, give him the situation, and tell him what we need to know."

"I haven't got it with me here," Leaphorn said. "But I remember it. Which wasn't much."

"We'll find out who paid his hospital bill. Who arranged to get him buried, if he had any criminal record back there in his home state, everything useful. Do it right now."

Rostic had reached into his jacket pocket and extracted a cell phone, punched some buttons, said: "Yep. Here he is. What do I ask him?"

"What I'd be happy to know," Leaphorn said, "is whether Mr. Totter is actually dead."

"Consider it done," Rostic said, and began punching in numbers.

Leaphorn watched, reassessing his opinion of cell phones. But probably this wouldn't work. He waited.

"Hello," Rostic said. "Mrs. Bradley? Well, how are you? This is Ted Rostic. Remember? Special agent with the bureau way back when. Is Carter available?"

Rostic nodded, grinned at Leaphorn, signaled the waiter for another coffee refill. So did Leaphorn. This would probably take a while.

It didn't take very long. A few moments of exchanging memories of screwups and mistakes, a few comments of the travails of becoming elderly and the boredom of retirement, and then Rostic was explaining what he needed to know about the Totter death, giving Bradley his telephone number and asking Leaphorn for his.

"Ah, you mean my cell phone number?" Leaphorn asked. What was that number? Louisa, conscious of his attitude, had written it on a bit of tape and stuck it on the phone, but the phone was in the glove box of his truck. Leaphorn pondered a moment, came up with the number.

Rostic relayed it. "Okay," he said. "Thanks, Carter. No, it's nothing terribly pressing, but the sooner the better. Lieutenant Leaphorn and I are digging back into an old cold case. Very cold. Fine. Thanks again." He clicked off, shut the telephone.

"Well, thank you for that," Leaphorn said.

"Take my number," Rostic said. "And, damn it, if he calls you first, don't forget to call me. I'm getting interested in this thing, too."

Leaphorn was pulling away from his parking spot at the diner before the unusual look of the Crownpoint school parking lot down the street caught his attention. Unusual because it was crowded with vehicles. Unlike most school lots in urban areas of the West, most Navajo students got to school by school bus or on foot and therefore did not jam school lots with student-owned vehicles. The lot content was also remarkable because relatively few of the vehicles in it were pickup trucks. Mostly newish sedans and sports utility vehicles, and many of them wearing non-New Mexico license plates. Leaphorn had solved this minor mystery even before he'd noticed this. Today was the second Friday of the month, which meant the Crownpoint weavers cooperative was holding its monthly rug auction in the school gymnasium. Which meant tourists and weaving collectors and tourist shop owners from all over had swarmed in looking for bargains.

He pulled into the lot, found a spot by the fence, fished out his cell phone, and called his home number. Maybe Louisa would be back from her University of Northern Arizona Ute history project earlier than she'd expected. She wasn't, but the answering machine informed him he had a message waiting. He punched in the proper code to retrieve it.

It was Louisa's voice. "I don't know if this is worth bothering you with," she said. "But after I headed up toward the southern Ute country, I remembered I'd forgotten the new batteries I'd bought for my tape recorder so I went back to get them. There was a car parked in front of your house and when I pulled into the driveway, a man came out from behind the garage and said he was looking for you. He said his name was Tommy Vang, and that he lived in Flagstaff, and he wanted to talk to you. Wouldn't exactly say about what, but it seemed to have something to do with Mel Bork and that old rug you're interested in. I think he works for the man who now owns the rug. Anyway, I told him I wasn't sure where he could find you, but you had talked about going to Crownpoint to see a man named Rostic. Maybe he could find you there. And he thanked me and left. He was maybe five feet six and slender. Probably in his thirties or early forties, well dressed. Looked like he might be from one of the Pueblo tribes, or maybe Vietnamese. Very polite. Anyway, this getting a late start means I probably won't be back in Shiprock as soon as I'd hoped. And by the way, it sort of looked like he might have been poking around in the garage before he heard me driving up, but after he left I checked and there didn't seem to be anything missing. Anyway, old friend, take care of yourself. See you soon, I hope. Will exchange progress reports with you."

Leaphorn clicked off the phone and sat looking at it, considering Louisa's tone when she said "Anyway, old friend." And thinking maybe she was right about cell phones. It was handy to have one with you. He slipped it into his jacket pocket. Unless he was kidding himself, Louisa's tone had sounded very affectionate, sort of sentimental, which was good. What was bad was that she wouldn't be at the house when he got home. It would be empty, silent, cold. He sighed. No reason to hurry home. Maybe he would find someone at this collection of tribal weavers and the buyers of their work who could tell him something additional about the tale-teller rug. Or maybe he'd meet some old timers to talk to. Maybe, for example, the auctioneer who always handled this might know something useful.

Leaphorn entered the auditorium and saw that conversation would have to wait. On the stage the auctioneer was a lanky, raw-boned middle-ager wearing the same oversized reservation hat with the same silver-decorated hatband Leaphorn remembered seeing him with at earlier auctions. He was instructing two teenagers who were helping him sort out weavings on the table beside his podium. Leaphorn stood just inside the rear entrance door of the auditorium and inspected the crowd.

As was customary, both sides were lined with chairs, mostly occupied by women—about half were the weavers who had come to watch the rugs, saddle blankets, scarves, and wall hangings, on which they had spent untold hours creating, have their value measured in *belagaana* dollars. And, as was usual, the other half of the audience was composed of potential customers holding the white paddles marked with the big black numbers that would be recorded with their bids. Leaphorn gave that group only a cursory scanning, and focused on the tables by the entrance. There potential bidders were inspecting scores of weavings that would be moved to the stage for auctioning a little later. And there would be the old-time dealers of such items in the tourist shops of Albuquerque, Santa Fe, Scottsdale, Flagstaff, and all such places where tourists stopped in to find themselves a relic of Native Americana. Among those old timers, Leaphorn hoped to locate someone he knew, and someone who might know something about what he had come to think of as "that damned rug."

He spotted two such men. One, a tall, slender man

wearing a black turtleneck sweater and a neatly trimmed
goatee, was heavily engaged in discussing a very large
and ornate New Lands rug with an elderly woman. Probably not helpful because Leaphorn had once testified on
the other side of a legal action involving sale of Navajo
artifacts in his Santa Fe shop. The other man was exactly
the person Leaphorn had hoped to see—the operator of
Desert Country Arts and Crafts in Albuquerque's Old
Town district. He was short, substantially over the recommended weight for his height, and was bent over a Two
Grey Hills carpet, examining it with a magnifying glass.
Burlander was his name, Leaphorn remembered. Octa-
vius Burlander.

Leaphorn stopped beside him, waiting. Burlander
glanced at him. His eyebrows raised.

"Mr. Burlander," Leaphorn said, "if you have a little
time, I have a question for you?"

Burlander straightened to his full five feet five inches,
smiled at Leaphorn, stuck his magnifying glass in his
jacket pocket. "Officer," he said. "The answer is, I am not
guilty. Not this time anyway. And, yes, this rug is a genuine Two Grey Hills weaving, unimpaired by any chemical
dyes or other indecencies."

Leaphorn nodded. "And my question is whether you
could tell me anything about an old, old rug supposedly
woven about a hundred and fifty years ago. It was apparently a tale-teller rug, full of sorrowful memories of the
Navajo Long Walk, and was supposed to have been destroyed in a trading post fire a long time—"

"At Totter's place," Burlander said, grinning at Leaphorn. "But us people in the business always figured the
bastard looted his place himself before he burned it down,

and that famous Woven Sorrow rug was the first thing he stole."

"You have time to tell me about it?"

"Sure," Burlander said. "If you'll tell me what you're doing here. Which one of us in this crowd—" Burlander used both of his short, burly arms in an all-encompassing gesture—"is being investigated by the legendary lieutenant of the Navajo Tribal Police."

"Nobody," Leaphorn said. "I'm a civilian now."

"Heard you'd retired," Burlander said. "Didn't believe it. But what about that rug? I never did believe Totter let it burn."

"Did you know him?"

Burlander grinned. "Just by reputation. He was a relative newcomer out here. Supposed to have come in from California. Bought that old half-abandoned trading post, put in the art gallery. Had a reputation for faking stuff. You know they say bad news travels fast and far. But I hadn't heard anything about him since the fire."

"Obituary notice in the *Gallup Independent* reported he died in Oklahoma City, a few years after that fire. It said he was a veteran, was buried in the VA cemetery."

"I never heard about that. Guess I shouldn't have been talking ill about the dead. But what do you want to know about that old rug?"

"First of all," Leaphorn said, "do you think it survived that fire? If it did, do you think it could be copied? Do you think what I heard about it being sold at the Santa Fe Indian market after the fire could be true? And anything else you know."

Burlander was laughing. "Be damned," he said. "I haven't heard that old rug mentioned for years until this

very morning. Then old George Jessup over there—"
Burlander nodded toward the Santa Fe dealer whom
Leaphorn had noticed checking New Lands rugs "—well,
he asked me if I'd heard it was going to be for sale. Going
to be auctioned—e-Bayed, maybe, or maybe Sotheby's, or
some other auction company like that. He asked me if I'd
heard about it. I hadn't. He said all he knew was what a
fellow he knows in Phoenix had told him about it. Wanted
to know what I thought it would be worth. And if I would
bid on it."

"Would you? And how much would it be worth?"

"No," Burlander said. "Well, I don't think so. But if
there could be any sort of documentation of all those tales
that are told about it, it would bring big money from some
collectors." Burlander made a wry face. "There's some
real freaks out there."

"A man in Flagstaff owns it now," Leaphorn said.
"That, or a copy of it. He told me he was thinking about
getting rid of it. Which brings me to my other question.
He said he had bought it a long time ago at that market
under the porch of the Palace of Governors in Santa Fe.
Where the Pueblo Indians hold their market. What do you
think of that story?"

"Well," Burlander said, frowning, "it sounds sort of
wild to me. You don't see the really old, really expensive
things being dealt with there."

"That occurred to me," Leaphorn said.

"But, hell, anything's possible in this business That
would seem to mean that Totter had sneaked it out of his
gallery before he burned the place. Got somebody to sell
it for him. Who did this Flagstaff owner buy it from? And
who is he?"

"His name's Jason Delos," Leaphorn said. "Elderly fellow. Wealthy. Does a lot of big-game hunting. Came from the West Coast, so I hear, and bought a big house up in the San Francisco Peaks just outside Flagstaff."

"Don't know him. Did he say why he wants to sell it?"

Leaphorn considered how to answer that. Shook his head. "It's sort of complicated," he said. "A picture of his living room was printed in a fancy magazine. Somebody who knew it was supposed to have been burned came to see it and ask about it. And on his way back to Flagstaff his car skidded off that mountain road."

Burlander waited, gave Leaphorn a moment to finish the paragraph. When Leaphorn did not continue, he said, "Fatal accident? Killed the man?"

"They found his body in the car two days later," Leaphorn said.

Burlander grunted. "Well, that would sure fit into the stories I've heard about that rug. You know. About it being cursed by your shaman, and causing misfortune and disaster to whoever gets involved with it. Well, maybe that's why this Delos wants to dump it."

He produced a wry laugh. "And maybe it's the reason I doubt if I'll bid on it if it really is up for sale. I've got enough problems already."

The bell signaling resumption of the auction put a stop to their conversation. Leaphorn was handed a bidding paddle (number 87), found himself a seat, and began scanning the row of weavers along the walls, hoping to spot a woman who looked old enough to add something to his collection of information about the Totter rug. Many of them were elderly, several were ancient, and relatively few were young—a glum sign, Leaphorn thought, for the prospects of maintaining Dineh culture when his generation was gone. But that conclusion caused Leaphorn, being Leaphorn, to consider the other side of the issue. Maybe that just meant the younger generation was smart enough to notice that the pay scale for working half the winter to weave a rug—such as the one the auctioneer was now offering—that would sell for maybe $200 was not only unwise by *belagaana* standards but way below the legal minimum wage.

It was a pretty rug, in Leaphorn's judgment, about six feet by four feet, with a pattern of diamond shapes in muted reds and browns. The auctioneer had noted its good features and, as rules of the association required, noted that some of its yarn was not quite up to collector standards and that some of the color might be "chemical." But the weave was wonderfully skillful, tight and firm, and it was worth far more than the minimum bid of $125 the weaver had applied to it. Far more, too, he said, than the current bid of $140.

"You look at this in a shop in Santa Fe or Phoenix or even in Gallup, and they'll charge you at least five hundred dollars for it, and then put seven percent sales tax on top of it," he said. "Who's going to offer one-fifty." Someone did, and then a woman in the row ahead of Leaphorn waved her paddle and jumped it to $155.

The auctioneer finally closed it off at $160. The assistants brought out the next rug, held it up for the audience to admire, and the auctioneer began his description. Leaphorn reached a sensible conclusion. He was wasting his time in here. Even if some of the waiting weavers were ancient enough to know something useful about the Totter rug, they would almost certainly be traditionalists.

Therefore, they would not want to talk to a stranger about anything so enveloped in evil. Anyway, what possible good was knowing more about that damned rug going to do. Besides, it made more sense to move around through the crowd, in the auditorium and out of it, to see if Tommy Vang had come here looking for him. Why would Vang do that? Because Mr. Delos had told him to. And why would that be? A question worth getting an answer for.

Leaphorn walked out into the parking lot, stretched, enjoyed the warm sun and the cold, clear air, looked around. He heard someone shouting, "Hey, Joe." That would not be Tommy Vang; he would never shout and would never call him anything less dignified than Mr. Leaphorn.

It was Nelson Badonie, who about half a lifetime ago had been a sergeant in the Tuba City Tribal Police office. He was trotting toward Leaphorn, grinning broadly. "I saw you in there," Badonie said. "How come you didn't bid on that rug my wife wove? I was counting on you to run it up to about four hundred dollars."

"Good to see you, Nelson," Leaphorn said. "Looks like you've been eating well since your Tuba City days."

Badonie patted an expansive belly, still grinning. "Just got back to my natural weight," he said. "How about you, though? You slimmed down to mostly bones and gristle. And I heard you've been thinking about retiring."

"I have," Leaphorn said.

"Have thought about it? Or have quit?"

"Both," Leaphorn said. "I am now unemployed."

Badonie was looking back toward the entrance at a woman standing there. "I'm not," Badonie said. "That's my boss calling me right now." He waved to her. "By the way, Joe, you remember that Arizona deputy who used to work around Lukachukai, and Teec Nos Pos, and around the west side of the Chuska range? Back when we were younger? Deputy Sheriff Bork, it was then."

"Yes," Leaphorn said. "I remember him."

"Did you hear he got killed the other day over near Flagstaff. They thought it was just a car accident, but I just heard on the noon news it wasn't. It turns out he was poisoned."

"Poisoned?" Leaphorn said. "Poisoned how?" He had a sick feeling that he already knew the answer.

"The radio said the fellow at the sheriff's office reported they had an autopsy done. Didn't say the reason for doing that in a car wreck. But it seemed to show some poison had killed our Mr. Mel Bork before his car went off the road." Badonie shrugged. "Thought it might be some sort of violent food poisoning." Badonie chuckled. "Too much of that good, hot Hatch green chile, maybe," he said. "But it does seem funny, doesn't it? I mean, how something like that could happen."

"Did they say anything else about it? Have any suspects? Anything like that? Like any other reason why they didn't think he just skidded, or passed out and ran off the road?"

"All the newscaster said was they were investigating the case as a homicide," Badonie said. "Poison in the blood, I guess." Now Badonie was looking over his shoulder again, at his wife summoning him.

"See you later," he said, grinning, and trotted off wifeward.

Leaphorn didn't look after him. He extracted the cell

phone from his jacket, stared at it, remembered he had loaded a long list of Four Corners area police telephone numbers into it, then worked his way down to Sergeant Garcia's and punched it in.

A woman's voice responded to the ring. Yes, she said, he's here. Just a minute.

In about three minutes Garcia's voice was saying "Sergeant Garcia" in his ear, and he was asking Leaphorn what he needed.

"I need to know more about that autopsy report on Mel Bork," Leaphorn said.

"All I know is what I heard on the radio," Garcia said. "They think Bork was poisoned. Probably had that wreck because of that."

"Do you have the number for the coroner who did the autopsy? I think you said the pathologist was still old Dr. Saunders. That right?"

"Yeah. It's Roger Saunders," Garcia said. "Just a minute and I'll dig out his number for you."

Leaphorn dialed it, identified himself to a secretary, was put on hold, was told by another older-sounding woman that Dr. Saunders wanted to talk to him and could he hold another minute or two? He held. He switched the phone from right ear to left to allow his aching arm to dangle for a while. He looked around for a shady place to stand out of the warm autumn sun, found one that also allowed him the comfort of leaning on a car fender. He heard a voice saying hello and shifted the phone back to his better ear.

"Dr. Saunders," he said, "this is Joe Leaphorn. I wondered—"

"Great," Saunders said. "Aren't you the cop Garcia

told me about? The one who had suspicions about that Bork death? I've got some questions for you."

"It's mutual then," Leaphorn said. "You want to go first?"

"What made you suspicious? That's the big question. It sure as hell looked like just another guy driving too fast, skidding down into the ditch. The crash would have killed him even if he hadn't been poisoned."

"Mel was investigating an arson fire. Well, it had been ruled not arson, but it was suspicious-looking, a man burned in it, and just a bit before this wreck happened, a death threat turned up on his answering machine."

"Death threat," said Saunders, sounding both pleased and sort of excited. "Really? Tell me about that. Who was doing the threatening? I know he had been up in the San Francisco Peaks area talking with somebody up there just before it happened. Was that who was making the death threats?"

Leaphorn sighed. "A lot of this we don't know yet," he said. "When we find out, I'll fill you in. But what I need to know is how the poison got into him, and how fast it might have worked. Things like that."

"This is likely to sound odd," Saunders said, "but it appears that Mr. Bork managed to eat, or possibly drink, something we used to call 'rat zapper' back in the days when it was legal to use the stuff. You know anything about toxicology?"

"Not much," Leaphorn said. "I know arsenic is bad for you, and cyanide is worse."

Saunders laughed. "That's what most people know, and I guess that's why the books on the subject are full of cases using those, and a few others about as popular. The stuff that killed Bork is sodium monofluoroacetate. People have trouble pronouncing that, so toxicologists just call it compound ten-eighty. Back when it was on the public market it was called Fussol, or Fluorakil, or Megarox, or Yancock. For the past thirty years or so, owning it has been illegal except by licensed varmint-control people. We've never run into it here before, and none of the people I know in this business have either. You know, I think this case may get me invited to do a paper on it at the next meeting of our national association of folks who poke into corpses."

"This has me wondering how the poisoner got his hands on it," Leaphorn said. "Any suggestion?"

"Wouldn't be too hard out in this part of the world," Saunders said. "Lots of ranchers and farmers and so forth used it routinely to keep down the rat, mice, and gopher populations. They even used it in coyote bait in some places. Easy to use. It's based on a extremely toxic substance called . . ." Saunders paused, "—you ready for some more impossible words? Called dichapetalum cymosum, which they get out of a South African plant. If you found it in a drawer in an old barn, it would probably be in a box, or mason jar, and it would look a lot like regular wheat flour. Very easy to use. Just a tiny amount would be lethal."

"How tiny?" Leaphorn asked, thinking of Tommy Vang and the fruitcake cherries.

"Well, say you had about the volume equal to the amount of sulphur on the tip of a kitchen match. I'd say that would be enough to kill about ten or twelve men the size of Mr. Bork. But look, Lieutenant, if you want to know more, you could call the absolute national expert on it, a Dr. John Harris Trestrail. Lives in Michigan. I could give you his telephone number. Or you can get it out of one of his books. Best one I know about is called *Criminal Poisoning*, and it's sort of the international guide for forensic scientists. People like me."

"I'll look for it," Leaphorn said. "But you have any thoughts about how that poison got into Bork?"

"Something he ate, probably. Maybe something he drank."

"You could mix it into a cake batter? Something like that? Put it in coffee?"

"You could put it in, I'm sure, because it's water soluble. Maybe not coffee. It's odorless, but it might give the coffee a wee bit of an acidic taste. Cake? I don't know if the baking heat would have any effect."

"How about one of those fat maraschino cherries like people drop into their cocktails," Leaphorn asked. "Or stick on top of little cakes. Could you inject a little shot of that stuff into one of those?"

"Sure," Saunders said. "Perfect. In a cherry the victim would never taste it. Or not until it was too late. Soon as it hits the bloodstream it starts screwing up the nervous system, shutting down the heart. Victim goes into a coma in a hurry."

"From what I know about this case, the poison must have acted awfully fast. He left the house of a man he'd been questioning outside of Flagstaff and was driving home. He'd been given a lunch bag there while he was leaving, and he only got about twenty miles down the road before he ran off into the canyon. Now, given the fact he was a retired cop, and a very experienced mountain driver, I'd say it would be a matter of a very few minutes."

"Well, I'd say that fits very well," Saunders said. "And when you catch the man who doctored up the cherry, I want to hear about it."

16

While this conversation was winding down, Leaphorn had been keeping a casual eye on various auction attendees milling in the parking lot, hoping to see someone he recognized from his distant past, and failing at that. But as he slid the cell phone back into his jacket pocket he noticed that a young-looking man seemed to have taken an interest in his pickup truck. He was standing right beside it now, peering into the truck bed.

Leaphorn crossed the lot at something close to a trot, passed the hulking Ford 250 King Cab parked at the end of the row, an equally bulky Dodge Ram, and an SUV whose heritage he didn't identify. Beyond was his pickup, with a slender man leaning way into its bed, and then coming out of it looking at something in his hand. The man was Tommy Vang, and Tommy Vang was holding a paper sack, carefully unfolding its top, preparing to open it.

"Ah, Mr. Vang," Leaphorn said, "Professor Bourbonette told me you might be coming here to see me."

Tommy Vang had spun with remarkable agility. He
stood, feet spread, facing Leaphorn; his eyes were wide
as he sucked in a breath.

"And what have you found there?" Leaphorn asked.
"That looks like that lunch sack you so kindly prepared
for me at your place." Leaphorn was talking slowly, intent
on Vang's expression. It had varied from stunned to an
unreadable blank.

"That was very polite of you," Leaphorn added. "I'm
sorry to say I've been too busy to enjoy it."

Vang nodded, holding the sack against his chest,
looking like a little boy caught stealing.

"What caused you to think of making me a lunch?"
Leaphorn reached for the sack, lifted it from Vang's un-
resisting hand. "Professor Bourbonette told me you had
come to see me in Shiprock. She said you might come
here looking for me. Is that correct?"

Vang had regained his composure. He swallowed.
Nodded. "Yes," he said. "I came out to here hoping I could
talk to you."

"Why?"

Vang swallowed again. "To tell you that your friend—
that Mr. Bork who came to see us just before you came.
To tell you he was killed in a car accident. I thought you
should know about that."

Leaphorn waited, eyes on Vang. "Oh?" he said.

"Yes," Vang said, producing a smile. "You had come
to our house looking for him. Remember?"

"Did Mr. Delos send you?"

Vang hesitated. Thought. "Yes," he said. Grimaced.

Shook his head. "No," he said. "He has gone to hunt for another elk. But I thought I should come when I heard on the radio how Mr. Bork died."

Leaphorn unfolded the sack, looked in, saw a neatly made white bread sandwich wrapped in waxed paper and a Ziploc kitchen bag containing what seemed to be a V-shaped slice of something that must be fruitcake.

"This cake of yours looks very good," he said. "But remember what I told you and Mr. Delos, I never eat it very much because—" he smiled at Vang, and rubbed his stomach "—because for some reason it makes me sick. Ever since I was a boy. We Navajos never did eat much fruitcake. I guess we're not used to it."

Vang nodded, looking less tense, suddenly looking pleased. He held out his hand. "Then I am glad you didn't eat it," he said. "I will take it back now. It will be stale pretty soon." He shook his head, frowned disapprovingly. "Not so good anymore anyway, so I will take it away and get rid of it."

Leaphorn opened the Ziploc bag, slipped out the slice, and inspected it. It was stiff, firm, multicolored from the fruits mixed into it. He noticed a bit of yellow, probably pineapple, and what might be a bit of apple, and a chunk of peach, and lots and lots of dark red spots. Cherry red, Leaphorn thought. And another cherry, a great big one, sat atop the slice.

"I must say it does look delicious," Leaphorn said. "I think if I had taken it out and looked at it, I would have loved it." Leaphorn spent a moment admiring the cake, smiling at Tommy Vang. "Where did you learn how to cook like this, like this wonderful cake? Mr. Delos told me that all of your cooking is excellent."

Vang shrugged, produced a sort of shy, half-embarrassed smile.

"Mr. Delos, he sent me to cooking schools. At first when we stopped in Hawaii, and then again in San Francisco." The smile broadened, became enthusiastic. "It was a great school there. We baked pies. All kind of pies. And muffins and biscuits. Learned how to bake fish, and make kinds of chowder, and stews with vegetables. Learned just about everything. Even pancakes. Even jackflaps."

"And this fruitcake." Leaphorn displayed the slice. "Is this your production?"

"Oh, yes," Vang said.

"Well, it's a very pretty piece of work."

"All but that big cherry on the top. I chop up cherries and mix them in with the batter before I bake, but Mr. Delos, when it is for someone special, then he buys these big, expensive cherries and he decorates the top with them when I take the pan out of the oven."

Leaphorn considered this a moment.

"This slice here, was this for someone special?"

"Yes! Yes!" Tommy Vang said with a huge smile. "That was specially for you. Mr. Delos came into the kitchen, and he told me a very famous policeman was coming to visit us. He had me take out the cake I had baked for Mr. Bork, and cut another nice slice of it, and then he brought in his bottle of those big cherries he use in his Manhattans, and he decorate it for you."

"And this is one of those," Leaphorn asked, touching the cherry on the slice with a fingertip.

Tommy Vang nodded.

Leaphorn removed the cherry, noticed it had lost some of its plumpness, turned it in his fingers, pursed his lips. "It looks delicious," he said, and opened his mouth.

"Ah," Vang said. "Mr. Leaphorn." He held up his hand.
"No, I think maybe those special cherries are maybe
not carefully preserved. I wonder if maybe they are not
so good after they've been in the bottle too long. If they
haven't been kept sealed up, in cold storage."

"Why would you think that? It's a very good-looking
cherry," Leaphorn said, and held it out toward Vang. "Did
you notice this little puncture hole here in the side? I
wondered what would have caused that."

All the good nature was gone now from Tommy
Vang's face. And the tension was back. He leaned forward,
staring at the cherry perched between Leaphorn's thumb
and forefinger.

"Right there," Leaphorn said. "See the puncture
mark?" The wind had become gusty now, blowing leaves
across the lot, ruffling Vang's hair. Leaphorn protected
the cherry from the dust with his other hand.

"I see it," Vang said. "Yes. A little hole."

"Maybe you made it when you put it on the slice of
cake. Did you use any sort of pin to do that?"

"No." Vang said, sucked in a deep breath, and sighed.
"Maybe when they put it in the bottle, the cherry people.
Maybe that's what did it?"

"I'll bet they just pour them into the bottle. Wouldn't
you think? I can't think of any reason they'd stick a needle
into them."

"I don't know," Vang said. He stood, arms folded against
his chest, looking at Leaphorn with a sad expression.

Leaphorn replaced the cherry on the slice, deposited
the slice into the Ziploc sack, zipped it shut, dropped it
into the sack, and folded the sack shut again.

"You said you came to see me about something,
Tommy. So let's sit in my truck awhile, get out of the wind,
and let me know what you want to talk about. And I'd
like to know more about why you drove all the way out
here looking for me. I don't think it was just to tell me
about Mr. Bork being killed because I bet you'd know I
probably already had heard about that from the news
broadcasts."

Leaphorn opened the passenger side door, held it.

Tommy Vang stared at him, expression doubtful.

"Please, Tommy. Get in. Something is bothering you.
Let's talk about it. It shouldn't take long, and then you can
go home again."

"Home," Tommy said, shaking his head. He climbed
in, and Leaphorn took his own seat behind the wheel.

"What's worrying you, Tommy?"

Tommy was staring at the windshield. "No worry," he
said. "No worry."

"But it seems to me that something is just sort of
bothering you?"

Tommy laughed. "I have a puzzle," he said. "You are a
policeman. You caught me stealing something from your
truck. All you do is just talk to me, very polite. You could
have arrested me."

"For stealing a piece of stale fruitcake?"

Tommy ignored that. Just shrugged.

"Then I have a puzzle, too. I don't know if you heard
that the sheriff had an autopsy done to find out what
caused Mr. Bork to let his car run down into that canyon.
They announced that Mr. Bork had been poisoned. Apparently the poison gets the blame for his car running off
the road. He didn't die in the accident. He was already

dead. Did you hear that? Did you think your cake might have made him sick?"

Tommy Vang was looking down, thinking.

"I've been wondering if you might have come here to warn me. Just to keep me from eating it?"

"Not the cake," Tommy said. "The cake wouldn't have hurt Mr. Bork. The cake I make is good."

"Then is it the cherry? Is that it?"

"The cherry might be spoiled. Out in the heat. Fruits get rotted, not preserved properly," Vang said, his voice so choked that Leaphorn could barely understand him. "Maybe that was what got the people sick."

The people, Leaphorn thought. Other people? Tommy's command of the nuances of English was somewhat shaky, but he seemed to have more people than just Mel Bork in mind. Leaphorn considered that, decided to let it wait and come back to that question later.

"Well, let's not worry about that then," Leaphorn said. "I'm curious about how you got acquainted with Mr. Delos. I guess he worked for our government in Southeast Asia during the Vietnam War. Is that where you met him?"

"In Laos," Tommy said, staring at the windshield. "In our mountains. A long, long time ago."

Laos? Leaphorn considered that, wishing he had a better recollection of Asian geography and the pattern of that war. If his memory was right, Laos would be on the border of about everything. It would fit Delos's presumed role as a CIA operative. The CIA was working on all the edges there.

"Is that where you started working for Mr. Delos?"

"My father did," Tommy said. "And my uncles, and—" he exhaled, shook his head, broke off his study of the windshield to look at Leaphorn "—and about everybody in our village. All the Vangs, and Thaos, and the Chues anyway. All the families except the Cheng men. They had mostly joined the Vietcong. And the Pham. I don't know about them, but I think they were maybe working with the Pathet Lao."

"You're not Vietnamese, then?"

"We were Hmong," Tommy said. "Our people were running out of China. Getting away from the wars that always went. Coming down into the Laos mountains, I think maybe same time Europeans were migrating into America. My older kinfolks still used Chinese words. But the CIA didn't mind. They recruited the men in our village. We were already having to fight both the Vietnamese and the Pathet Lao. Trying to protect our villages. And then the Americans came in and wanted us to help them fight their war. That how I got acquainted with the colonel. He wasn't Mr. Delos then. He was Colonel Perkins. He was recruiting my family members."

"What did this colonel want you to do for him?"

Tommy produced a wry-sounding laugh. "I guess you would say he was a collector of information. He would come into our house, and my father and uncles, and the men from the Thao and Chue families would come in and talk. And Mr. Delos would tell each one of them where he wanted them to go, and what he wanted them to watch for. Mostly he would be sending them back into Vietnam to watch the trails the Congs were using. When they got back, Mr. Delos would come again, and they would tell him what they had seen."

"Did he have you doing anything for him?"

Tommy shifted in his seat, wiped his hand across his eyes. "I was too young to be useful at first, and my mother wouldn't let me go anyway. Then one night my uncle came back, and he said some North Vietnam soldiers had seen them and they had killed my father and my youngest uncle. Or maybe just took them captive. He wasn't sure, and I never did find out. But after that, the Vietcong came to our village, and my mother and sister and I, we had to hide out in the mountains."

With that Tommy resumed his study of the windshield, lost in his memories.

Leaphorn waited, as unwilling to interrupt such thoughts as he was to break into a conversation, and just studied Tommy Vang. Very slender, Leaphorn noted. Very neat. Trimmed. Buttoned. Clean shaven. Shirt cuffs correct. Trousers somehow still properly creased. Vang raised a hand, and wiped the back of it across his cheek. Wiping away a tear, perhaps. The wind rattled dust against the truck door. Two women hurried past, one carrying a blanket. Tommy sighed, shifted in his seat.

"We were living in a sort of a cave shelter up there in the high ridges after that. The American planes, they came over, very loud, very low, and they bombed our village with napalm. I guess they'd got the word that the Cong had moved in." He laughed. "I always wondered if Mr. Delos told them. Anyway, we went back down later to pick up what was left."

With that Tommy lapsed into silence, looking straight ahead.

Overcome with memories, Leaphorn guessed.

"Not much left," Tommy Vang said. "Even the pigs. The napalm fire had flooded right over all their pens so they couldn't get away." He sighed. "All burned up. I still remember. It smelled like a huge roast feast like we'd have for a wedding banquet. That is sort of special with the Hmong elders." He glanced at Leaphorn, looking doubtful. "I think the way we are supposed to be taught God gave us multiple souls, or maybe I should say duplicate souls, and the duplicate souls live on in our animals."

"I read about that when I studied anthropology. In an article about Hmong funeral rituals."

"I don't know enough about it," Vang said. "I was too young. The elders were busy with fighting the Vietcong and the others. And hiding. Too busy to teach the children. You understand?"

"I do," Leaphorn said. "It happened in a different way to some of us. We were hauled away to boarding schools. But I'd like to know when you finally got reconnected with Mr. Delos?"

"That was later. My mother died and I got put in a refugee camp. Mr. Delos found me there and started paying me a fee to get him information on anyone in the camp who was—" Tommy paused, trying to decide how to explain. "People who were what he called 'Cong-connected.' I did that, and then, it was the next summer I think, he came and got me and took me Saigon. I worked for him there. We stayed at a big hotel and he went to work down at the U.S. embassy until the North Vietnamese came in, and the helicopters came in and the Americans got on them and went home. I told him I could find my way back to Klin Vat. I would help rebuild our village and get back with my relatives in the Vang family. Not a good idea, Mr. Delos said to me."

Tommy held up an open hand to demonstrate how Mr. Delos had made his case.

"In the first place, Mr. Delos said, he had done some

checking and he had learned that between the Pathet Lao and the North Vietnamese army getting their revenge, there didn't seem to be any Hmong people left from that village." With that Tommy pulled down one of his fingers. "In the second place, there wasn't anything left of the village." A second finger came down. "It had been hit with that napalm again. And in the third place, Mr. Delos said there didn't seem to be anyone left in that part of our mountains. He thought the Vangs, and the Chengs, and the Thaos must have all scattered elsewhere to escape the Pathet Lao and the Vietcong."

Tommy Vang closed his hand, looked down at it. Expression sad.

"But you still want to go back?"

Tommy Vang turned in the seat, and stared at Leaphorn, his expression incredulous. "Of course. Of course. I am all alone here. Alone. Nobody at all here. And there, I know I could find some of my people. Not many maybe. But there would be somebody there. I think so. I am pretty sure of that."

He turned away, stared out the side window, silent. Then he raised his hands, a gesture that encompassed all he was seeing. The dusty wind, the desiccated landscape of high country desert with winter coming on. "It is cold here," said Vang, talking to the glass. "And there is the green, the warmth, the ferns, the moss, the high grasses, and the waving bamboo. There is the sense of everything being alive. Here all I see is dead. Dead rock, cliffs with snow on them. And the sand."

A tumbleweed bounced off the windshield. "And that," Tommy added. "Those damned weeds that are nothing but brittle stems and sharp stickers."

"So you're going back?" Leaphorn said. "You're planning that? Have you made your plans? Arranged it?"

Tommy Vang sighed. "Mr. Delos has told me he will make the arrangements. When the proper time comes, he will send me home."

"Has he made any plans for that?"

"I don't know. He doesn't talk about it. But he said that when he is finished with everything here, he will send me back. Or maybe he will go back with me."

Finished with what? Leaphorn thought. But that question too would wait. Anyway, he thought he knew the answer.

"Would you be going back to Vietnam? Or Laos? I don't imagine the Hmong have any sort of passport, or entry visas, or that sort of paperwork."

"If they ever did, they probably wouldn't by now," Tommy said. "I guess our mountains are not ours anymore. We fought for the Americans, and the Americans went home."

"Yes," Leaphorn said. "We sometimes do things without really knowing what we are doing. Then we say we're sorry about that. But I guess that doesn't help much."

Tommy Vang opened his door. "Would you give me back my piece of fruitcake? I must be going now. I have more things to do."

"It's still early," Leaphorn said. "You said you had come here to talk to me. We haven't talked much. Did you find out what you wanted to know?"

Vang settled himself into the seat. "I guess I don't know. I think I found things I didn't expect."

"Like what?"

Vang smiled at Leaphorn. "Like you are a nice man. I didn't expect that."

"You didn't like me?"

"No. Because you are a policeman. I didn't think I would like a policeman."

"Why not?"

"I have sometimes heard bad things about them," Vang said. "Probably not true. Maybe some policeman are bad and some are good." He smiled, shrugged. "But now I have to go. I have to find a place out here—" he waved both hands in a widespread gesture. "I know its name, but its name is not on my map."

"Maybe I can help you with that." He patted Vang's shoulder. "Maybe that would prove to you that I'm one of the good policemen. What's the name of the place?"

Vang extracted a folded postcard from his shirt pocket. Unfolded it, read from it.

Leaphorn understood "chapter house," but the rest was lost in Vang's Hmong interpretation of the message.

"Let me see it," Leaphorn said, and took the card.

On it was written:

Tomas Delonie. Torreon. Chapter house. Use 371 north, then Navajo 9 east to Whitehorse Lake, then 12 miles northeast to Pueblo Pintado, the 9 southeast about 40 miles, then 197 short distance northeast. Look for Torreon Navajo Mission signs. Ask directions.

"I think you will have troubles finding that place," Leaphorn said. "I think I should help you."

"Yes," Vang said. "This place. Torreon. I not find on my map. Nor some of these roads. They're not included.

Not marked." He showed Leaphorn his map. It was an old Chevron Service Station version.

"An old map," Leaphorn said. "I have a better one." Tomas Delonie, he was thinking. Why was Tommy Vang making this trip?

"Mr. Delos gave you these directions, I guess," Leaphorn said. "He didn't have a new map. And I would doubt that he knows this eastern side of the Navajo Reservation very well."

"I guess he wouldn't," Vang said.

"But he wrote these directions for you?"

"Oh, yes," Vang said.

Leaphorn opened his mouth intending to ask why. To learn if Vang would tell him if Delos had explained the reason for this trip and just what he wanted Vang to learn about Delonie. But he wanted to approach that carefully with Vang.

"I guess he wanted to be sure he knew just where Mr. Delonie lives, and where he works, and things like that. Things he'd need to know if he wanted to come and visit him. He didn't explain it, but it was about like that, I think. He told me just to sort of act like I was a tourist. You know. Asking about things, looking all around. But then he wanted me to be able to tell him what sort of vehicle Mr. Delonie drove—car or truck, what kind, what color. If he lived alone. Things like that. When he went to work. When he came home. If he had a woman, or anybody else, living with him."

Vang paused, reached into his jacket pocket. "And he gave me this."

Vang extracted a very small camera and showed it to Leaphorn.

"It is one of those new ones with the computer chips," Vang said, smiling proudly. "Very modern. You look through the finder, and see what you are photographing, and click it. Then if you don't like it, you can erase it, and shoot again until you get good pictures. What you think? Pretty nice?"

"He wanted you to photograph Delonie?" That thought surprised Leaphorn.

"No. No. Not like taking his portrait, not anything like that. He said just take casual pictures. Of his house, his truck, things like that. But he didn't want Mr. Delonie to see me taking pictures. He told me that lots of people don't like having their pictures taken."

"Did he want you to question Mr. Delonie about anything?"

"Oh no," Vang said. "I was just to be acting like a tourist. Just curious. Just looking around. It would be best, Mr. Delos said, if Mr. Delonie didn't even notice me."

"Did he tell you anything about Delonie? About whether he was an old friend? Anything like that?"

"No," Vang said, "but I don't think he was a friend."

Leaphorn studied Vang. "What causes you to think that?"

Vang shrugged. "Nothing, really. Just the way he looked when he talked about him. It make me think that Mr. Delonie made Mr. Delos feel nervous. Or something like that, I think."

Exactly, Leaphorn thought. Mr. Vang is short on information but well armed with an astute intelligence. Smart enough to try to look beyond the bright and shiny surface of external appearances.

"You know, Tommy, I think the only sensible thing for

us to do is for me to take you there," Leaphorn said. "We can leave your car here in Crownpoint. Lock it up. We'll tell whoever's at the Tribal Police office. They'll take care of it."

Vang looked doubtful.

"Otherwise, you'll probably get lost," Leaphorn said.

"I think I have to take the truck I came in," Vang said. "Have to have it."

Leaphorn noticed Vang was looking tense, frightened.

"Why not just ride with me?"

Vang looked at Leaphorn, looked away, then down. "After I go where Mr. Delonie lives, ah—. After I do what Mr. Delos told me to do, then I have to drive over to that place where he will be shooting the elk, and wait for him there, and he will be looking for this truck, and if I am riding in another truck, I think then he would think that I have been disobeying him."

"Oh," Leaphorn said. And waited.

"Yes," Vang said. "I think I had better be there in that truck I drive for him."

"Are you sort of afraid of him?"

"Afraid?" Vang asked, and thought about it. Nodded. "Yes," he said. "Very afraid."

Leaphorn considered that for a moment. Of course he would be afraid. Everything in Tommy's life depended on Jason Delos. Going home to his Hmong mountains, most of all.

"Okay," he said. "Then we will turn the arrangement around. We'll leave my truck at the Tribal Police office and we'll take this one."

And so they did. Vang pulled his King Cab pickup

into the Tribal Police parking lot behind Leaphorn, then turned off the ignition and waited while Leaphorn went into the office.

Inside, Leaphorn shook hands with Corporal Desmond Shirley and explained what he was doing. Then he returned to his pickup and removed his cell phone and his police issue .38 pistol from the glove box. He dropped both into his jacket pocket, locked the door, and walked over to where Vang was sitting in his vehicle, watching.

"I think I should drive," Leaphorn said.

Vang looked surprised.

"Because while you know the truck better, I know the roads, and all these pickups are pretty much alike."

Vang scooted over.

He took them north past the Crownpoint airport, then eastward across twenty-five miles of absolutely empty country toward Whitehorse. For the first half hour they drove in a sort of nervous silence, with Vang keeping his eye on his own road map—apparently making sure Leaphorn was taking them where his instructions told him to go. At the little settlement of Whitehorse, the pavement of Navajo 9 swerves northward to climb Chaco Mesa en route to the ancient ruins of Pueblo Pintado before swerving back southward toward Torreon. Leaphorn turned off the pavement onto the twenty-three miles of dirt road that goes directly to Torreon without the wide detour.

"Ah, Mr. Leaphorn," Vang said, sounding uneasy. "You are leaving Highway 9. But my map says Nine takes us to Torreon. Takes us to find Mr. Delonie."

"It does," Leaphorn said. "But this dirt road takes us there directly, without going way up on Chaco Mesa. This way we get there quicker, and right to the Torreon Chapter House. We should stop there and ask where we can find Delonie."

"Oh," Vang said. "Would he maybe be at the chapter house? Is that like a government office? For the Navajos who live around there?"

"It is," Leaphorn said. "But Delonie isn't a Navajo. I know he's part Indian—Pottawatomie and Seminole—because the name sounds French."

"French?" Vang's tone suggested he would like an explanation.

"Both of those tribes once lived in the part of America where a lot of French people settled. Like Louisiana and that southern coastal country. Then the Pottawatomies helped General Jackson defeat the British in the War of 1812. The fight for New Orleans. And when Jackson was elected president, he granted citizenship to the Pottawatomies who helped him. Made them the 'Citizen Band.' Then when the white people wanted the land they were living on, he had the army round them up and moved them to Kansas."

Leaphorn glanced at Vang, noticed that Vang was not following his explanation and decided to hurry through it.

"Anyway, then the railroad built a transcontinental line through there, and the land in Kansas got valuable and the white people wanted it. So the Pottawatomies were rounded up again and moved down to Oklahoma. They called it Indian Territory then. A lot of Seminoles got there, too, but I don't remember how that happened."

Vang considered this.

"I think this is something like what happened to our people, too. My parents said our ancestors started way up north, in China, and kept being pushed south, and finally got chased up into the mountains. But if Mr. Delonie is not a Navajo, why then would those at the Navajo Chapter House be likely know where to find him?"

"Because when there aren't many people around, everybody gets noticed. I guess you've seen that very few people live out here." He glanced at the odometer. "In the thirty-one miles since we left Whitehorse we have not passed even one residential place. And just about forty people live at Whitehorse. Where there are very few people, the people who are there all seem to know one another, no matter their tribe or their race."

"It was that way in our mountains, too. But just in the mountains. Out of the mountains where there were more people nobody liked the Hmongs."

"Look to the south," Leaphorn said, gesturing to the mountain dominating that horizon with enough early winter snowpack to provide a glittering reflection of afternoon sunlight. "The map you have calls it Mount Taylor; it's fifty miles from here, and there is absolutely nobody between us and that mountain."

Vang considered that. "It looks so close."

"It's an old volcano," Leaphorn said, finding himself lapsing into his habit of becoming a tour director anytime he was driving with anyone unfamiliar with his territory. "Biggest mountain in this part of the reservation. Eleven thousand three hundred and something feet high. It has a lot of historical and religious significance for us. In our people's origin story, it was built by First Man when the Navajos first got here. It's one of our four sacred mountains. Four mountains that mark the boundaries of our land. We have several names for that one. The Navajo ceremonial name is *tsoodzil,* and the formal title is *dootl'izhiidzii,* which translates to 'Turquoise Mountain.' And then on the map it's named after General Zachary Taylor, and we also call it 'Mother of Rains' because the west winds pile clouds on top of it and then drive out over the prairie."

Leaphorn noticed Vang had been trying to suppress a grin. Recognized what might be an opportunity to get closer to this man. To understand him. To be understood.

"You're smiling," Leaphorn said. "What?"

"The way you say those two Navajo names," he said, grinning again. "Our Hmong language has words like that. You have to make funny sounds when you say them."

"Some of our words don't fit well with the white man's alphabet," Leaphorn said. "And since your people originated in China—well, at least a lot of anthropologists believe you did, and there's pretty good evidence that was your point of origin, too. So it wouldn't surprise me if we had some connections way back in time. How about your tribe's stories of how it originated?"

Vang looked surprised. Raised his eyebrows. Said, "I don't anything know about that. About what you mean."

"I mean like what we call 'origin stories.' For example, in the Judeo-Christian culture—the Europe-based white culture—in that one God created the universe in a series of six days, and then said we should rest on the seventh one." Leaphorn summarized the rest and mentioned the Garden of Eden.

"Adam and Eve," Vang said. "I've heard about that." He smiled, touched his side. "And that's why we have one less rib on one side of our chest."

Leaphorn paused, glanced at Vang, his facial expression a question. Vang nodded. Yes. He was interested.

"Well, Navajo tradition, at least the way I was taught it in my clan, doesn't give us such a clear statement of the creating power, or the sequences of how it happened. We believe we first existed in a series of previous worlds, but not exactly as flesh and blood humans. We were more like concepts, sort of the notion of what we would eventually be. Anyway, in our first world we do evil things and the Creator destroys it, and we escape into a second world. These early humans . . ." Leaphorn paused again, studying Vang. "Am I getting too confusing?"

"Go on," Vang said.

"Let's call this early version of humans prehumans," Leaphorn said. "Anyway, bad conduct again, and the second world was destroyed, and they escaped into the third world. Now our origin stories get more detailed. We learn how the prehumans were separated into the sexes; men and women. Men doing the hunting and fishing and being the warriors, and the women raising families. The selfish, mean, greedy behavior was going on again, and the Creator repeated the process. The way my clan teaches the story, a sort of super-version of Coyote kidnapped the baby of another of these primal beings—one we call Water Monster—and he was so enraged he produced a terrible flood and drowned the third world as punishment. So we climbed up through a hollow reed and escaped into this world."

Leaphorn gestured at the landscape they were driving through, the eroded slopes of the butte they were passing, the distant mountain ridges, the high, dry, semidesert landscape of rabbit brush, snakeweed, bunchgrass, and juniper and, above it all, a scattering of puffy clouds decorating the clear deep blue of the high country sky.

"Our Fourth World," Leaphorn said. "We call it Glittering World."

He glanced at Vang, who was staring out the windshield.

It was a longer statement than Leaphorn had intended, but Vang's expression showed he was interested. Maybe even intensely interested.

"You have any questions?" Leaphorn asked.

"Oh, yes," Vang said. "You climbed up to here—" Vang indicated "here" with a wave of his hand at the landscape. "Climbed up a hollow reed?"

"Well, as I understand it, we weren't really humans yet. But they had human characteristics. The same tendency to push and shove, try to get on top, try to get out in front, and they still had to get revenge, for example, if someone hurt them. The habits that always got them into trouble. I guess you could just call it selfishness. Being greedy."

Vang considered this. Nodded. "All the bad things that were the reason the Creating Spirit punished them for. The reasons the Creator made the flood. To destroy all that. That's what it means?"

"I think so," Leaphorn said. "That's all that seems to make any sense, anyway. In any of these various religions, the Creator seems to have started mankind, to have given humans a bunch of lessons on how to live the good life, be happy, stay happy by loving your neighbors, feeding the poor, not being selfish. Not chasing after fame, fortune, three car garages, all that. But he didn't make us slaves. He gave us a way to tell good from evil, but he also gave us free will. You know. Do you want to get rich, or do you want have a good life. It's our choice."

"I think our people got created a lot like that, too. But I never really had much chance to hear our stories. And I don't think the Hmong ever had much chance to get rich." He sighed. "Didn't even have any chance to teach their children about all that."

Vang's voice faded into a sort of sadness when he said that, and he looked down at his hands.

Something like me, Leaphorn was thinking. Tommy Vang sitting there beside him was another product of childhood interrupted. Vang's by war. Joe Leaphorn's by that old assimilation policy of the Bureau of Indian Affairs. By the school buses that hauled Indian kids away to boarding schools. Away from our hogans where the old people would have been teaching us all the ancestor stories—of the first, second, and third worlds. The buses brought them home when summer came, of course, to help with the herding, and their other duties, but the summer was the time tradition allowed for another set of stories, about hunting, relations with the animal worlds. The origin stories could be told only in the cold times, during the season when the thunder sleeps, when it was quiet, and the snow kept them in the hogans, and there was nothing to distract them, nothing to keep the children from listening, and thinking, and understanding.

And thus, Leaphorn was thinking, the assimilation program had cost much of this generation the heart and soul of the Navajo system of values. And this led him to another thought. Why younger, much more modern Officer Jim Chee, who had been born late enough to escape assimilation, was much better tuned to the Navajo Way than he was. Why Jim Chee still believed he could be both a policeman enforcing most *belagaana* laws and a

shaman conducting the ceremonies that cured people
who violated Navajo cultural rules and restored them to
harmony.

"Why don't you tell me what you remember,"
Leaphorn said. "When I was a lot younger and a student,
I studied anthropology at the university. I learned just a
little, very, very little, about the cultures of your part of the
world. Didn't your Creator have an emissary, sort of an am-
bassador, who he sent down to sort of govern humanity?"

"Ah, yes," Vang said, looking delighted. "How you
know about that?"

"Mostly just from books," Leaphorn said. "We used
one called"—Leaphorn paused, probing his memory—"I
think it was *Hmong, A History of a People.*"

"Did it tell about Hua Tai?"

"I have to think," Leaphorn said, noticing that Vang's
attitude had changed abruptly. His patient, enduring leth-
argy had converted into enthusiasm.

"As I remember it," Leaphorn said, "Hua Tai was the
God who created the world and the people. But most of
the little bit we learned was about his lieutenant. I think
'Harshoes,' or something like that. I sort of thought of him
as being like Mohammed. You know, the prophet who
represented God to the Arabian world."

"You say his name 'Yer Shua,'" Vang said, pronouncing the syllables very slowly and repeating them. "I have
heard about Mohammed. They talk about him some on
the television news. About the war in Iraq. But Yer Shua
was different, I think. He was part God and part man, I
think. I remember they told about him being a farmer
like the rest of the Hmong people, and raising pigs and
having a whole lot of wives. And he was the one who tried

to take care of the Hmong people. I mean he tried to protect them."

"We Navajos have what we call *yei,*" Leaphorn said. "Powerful, like spirits, but good. And the *belagaana*—white people—they have . . . well it depends on whether they're Christian, or Jewish, or what. Anyway, their bad supernatural beings are devils, or witches, or some other names. Good ones are angels."

They crossed the Continental Divide on Navajo Route 9 as Leaphorn was covering this side of theology, and now the Torreon ridge rose about six miles ahead, and beyond it Torreon arroyo and Torreon itself, with its chapter house and maybe, Leaphorn guessed, something like 150 residents scattered around the valley. Above it all, rising like a great sunlit thumb against a background of scattered clouds some thirty miles to the southeast, was Cabezon Peak. The thoughts Leaphorn had been forming jelled into a sudden decision. He slowed, pulled the vehicle off to the side where a ranch entry road had widened the shoulder.

"There's Torreon," he told Vang, pointing at the scattered buildings far ahead. "Before we get there, let's talk about what we're doing there." He released his seat belt and opened the car door.

"Talk?" Vang said. "What we talk about?"

"I want to hear some more about what you've been telling me about the Hmong, for one thing," Leaphorn said. "And if you're interested, I'll tell you more about the Dineh and about our traditional relationship with God and the spirits. And then we ought to plan what we're going to do about finding Mr. Delonie. And we should stretch our legs a little. I'm getting old, and I get stiff."

"Sure," Vang said.

Leaphorn got out, stretched, leaned against the fender, admired the view, planning his tactics. Vang joined him, glanced at Leaphorn inquiringly, and leaned against the car door.

"Not many people," Leaphorn said. "A few down below, then miles and miles and miles in every direction, no sign of people." He pointed down the road toward the village. " 'Torreon' means tower, and when that little valley was first occupied by people, they built one out of stones because enemies kept attacking them."

Vang considered that. "Like what they say about Hmong. Everywhere we went people attacked us." He glanced at Leaphorn, a wry smile. "We even had a god like that. His name was Nau Yong, and they called him 'the Savage One' because what he liked to do was capture lots of Hmong people, and tear them apart and drink their blood." Vang grimaced. "Like he was a great tiger in the forest. They said he was the chief of all the bad spirits. Sort of like their king."

Leaphorn considered this. "Did he live on top of a mountain?" Leaphorn asked.

Vang looked surprised. "How did you know?"

"Maybe I read it somewhere," Leaphorn said. "But that's usually how it worked."

He pointed toward the south, where Mount Taylor's crest was visible against the horizon. "That's our Sacred Mountain of the South, our boundary marker. According to my clan's traditions, it was the home of a supernatural named 'Ye-iitsoh.' He was our version of your, ah, Nau Yong. Sort of in charge of all the vestiges of greed, hatred, malice, selfishness, cruelty, and so forth. The way our origin worked, our First Man spirit when he was escaping the flood that forced us to move up here, he sent a diving bird back into the water to recover what he called his 'way to make money.' In other words, it contained everything that caused the greed and selfishness."

Leaphorn was watching Tommy Vang's expression through every word of this.

"Do you understand?" he asked.

"Sure," Vang said. He threw out his hands. "Everybody fighting everybody else to collect more money, bigger car, bigger house, get famous on television. Get to the top of that mountain yourself. Step on the Hmong people. Climb over them."

Leaphorn chuckled. "That's the general idea."

"I heard that you Navajo say the way to find witches, anybody evil, is to look for people who have more than they need and their kinfolks are hungry."

Leaphorn nodded. "And also according to our origin story, two good *yei* decided to go around this glittering world and eliminate all the bad *yei* to make this place safe for regular humans, like you and me, to live here. They killed the Ye-iitsoh up on the mountain, cut his head off."

Leaphorn pointed at Cabezon Peak. "That's his head," he said. "It rolled all the way down there and turned into stone. And Ye-iitsoh's blood flowed down the other side of the mountain and dried into all the back lava flow along the highway around Grants."

"So I guess everybody has this idea about evil. Pretty much alike," Vang said.

"And people who fight evil, too," Leaphorn said. "Sometimes that's got to be policemen."

Vang looked at him. "Like you?"

Leaphorn considered that. "Maybe like both of us," he said. "I'm going to ask you a bunch of questions."

"Oh," Vang said. And thought for a moment. "What do I know?"

"First, when Mr. Delos brought you from Asia, you came to San Francisco, right?"

"Yes. We stayed in a hotel there."

"What year was that?"

"Year?" He shook his head.

"Then how old were you?"

"I was ten. Or maybe eleven. Mr. Delos had to buy me some new clothes because I had gotten a little bigger."

"And what did you do at the hotel?"

"A woman came in every day. A Chinese woman. And she would help me some with learning better English. Like we would watch the children's program on television, and she would help explain. And then she started teaching me how to cook, and how to iron shirts, and how to keep everything neat and clean. Things like that. And sometimes she would take me out in a taxicab and show me the city. And every evening we would sort of plan a dinner if Mr. Delos was going to be home, and she would teach me how to cook it. And then I would put out the plates and the silver, and she would go." Vang looked at Leaphorn, smiling. "That was fun. And good, good food."

"She didn't stay at night."

"No. No. Just daytime. Five days a week. That was for maybe the first year. Then Mr. Delos thought I was ready to go to cooking school and I would spend my daytimes at a sort of restaurant-bakery and food store. The boss there was from Manila. A nice man, and he knew something about Hmong people, but the other language he spoke was sometimes Spanish and sometimes a sort of tribal speech. From his island, I think."

"Were you still living in the hotel?"

"Oh, no. We moved into an apartment building. Close enough so I could walk down to where I was working."

"And what was Mr. Delos doing?"

"He was gone away most of the time. Sometimes people would come there to see him, and Mr. Delos would tell me to plan a meal for them, buy the wine, all that. I would put flowers on the table. Make everything nice. Put on this sort of apron and white cap he bought for me, and be the waiter. I enjoyed that."

"Gone most of the time?" Leaphorn said. "For days, or weeks, or months? Do you know where?"

"Usually just a few days, but sometimes for a long time. Once for more than a month. I think that time, he had gone to Phoenix, and another time he was in San Diego, and once it was Albuquerque."

"Did he always tell you where he was going?"

"No, but usually, after he had taught me how to do it, he was having me arrange the trip for him." Vang was smiling again. "He said I was his butler-valet. Like the man in the hotel lobbies who does all the arranging for you."

"You called the travel agencies, worked out the schedule, bought the tickets, everything?"

"Sure," Vang said. "Mr. Delos always had me call the same agency. There was a woman there. Mrs. Jackson. Always first class. And she knew all about where he liked to sit, that he liked late flights. If he wanted to have a car waiting for him. All those sort of things."

"You just gave her the credit card number? Or what?"

"Yes. Well, no. She had the number. She say: 'Mr. Vang, do I just put this on his regular business card.' And then she would e-mail the paper to get him on the airplane and I would print it out for him."

"Overseas flights, too. Or was he making any of them?"

"Yes. Not many though. One to Mexico City. One to Manila. One to London, but I think he had me cancel that."

"She handled the visas, too. "

"Sure," Vang said. "Very nice lady."

Leaphorn nodded, thinking of the benefits of the very rich.

"Sometimes there would be two tickets. Because he would take me along to take care of things for him if he was staying several days."

Leaphorn was silent a moment, considering that.

"She handled your visa for you when you needed one? Tommy, did Mr. Delos get you naturalized. As an American citizen, I mean. Were you sworn in and all that?"

"Oh yes," Tommy Vang said. "That was exciting. It was when I was twenty-one years old. The same day I registered so I could vote."

"Several years before that—I'd say when you were about fifteen or sixteen—was Mr. Delos away for a long period of time? Maybe as long as a year?"

"Oh, it was longer than that," Tommy Vang said. "For about five years, he was gone most of the time. Sometimes he'd call about the mail, or messages. And then he would call and tell me to meet him at the airport, and he'd be home for maybe a week and then he'd have to leave again."

"You just stayed at the apartment?"

"And worked for Mr. Martinez, at his bakery, restaurant place." He produced a wry sounding laugh. "Not good times. I watched television, and went for walks, and worked a lot. Nobody to talk to. Spent some time at the library trying to learn something about what had happened to the Hmong people."

"And thinking about going home?"

"No money," Tommy Vang said. "Sometimes I tried to talk to Mr. Delos about that, but he would just say when everything was finished here, he would take me back himself."

"He never paid you any salary?"

"He said it was just like he was my daddy. He gave me my clothes, my home, my food, everything I need. Had me taught things. Just like I was his son."

Leaphorn looked at Tommy. Yes, that statement seemed serious. It also seemed terrible.

"Time to get moving again," he said. "Mr. Delonie will be getting home from wherever he works about now. Time to get back on the road. Get down to Torreon and find out where he lives."

Fastening his seat belt, Leaphorn noticed Tommy was staring at him. Tommy frowned, gestured toward the glove box.

"Your telephone," he said. "I think I hear it ringing in there."

Leaphorn got it out, flipped it open. Punched the wrong button. Punched the proper one. Listened. "Hello?"

"Is this Lieutenant Joe Leaphorn?" a voice asked. "Ted Rostic asked me to call you about an obituary. I'm Carter Bradley, and I guess I've got some bad news for you." Bradley chuckled. "Or maybe it's good news."

"About Totter?" Leaphorn said.

"Yeah. Saint Anthony's Hospital records said they hadn't admitted anyone named Totter. Not that year anyway. Hope I got the date right." He repeated it.

"That's right," Leaphorn said.

"Had a Tyler die a few weeks after that date," Bradley said. "But that was a woman."

"I wonder if whoever sent the obituary to the paper had the hospital right. Seems unlikely, but you—"

"Well, the obituary said this Totter was buried in the Veterans Administration cemetery. Turns out he wasn't. No record of it, and the VA keeps good records."

"Well, I thank you," Leaphorn said. "I can't say I'm surprised."

"I am," Bradley said. "Why would anybody pull a stunt like that?"

"I'm afraid I don't know," Leaphorn said. "Did you call Ted Rostic?"

"I did," Bradley said. "He didn't know either. But he didn't sound surprised either."

Leaphorn pulled back onto the highway, heading for Torreon, thinking how he'd have to handle this. Tommy Vang was watching him, looking curious.

Leaphorn sighed.

"Tommy," he said. "I am going to tell you some very important things. Very serious for you and other people, too. That call was about Mr. Totter, the man who had that famous rug hanging on Mr. Delos's wall. You know about that?"

"I heard something about it," Tommy said. "About his gallery being burned, but somehow the carpet being saved. And about Mr. Totter going away and dying, and being buried."

"That call was from an old retired newspaper reporter. Somebody about like me. He checked for me back in Oklahoma where Mr. Totter was supposed to have gone. But Mr. Bradley found out that Mr. Totter didn't die in that hospital there. And he hasn't been buried."

"Oh," Tommy said, looking surprised, awaiting an explanation.

"I think he is still alive. And I think he is a very dangerous man."

"Ah," Tommy said, and raised his eyebrows.

"You're not going to like hearing what I'm going to tell you, Tommy. And I can't prove a lot of it. But when we find Mr. Delonie, I'm going to tell him all this, too. And maybe he's the one who can prove whether I'm wrong or right." He shrugged. "Probably the only one, for that matter—"

"I guess this is all about what Mr. Delos has been doing with those cherries?" Tommy Vang said. His tone sad.

"Yes, and more than that. In a way, I guess it's about all these religious things we've been talking about. About the chief of the evil spirits you Hmong call Nau Yong."

"All right," Tommy Vang said. "I will listen."

"Let's start way back when you were still a teenager, living in San Francisco. By yourself then, because Mr. Delos was mostly away on his long business trips. We move to this area. To a service station-tourist gallery-food store beside the highway, run by a couple named Handy.

One day, a man showed up there. He gave his name as Ray Shewnack, a big, good-looking man, great smile, made friends fast."

Leaphorn described what happened next, how Shewnack killed Handy and his wife, betrayed his new friends, and vanished with the money.

"Now we skip ahead to when you are a mature man, living mostly alone in California with Mr. Delos often away on a business trip. A man who calls himself Totter buys a roadside store, adds an Indian art gallery to it, does some business. Time passes; the three who went to prison for the Handys' murders are now getting out on parole."

Leaphorn paused, studied Tommy, who had his lips pursed, staring ahead, seeming deep in memories. Putting things together, Leaphorn hoped.

"I want you to remember the time element and the places. These three people the man called Shewnack had betrayed would be getting out of prison. Coming back right into this very empty country where everybody knows everybody. Think about that. Remember these three would recognize Shewnack if they saw him. Okay?"

Tommy nodded.

"So then this Totter hires a man, a stranger so it would seem, to help him at the store. Fire breaks out, the man is burned beyond recognition but left behind a bunch of stuff to identify him as Shewnack, who by then is on the FBI Most-Wanted-Fugitives list. Shewnack is declared dead. Totter collects fire insurance, sells the place, disappears. Then the death notice is published declaring Totter also dead."

"Okay, okay, okay," Tommy Vang said. "But he isn't dead. And you are pretty sure that the man who was called Shewnack became Mr. Totter and got rid of Shewnack, and then announced that Totter was dead, and now he has disappeared again."

"Not exactly vanished this time," Leaphorn said. "I think we know the name he is using now." He was staring at Tommy. "Do you agree?"

Tommy exhaled. "Like it would be Mr. Delos, the man who poisons people with fat red cherries?"

"And who, with the latest little packages of cherries, has fixed it very carefully so that if they kill Mr. Delonie, it will be Tommy Vang who brought the poison to the victim, whose fingerprints are all over the bottle, and whose handwriting is on the delivery note."

Leaphorn waited a reaction to that. Got none.

"Does that make sense to you?"

Tommy nodded. "I am thinking how he had me press my thumb down on the top of the bottle cap. He said it was to make sure it was tight, but it was screwed on tight." He held up his thumb, inspected the tip, rubbed his hand against his shirt.

"It makes me remember what he told me once, about people. About me. He said when God created humans he let them grow into two groups. A few of them—very few and only males among them—they are the predators. They are like our God of the devil spirits who ate the souls of the others. And the other people. Just about everybody else. They are the prey. The weak ones, he called them. Helpless ones. He said nearly all the Hmong were the prey. But maybe I was the exception. Maybe he could teach me to be one of the powerful ones." Tommy paused, shook his head.

"Did he try to teach you how to be powerful?"

"At first, when we were living in that hotel. But pretty soon, he got very angry and gave up. Told me to just forget about it. And then after a while, he would try to teach me things again."

"Did things happen to cause that?"

"I guess I just kept disappointing him. But finally, I came into the dining room where he had all the silver stuff, and I saw the old woman who worked for him putting some of the big serving spoons into her purse. I told her she better put them back because Mr. Delos would miss them, and he'd call the police, and she'd be put in jail. And then—"

Leaphorn violated one of the key rules of Navajo courtesy. He held up his hand, interrupting. "Let me guess. He was angry. He told you that you should have let her take the stolen stuff down to the exit, catch her there leaving, get hotel security involved, and then let her know that she was thereafter at your mercy. Anytime she didn't follow your orders, you could bring charges against her."

Tommy was nodding. "That's the way it was. He sat me down, told me how powerful people get to be powerful. How they get control. But I think he saw it might not do any good, so he just got up and told me he guessed I would always be a prey. That I better start learning. And he walked away."

"No more trying to make you a powerful person?"

"Not since then. Not hardly any."

"Well, let's go then and see if we can find Mr. Delonie."

Two pickup trucks and an aged Chevy sedan were parked at the Torreon Chapter House, but the owner of one truck was leaving. No, he hadn't seen Delonie today and wasn't sure where he would be. The other truck, on closer inspection, proved to have been left there with a blown rear tire, and no one was inside the building except Mrs. Sandra Nezbah, a sturdily built, middle-aged woman who greeted them with a warm smile. But no, she wasn't sure where Delonie might be found now. She looked at her watch. Probably at home. And where was that? She took them to a side door and pointed eastward, toward the slopes of Torreon ridge. His was the little house with the flat roof and the big barn behind it, and that vehicle by the barn looked like it might be his. "That great big Dodge Ram truck," she said admiringly. "Has diesel power, four-wheel drive. Quite a truck."

17

The truck was still there when Leaphorn pulled up by the driveway, turned off the ignition, and waited the polite Navajo moment for the residents to recognize his presence. Short wait, because Delonie had heard them and stood by the barn door looking out at them.

"*Ya eeh teh*," Leaphorn shouted as he got out. "Mr. Delonie. We are happy we found you at home."

"Well," said, Delonie, still standing at the barn door and looking uneasy. "Is it Lieutenant Leaphorn? What brings you out here? You working for my parole officer these days?"

"I want you to meet Tommy Vang," Leaphorn said, gesturing to Tommy, who was climbing out of the truck. "We want to provide you with some information, and see what you think about it."

Delonie considered that. Produced a skeptical-looking grin. "I'll bet you're not about to tell me you found all the loot Shewnack took from the Handy's robbery. Did you dig that up?"

"More important than that," Leaphorn said. "We want to tell you some things and see if you will agree with us that this fellow we've been calling Shewnack is still alive. In fact, still in operation."

Delonie took a deep breath. "Still alive? Shewnack? You telling me that son of a bitch didn't burn up at Totter's? Who was it then? What do you mean?"

"It's going to take a few minutes to explain what we're talking about. You have some time?"

"I've got the rest of my life for this," Delonie said. He ushered them into his house, gestured around the front room, said, "Make yourselves comfortable." Then he disappeared into what seemed to be the kitchen. "Got about half a pot of coffee in here, and I'll warm it up a little and see how it tastes."

A glance around the room showed Leaphorn that Delonie was not better than most in bachelor housekeeping. For seating it offered a massive old sofa, its sagging cushions partly hidden by an army blanket; a recliner chair upholstered in cracked black plastic; a rocking chair with a well-worn square cushion; three straight-backed wooden dining room chairs, two waiting at a cluttered table and the third leaned against the wall. The floor surface was a linoleum sheet patterned with blue-green tiles, but the effect was marred by too many years of hard wear. Beyond all this, a double-width sliding glass door looked out into a walled patio.

"Take a seat in there," Delonie said. "This java is a little stale but drinkable and I'll have it hot in a minute."

Leaphorn was looking at Tommy Vang, hoping to use

that available minute to plan how they'd communicate with Delonie. But Vang's eyes—and his attention—were focused on the view out the window, where a busy squadron of hummingbirds was zipping, drinking, pushing, and waiting around a cluster of feeders hanging from the patio rafters. Maybe a dozen of them, Leaphorn estimated, but they were moving too fast for an accurate count. But he thought he recognized at least three species.

In the little yard beyond the dangling feeders, a larger gaggle of birds were at work. Delonie, or whoever was responsible, had converted the patio into a disorganized forest of fence posts, each topped by grain feeders. These were augmented by a variety of others, some hanging from the limbs of pinyon trees, some attached to the yard wall, and the largest one—a log partially hollowed to hold more bulky bird food and fitted with a birdbath of cast concrete shaped to look like someone's version of an oversized clam shell. At the moment, two doves were drinking from it. Above and behind and all around the air was aflutter with avian activity.

Tommy Vang was grinning at Leaphorn, pointing at the aerial show.

Delonie emerged from the kitchen. On his right hand he was balancing a tray that held a can of condensed milk, a sugar sack from which a spoon handle emerged, and three cups. His left hand held a steaming coffeepot. He put the tray on the table and poured the coffee.

"Grab one and doctor it up the way you like, and then I want you to tell me how this son of a bitch Shewnack has raised himself from the dead."

Delonie chose the recliner as his spot for this conversation, but he sat on the chair's edge, making no attempt to get comfortable. He had poured a bit of condensed milk and a dollop of sugar into his cup, and now he swirled it around. He glanced at Vang now and then, but mostly kept his eyes on Leaphorn.

Leaphorn was drinking his coffee black. He took a sip, suppressed a startled reaction, and smiled at Delonie over the rim. It was stale, but it was hot. And it was the first coffee he'd had for a while.

"First, I want to tell you about Tommy Vang here," he said. "He's a part of this story, and he brought you a present. He'll give you that later, after we do some explaining. Tommy has got to tell you about his part, and that goes all the way back to the Vietnam War."

. Delonie nodded at Vang, took a sip of his coffee, and waited—still on the very edge of the chair. "Yes," he said.

"Go ahead, Tommy," Leaphorn said. "Tell Mr. Delonie about the CIA agent, and how he was working with your family in the mountains, and about his taking you out of the refugee camp. All that."

Tommy Vang did as he was told. Hesitantly at first, and in a low voice that grew louder as he began to see that Delonie was interested—even in hearing about his cooking lessons and his valet duties. When he reached the times when he was often left alone and his boss was away week after week, he hesitated, glanced at Leaphorn for instructions.

"Now we are getting to the time when you are about to be involved. About now this fellow has disappeared from San Francisco and a fellow who calls himself Ray Shewnack has showed up out here. You remember?"

Delonie's expression had changed as Leaphorn was saying that. He bent forward, eyes intent.

"Damn right," Delonie said. "I remember that day. Cold day. Ellie and me had been over to the Sky City Casino. Having some lunch, talking to some people, and Bennie Begay saw us, and Bennie brought this Shewnack over. They'd been playing seven card stud in the poker room, as I remember it, and Begay introduced us. Said Shewnack was from California, was a detective with the Santa Monica Police Department. Out here on vacation. Just looking around."

Delonie nodded to Leaphorn. "How about that? A policeman on vacation."

"I guess it sort of fits into what we're going to be telling you. Changed names, changed places, never the same twice."

"Evil son of a bitch," Delonie said. "Like those worst kind of witches you Navajos have. The shape shifters."

"To tell the truth, I'd thought of that myself," Leaphorn said.

"I could tell he was interested in Ellie right from the start. Sat down, talked about how much he admired our part of the country, said he was going to move out here, wanted to know where we lived. Where we worked. You couldn't imagine anybody being any friendlier." Delonie took a drink of his coffee, slammed the cup down on the table. "If I'd just been smart enough to see what was coming. If I just had a gun with me and been that smart, I'd a killed the bastard. Would've been a lot better off."

The sound of rage in this produced a moment of silence. Leaphorn noticed that Tommy Vang's expression went from startled to nervous.

"But how can anyone read the future?" Leaphorn asked. "Here you are, being friendly to a stranger."

"Yeah," Delonie said, and laughed. A bitter sound.

"So what happened next?"

"He keeps showing up at the Handys' place. Driving a pale blue Cadillac four door. Bought gasoline the first time and got out and checked his tire pressure and his oil." Delonie produced a wry smile. "Remember when people did that? I mean ask the gasoline pumper to do it for them? Well, he did it himself. That's how friendly he was. And then he went in, got himself some cigarettes, talked to Ellie and Handy. Did a lot of smiling, being friendly. That kept on happening for a while."

Delonie stopped. Stared out the window. Shook his head. "Pretty soon, dumb as I am, I could see Ellie was a hell of a lot more interested in Shewnack than she was in me. And pretty soon he'd be coming about quitting time, and we'd go down the road a ways, or maybe back over to the Acoma tribes casino, and eat something and socialize. Sometime play a little poker. And Shewnack was filling us in on his career as a policeman, mostly talking about how really dumb criminals made the job so easy for the cops. He was full of stories about that. Then he would tell us how easy it would be out here in the wide open country to get a lot of money by pulling stuff off. Not so many cops out here. Not well trained. Not all that smart, either. Said the secret was knowing how to not leave any evidence behind. So on, so forth. Full of good yarns about how it happened, and how cops really weren't all that interested in doing the work to catch people. Underpaid, underappreciated, and overworked. We heard that a lot from Shewnack. Just let nature take its course and the dumb criminals will catch themselves. Anyway, I admit it was kind of interesting, and Ellie got real caught up in it. One day she asked him how he would organize one if he wanted to rob a place, and he said, you mean like where you guys work, and she said yeah, how would you do that? And he said, well the real pros we run into now and then in California do a lot of planning. First, will there be enough profit involved for it to be worth the time. And he said Handy's store wouldn't be a prospect, because the day's take would just be a few hundred bucks."

Delonie stopped, drank coffee, stared out the window at the bird activity.

"Knowing what I know now, I'm sure he knew better even when he said that, but Ellie fell for it. She told him that Handy never takes his money into the bank more than once a week, and sometimes it's a whole month before he drives it into the bank in Gallup. Told him he keeps the money in a hidden safe. So forth. Anyway, sweet Ellie wasn't deceptive at all. Any question Shewnack had, she answered. And then, when the time came, what does he do to her?"

Delonie left that question hang, staring out the glass door into the patio.

"Those birds get even livelier than that in the spring," he said. "Birds get to thinking about nesting, pairing up. Even the Gambel quails are coming in, laying their eggs under the heavy brush out there. And after the hatch, they bring the young ones into the patio sometimes. Daddy quail sits on the wall and keeps an eye out for cats or hawks or anything he thinks looks dangerous. And the mama quail sort of herds them around. Teaches 'em to run into the bushes or hide under things when she gives 'em the danger warning."

Delonie's lips had curved into a sad smile now, remembering this.

"I used to get Ellie to come out here sometimes and watch them with me." He shook his head. "Very good company, Ellie was. She should have married me like I asked her. I think she would have if Shewnack hadn't come along."

"I talked to the police who handled that case," Leaphorn said. "They told me how nice they thought she was."

"Prison changed her, I guess," Delonie said. "Did me, too. When I finally got out, I tried to find her, but she didn't want to see me anymore. I finally gave up. Then, just a while back, I heard she was dead."

"You knew Bennie Begay is dead, too?"

"So I've heard."

"That means you are a very important person to this man who calls himself Shewnack. The only one left who could identify him with that double murder."

"If he wasn't already burned up," Delonie said.

"You believe that?"

"Well, should I believe you or the famous old Federal Bureau of Investigation?"

"We'll give you a choice," Leaphorn said, and began connecting the dots of time and place between a man calling himself Shewnack leaving Handy's store with the loot, and a man who called himself Totter appearing back in the high, dry Four Corners Country and buying himself an old trading post and gallery. Then the fire destroying a man Totter had hired, who the FBI decided was Shewnack. Then Totter cashing in, disappearing.

"Then," Leaphorn continued, but Delonie held up his hand.

"And then we learn that Mr. Totter is dead, too," he said. "How does that work in this blueprint of yours?"

"It didn't, but then we checked on the obituary notice, turns out it was false. The man who called himself Totter didn't die."

"Still alive? Where?"

"Just outside Flagstaff now, if we're right. We think he's a man who used to be a CIA agent in Vietnam. Mr. Vang here knew him when he was calling himself George Perkins. The way this funny trail leads, he got caught stealing CIA bribery money, got bumped out of the CIA, took Tommy Vang here out of a Hmong refugee camp, settled—if we can call it that—in San Francisco. As Tommy told you, he was gone a lot on trips. He was gone, for example, in the long period before the Handys were killed, and he was gone again for a long time when Totter was taking over that trading post and doing his business from there. Then—"

Delonie held up his hand again.

"Let me finish that for you. Then, when those of us doing time for the Handys started getting out on parole, he decided we'd see him and turn him in. So he hired himself a helper, burned him up, left evidence to persuade the FBI this was Shewnack, thereby eliminating that problem. That it?"

"Just about," Leaphorn said.

"Pretty weak connection, seems to me. You want me to think this Jason Delos is Shewnack?"

Leaphorn nodded.

"You left out that rug," Tommy Vang said. "And you left out how Totter stole that pinyon sap so the fire wouldn't look like arson."

"Pinyon sap?" Delonie said. "And a rug?" He was grinning. "I know this Shewnack sort of proved I'm stupid, but I've learned some from that. What are you trying to sell me here?"

Leaphorn explained the rug, explained—rather lamely—the sap, the lard buckets, the very hot fire without any sign of those fire-spreading chemicals the arson investigators are trained to look for.

Delonie thought about it, nodded. "If I was the grand jury, I'd guess maybe I'd be interested in all this. But I think I'd be asking for more evidence. Isn't this all pretty much just circumstantial?" He laughed. "Notice that language I'm using. We learn that doing time in prison. Lots of guard-house lawyers in there. But I think I'd be wondering what you are trying to accomplish with all this."

Leaphorn was wondering, too. Wondering what he was doing here. He was tired. His back hurt. He was supposed to be retired. Delonie was right. If they had Delonie on the witness stand ready to swear Jason Delos was actually Ray Shewnack, the defense attorney would note Delonie was a paroled convict and repeatedly note the total, absolute, utter lack of any concrete evidence.

To hell with it, Leaphorn thought.

"I guess you'd have to say we're trying to save your life, Mr. Delonie. To keep this 'raised from the ashes' Ray Shewnack from erasing you as the only threat left."

He pulled the little gift box from his jacket pocket. Handed it to Delonie. "Here's the present he sent you."

"What do you mean, save my life?" Delonie asked.

He took the little box, held it gingerly, turned it over, read the note on it, tapped it with his finger.

"Who wrote this?"

"I wrote it," Tommy said. "Mr. Delos spoke it to me and told me to write it down."

"Who is it supposed to be from? From this Delos man?"

"I don't know," Tommy said. "It's a little bottle of cherries. The big ones he uses in the bourbon drinks he likes to make."

Delonie tore open the wrapping, pulled the box apart, extracted the bottle, examined it carefully.

"Nice thing to send somebody," Delonie said. "If I thought this Delos was actually that Ray Shewnack, I'd be very surprised. I never did think he had any use for me. He smiled at everybody, and slapped your back, but you could tell."

"It won't have any Delos fingerprints on it," Leaphorn said. "Neither that slick paper wrapping nor the bottle, nor the bottle top. Nobody handled it, except Mr. Vang here. Delos even had Tommy press his thumb down on the bottle cap. Perfect place for a thumbprint."

Delonie twisted the cap open, laid it aside, looked into the bottle, sniffed it.

"Smells fine," he said.

Tommy Vang was looking extremely nervous, leaning forward, reaching toward Mr. Delonie. "Don't eat it."

"We think it's poison," Leaphorn said.

Delonie frowned. "These cherries?"

He reached into his pocket, took out a jackknife, opened it, pried out a cherry, and let it roll onto the table. He stared at it, said, "Looks good."

"I think if you take a real close look at it, you're going to find a little puncture hole in it someplace. Where a needle gave it a shot of something like strychnine. Something you wouldn't want in your stomach."

Delonie used the knife to roll the cherry onto a piece

of paper, picked it up, studied it. Put it down, frowned at Leaphorn. "Little bitty hole," he said.

"A Flagstaff private investigator, former cop named Bork, went to see Mr. Delos about this rug we told you about. Asked a bunch of questions about how Delos got it when it was one of the art things supposed to be burned up in Totter's fire. Delos gave him a little lunch to take home with him. It had a slice of fruitcake with it, and Mr. Delos had put one of these very special cherries on the top of the slice. Hour or so later on the way home Mr. Bork died of poisoning."

"Oh," Delonie said.

"Then I came along to find out what had happened to Bork. I asked Mr. Delos a lot of questions about that rug, how he came to have it, so forth. He had Mr. Vang make me a little lunch, too. Put a slice of fruitcake in it, put one of these cherries on top."

"I didn't," Tommy said. "Mr. Delos did that always. Used them as decorations. Just for somebody special, he would say. And put it on top. I didn't know he was punching those holes in them."

"Why didn't it poison you?" Delonie asked.

"I don't like fruitcake and I didn't get around to stealing the cherry off the top, and finally Vang here heard what had happened to Mr. Bork. It made him nervous. So he found me and tried to take the lunch back."

Delonie rolled two more cherries out of the bottle, looked at them, then looked out the sliding glass door, considering the activity among the birds.

"About this time of day, we usually have a bunch of crows showing up. If I'm not home, they crowd out the smaller birds and pig out on the bird food. Not just eat it, they scatter it all around. I run 'em off. Used to have a shotgun I could thin them out with, but the probation officer wouldn't let me keep that."

"You thinking about poisoning them?" Leaphorn asked.

"Crows will eat just about anything. They'd gobble these up. If they really are poison, that would be fewer crows around to steal the eggs out of other birds' nests. Looks like a way to show whether you're telling the truth."

And so Delonie put the cherries back into the jar, slid open the glass door, and walked out into the patio. Some of the bigger birds fled, but Leaphorn noticed that most of the smaller ones seemed to recognize him as harmless. He placed four of the cherries in a line atop the wall, and one on each of the roofs of four of the bird feeders, came back through the door, turned to survey his handiwork, then hurried back out again. He retrieved the cherries from the feeder roof, put them back into the bottle, came in, and slid the door shut, and stood far enough inside to be invisible to the birds, watching.

"In case you wondered why I wanted those cherries back," he said. "While them cherries would be way too big for the wrens, and finches, and the little ones to handle, putting them right on the feeders might tempt the doves, or the bigger ones. Them birds have to deal with all sorts of predators. Hawks, crows, snakes, rats, stray cats. Killing a few crows just does my birds a favor, but I didn't want to kill any of the good ones."

Leaphorn looked at his watch. "How long would you guess we'll be waiting to see if this works?"

Delonie laughed. "Not long," he said. "Crows are

smart. They watch. In fact, there was a little flock of the local crows up in the trees back there watching when I came out. They're not here all the time because they know I have those feeders rigged so they can't get their big heads into most of them. But when they see me come out carrying something that looks like it might be food, they start flying in a hurry. They want to beat the little birds to it."

Even as Delonie was saying that, two crows arrived, landing in a pinyon just beyond the wall. Three others followed. One noticed the cherries, landed on the wall. Picked up a cherry, found it a little too large to swallow, and flew back into the pinyon with it. Minutes passed. The sight of the cherries attracted another crow to the wall. It speared a cherry and stayed on the wall and worked away at getting it torn up enough to swallow. Then he pecked another one, knocked it off the wall, and flew down into the patio to find it. A third crow grabbed the remaining cherry, held it in his beak briefly. Put it back on the wall, pecked at it. It fell into the grass below, and the crow flew down looking for it.

Leaphorn checked the time. How long had it taken the poison to kill Bork? No way of knowing, but it had apparently acted to affect his driving within a relatively few minutes. Bork weighed maybe two hundred pounds. A crow would be a matter of ounces. Did a crow have a craw, as chickens did, in which foods were ground before being dumped into the stomach? Leaphorn didn't know. But while he was pondering that, Tommy Vang touched his shoulder.

"Look," he said, pointing.

The crow that had carried its prize into the pinyon

was moving its wings. It seemed to fall from one branch to a lower one, recover itself, flap its wings, and begin a sort of frantic flight. A very short flight. Abruptly its effort stopped, and it dropped behind the wall.

"Poisoned, I guess," said Tommy Vang. "I guess you were right about those little puncture holes."

Delonie was standing beside them now, watching.

"That one on the ground there, too," he said. "Look at that."

The crow was on the grass, trying to stand, trying to get its wings moving. Dying.

"I guess that would have been me," Delonie said. "I guess I owe you gentlemen a thank-you or something."

"What we need from you," Leaphorn said, "is to tag along with us to visit Mr. Delos, make sure he is the man you remember as Ray Shewnack so we can get him arrested and indicted and get him put away."

But even as he said it, Leaphorn was thinking he'd need a lot of luck to make any of those things happen.

"Where we going to get me a chance to look at him?" Delonie asked. "That means driving to Flagstaff, I guess."

"Mr. Vang is going to help us with that," Leaphorn said. "Mr. Delos left home to go hunting. Hunting elk. He was going after a big trophy bull elk up on one of those hunters' ranch places along the Colorado-New Mexico border. Vang's supposed to drive up there tomorrow and give him a bunch of information about you. About where you live, alone or what, where you work, your habits, what your vehicle looked like. Stuff like that."

Delonie was studying Vang while receiving this information. "Supposed to get acquainted, sort of, or just snoop around?"

"He said better if you didn't see me," Vang said. "I was supposed to just find out when you weren't home and leave those cherries in your mailbox, or by your front door, and then go away."

Delonie considered this. "That son of a bitch," he said. "He sure had me all figured out, didn't he? He figured I'd be eating those cherries while I sat there wondering who the hell had sent them. He was right, too. I wouldn't have had the brains to stop and think about it."

Leaphorn shrugged. "Why would you? You didn't have any reason to be suspecting anything. You knew Shewnack was dead. Formally certified by the Federal Bureau of Identification."

Delonie nodded. "Now let's figure out how we're going to nail him. If we want to catch him out hunting, we'll need to get there early. That's when the elk and the deer are coming out of the cover to get themselves a wake-up drink of water. And that's when those hunting-camp-type hunters are all set up waiting for them. We need to start getting ourselves ready for this. It's a long drive up there."

18

Getting ready for the venture first involved cleaning off enough of the table so that Tommy Vang could spread out his old road map, let them inspect the marks Delos had drawn on it, and expose the notes of instruction he had written for Tommy. They sat in the three straight-backed chairs, with Delonie in the middle.

Delonie tapped the area Delos had circled.

"That's where he's doing his hunting? Is that it?" he asked. "If it is, then our best bet would be to drive over to Cuba on 550." He paused, shook his head. "But there we got a choice. Either the long way on pavement on 537 through the Jicarilla Apache Reservation, or take the short way. Just keep going north out of Cuba to La Jara on old Highway 112 straight up to Dulce. Both get you to the same place. The first way is a lot longer, but it's all paved road. That county road 112 gets you going over a lot of dirt."

Leaphorn was trying to remember the shorter route. Terrible when snow was melting, but probably not bad this time of year. While he was pondering this, Delonie muttered something negative about the old Delos map, got up, disappeared into what was probably a bedroom, and emerged with other maps. One was a bound volume of reproductions of U.S. Geological Survey section surveys, another was an oil field pipeline route map that Leaphorn didn't recognize, and the third was a copy of the AAA Indian Country map like the one Leaphorn used himself. Delonie put them all on the table, pushed aside the USGA volume and the pipeline maps, and folded the Indian Country version to expose the pertinent portion of the Colorado-New Mexico border. On it, he carefully pencil-sketched the circle from Delos's map. Checked his work with the Delos map, made some slight corrections, and stared at the Delos notes.

"Can you read this scribbling here," he asked Tommy Vang.

Vang leaned over the map, looking surprised. He picked up the pencil Delonie had dropped on the map.

"Sure," he said, and tapped a scribble with the pencil tip. "Right here he says 'Wash cuts across road here. Park in wash. Wait in car. I come.' And this right here that sort of looks like a big M. Those lines beside it is 'Lazy W.'" Vang laughed. "I think lazy because it's not an M but a W laying on its back."

"It's probably the rancher's cattle brand," Delonie said, studying Vang, frowning. "How long you been working for this man? Brought you over from Asia when you were a boy, did he? That would have been close to thirty years ago. Did you already know English then?"

Vang laughed. "I was just nine or ten, I think. Just talked Hmong, and a little bit of Vietnamese, and some words of Chinese. But I studied English on the television in San Francisco. On the programs they had for children." Vang laughed. "Funny stuff. Clowns and puppets and little things supposed to be like animals. But it taught you numbers and if you paid attention you could get the meaning of the words they were saying."

"Never went to any regular school then," Delonie said, sounding incredulous.

"But you learn a lot on television. Like you watch *Law and Order*, and *NYPD Blue*, and those other ones, and you learn a lot about how policemen like Mr. Leaphorn here do their work. And you learn about different kind of guns. The only ones we had when I was a boy were the rifles the Americans brought for us, and some my uncles had taken from the Vietcong and the Pathet Lao."

Delonie considered that, now looking grim. "Are you telling me that miserable bastard never put you into any regular school? You never did really have anybody teaching you anything?"

"Oh, no," Vang said, looking shocked. "Mr. Delos put me in a cooking school. I helped in the kitchen and the people there taught me how to make bread, and cookies, and soups, and . . . well just about everything."

"But nobody taught you how to read. Or write, or anything like that?"

"Well, not sit behind a desk in a regular classroom like I see they do on television. Not anything like that. But I learned all sorts of other things. Mr. Delos and the woman who ran the food place where I was learning how to cook, they got me into a dry cleaner's place. Where they work on making clothing fit better." Thinking of that caused Vang to smile.

"I learned how to mend, and patch, and iron, and do what they called 'destaining.' I was very good at that."

Delonie was looking somber. "Never did send you to a regular sort of school then," he said. "Just kept you home and you worked for him. Did his cooking, and was sort of like a housekeeper." He glanced at Leaphorn. "I guess that's about what you were telling me, wasn't it. But I wasn't taking it seriously."

"Well, that's the way it was," Leaphorn said. "Mr. Vang was Mr. Delos's cook, housekeeper, and sort of secretary, too. Arranged his trips. Things like that."

"Worked for the bastard about twenty-five years or so, then, I'd estimate. What kind of wages did he pay you?"

"Wages?" Vang asked. "Nothing much when I was just a boy, I guess, but later on when I went out to do the shopping for things, Mr. Delos told me to just use the charge for stuff I needed."

"For stuff you needed," Delonie said. "Like what?"

Vang shrugged. "Like socks and underwear, and when I got older, razor blades, and that deodorant for under your arms. Sometimes I would buy chewing gum, or candy bars, things like that. Mr. Delos didn't seem to mind."

Delonie recovered the pencil and began jotting figures on the corner of the map.

"I'm figuring minimum wage at an average of $5 an hour in California 'cause it goes up and down. Higher now. Lower then. Figure him a forty-hour, five-day week, even though he was working full time and seven days, just figure it at forty. That would be two hundred bucks a week. Now maybe we should cut that in half because he got room and board. Make it a hundred per week. That fair?"

Without waiting for Vang or Leaphorn to answer, Delonie was doing the math.

"I'm calling it twenty years—knocking off those years before Vang was in his late teens. Then knocking two weeks off each year for vacation time, even though Vang didn't get any vacation. That gives us an even thousand weeks. Right? Multiply that by a hundred dollars a week, and it comes out Delos owes Vang a hundred thousand dollars. Right? Now if we figure in some interest, compounded annually, then it means that Mr. Delos—"

Leaphorn, who almost never interrupted anyone, interrupted. "Mr. Delonie," he said. "We see your point. But don't you think we should be sort of changing the subject and getting back to what we've got to do tomorrow?"

Delonie stared at Leaphorn. Put down the pencil. Picked it up again.

"All right. I guess so. I can't get it in my mind though, that this Delos is really going to be Ray Shewnack. If I see him, and it really is Shewnack, what I think I'm going to do is just shoot him."

"You do that, you'll be right back in prison again," Leaphorn said. "And not just for parole violation."

Delonie nodded. "I know. But it would damn sure be worth it."

"Trouble is, I'd be going in there with you. Me and Tommy Vang here."

"You think you can go up there, catch him, take him in, and get him convicted of anything? Damned if I see how. Me, a convicted felon, as your only witness."

"Let the jury decide," Leaphorn said. "Anyway, you can't cook the rabbit until you catch it."

Delonie made a wry face, bent over the map again.

"Well," he said. "If Delos wants to meet Mr. Vang right here where he marked that spot, it must mean he'd have his hunting stand pretty close. I guess we can drive up there, though. He must know that area pretty well."

"Mr. Delos has been there before," Tommy Vang said. "He took me once, when I was a lot younger." He smiled at the thought. "I got to learn how to cook on the woodstove. Mostly just frying meat and boiling stuff and mixing drinks for people. But the cooking wasn't easy until you know how to control the heat. Be way too hot, or then too cold." He shrugged. "The way my mother had to do it."

"Has a kitchen then," Delonie said. "I guess they have a cabin up there handy for those permit hunters to keep dry and comfortable."

"A little log house," Tommy said. "Mostly just one big room and a little kitchen place and then there was a water tank on the roof. You turned a big valve and the water came down in a sink in the kitchen." His expression registered disapproval. "It didn't look very clean. Everything dirty. The water, too, I mean. Sort of rusty looking."

"You were a mountain boy, weren't you?" Delonie said. "Maybe that sort of reminded you of home. Log cabin, wood fire, and all."

"It did," Vang said, and looked down. "But we weren't dirty like that."

Delonie was staring at him, expression grim. "That son of a bitch," he said. "He should have taken you home again."

"He said he would," Vang said. "Said he was going to do that."

"Do you still believe that?" Delonie asked.

Vang considered. "I used to believe it. For a long time I believed it," he said. Then he bent over the map, either studying it or, Leaphorn guessed, not wanting them to see that he was about to cry.

"Right here," Vang said, tapping an ink dot beside a line which, in the map marking code, identified a road as "doubtful" and to be avoided in bad weather.

"I guess that's where we're going," Leaphorn said. "Shouldn't be any problem this time of year."

"I think that's going to be on the old T.J.D. Cater spread," Delonie said. "I hunted up fairly near to there when I was a lot younger. The old man owned a lot of his own land and then his grazing permit spread out over a bunch of National Forest leases. Went way up into the mountains, I remember. It was all posted. No trespassing. Had a deal with the Game Department people to let the deer and elk graze on his leased grass and drink his water. Then they'd give him a bundle of hunting permits he could sell."

"But Mr. Delos said he'd be hunting on the Witherspoon Ranch," Vang said. "And that's where he went last year. That mark he made right there, that little squiggle, he said that was a big sign by the road. It tells people that anybody who goes on the property without permission will be prosecuted. Big sign says Posted, and then there's what Delos said they call 'The Lazy W,' painted on a board nailed to a tree."

"Yeah," Delonie said. "When old Cater died, Witherspoon's the one who bought out the estate. And that

sounds like his brand. That's what I heard. Anyway, whoever has it, to hunt up there you still had to either sneak
in, or pay the bastards their fee."

"Okay," Leaphorn said. "Now let's figure out the best
way to get there."

Delonie pushed back his chair and rose.

"I'll leave that to you, Lieutenant Leaphorn," he said.
"I'm going to fix us some supper. Tomorrow's going to be
a long day and probably pretty interesting. We should eat
something and then get some sleep."

19

For Leaphorn, getting some sleep had been easier said than accomplished. After feeding them overfried pork chops with bread, gravy, and more coffee, Delonie had put him and Tommy Vang in a space once apparently used as a second bedroom but now stacked full of odds and ends of mostly broken furniture. Vang fit himself neatly onto a sagging sofa against the wall, leaving Leaphorn to retire upon a stack of three old mattresses on the floor.

It was comfortable enough, and certainly Leaphorn was tired enough, but his mind was occupied with setting up plans for the various unpleasant situations he kept imagining. Ideally, Delonie would get an early look at Delos, would clearly identify him as the man who called himself Ray Shewnack, the one who had murdered the Handys in cold blood and then gone on to earn high ranking on the FBI's list of Most Wanted felons. In that case, he would manage to persuade Delonie to choke down his long-building hatred and come back with Leaphorn to get a warrant for the arrest of Delos. An even happier outcome involved Delonie staring through his telescopic sight a bit and declaring that Delos was not Shewnack, that he didn't resemble Shewnack in any way at all, and asking what in the world had provoked Leaphorn into taking them on this foolish wild-goose chase. Whereupon Leaphorn would apologize to Delonie, head for home, and try to forget this whole affair.

But what about Tommy Vang then? And what if Delonie simply kept looking through that telescopic sight on his rifle until he was certain it was Shewnack and then shot the man? Even worse, what if Delos, who had clearly demonstrated his tendency to be cautious, saw them first, recognized the danger, and initiated shooting himself? Judging from the trophy heads on his wall, he was good at shooting. And Delos certainly knew Delonie was a dangerous enemy, and the fact that he had also poisoned one of those delicious-looking cherries for Leaphorn's own lunch made it clear that the name of Lieutenant Joe Leaphorn, retired, was also on his kill list.

Leaphorn had worked his way through a multitude of such thoughts, including whether Tommy Vang was still perhaps just a little bit loyal to Delos, how much he could be trusted, and how to handle the Vang situation in general. He was still thinking that when he finally dozed off. He resumed pondering it when the sound of Delonie clumping around in the next room and the smell of coffee perking jarred him out of an uneasy sleep.

He rubbed his eyes. Moonlight coming through the dusty window revealed Vang curled on the sofa, lost in the sleep of the innocent. Leaphorn stared at him for a moment, decided he would rule Tommy an ally with some reservations, and pulled on his boots.

By a little after three A.M., the coffee had been consumed, they had piled into the King Cab pickup Tommy Vang had been driving, they had slid through the sleeping town of Cuba while the moon was sailing high over the San Pedro Mountains, and now they were making pretty good time on County Road 112. Vang had suggested that he should drive, since he knew the truck, but Leaphorn had again noted that pickups were a lot alike and that he knew the roads. Thus Vang had settled in the jump seat behind them, and was occupying himself for the first thirty minutes or so examining Delonie's lever-action 30-30 rifle. He had seen lots of firearms, he explained—the U.S. Army rifles carried by the ARVN, the Russian models the Vietcong used, and the Chinese weapons carried by the Pathet Lao—but never one that loaded itself by pulling down a lever. Before many miles he somehow resumed his sleep on the jump seat behind them.

Delonie was riding up front, wide awake but deep in some sort of silent contemplation. Totally silent for miles, except for muttering a sardonic "heavy traffic this morning" remark when they met the first car they'd seen in about fifty miles. But now he stirred, glanced at Leaphorn.

"If we're where I think we are," he said, "that mountain is what they call Dead Man's Peak, and you've got a junction just ahead. If I read Vang's old map right, you're taking the left turn. That right? That takes you past Stinking Lake and then across a lot of Jicarilla Apache Reservation lands and into Dulce. Then what?"

"Then we turn east for about four miles or so on U.S.

84, back on pavement then for a few minutes, and then
north on gravel toward a little old village up there named,
ah, Edith, I think it is, and then we jog northwestward a
little—in to Colorado and winding under Archuleta Mesa,
and going very slow because we will have to be looking for
that little turnoff road Delos marked."

"Yeah," Delonie said, peering out the window. "That
hump over there, it's part of the San Juans, I guess, but
they call that long ridge the Chalk Mountain. I've hunted
up there a little in my younger days." He sighed. "Complicated country. You never knew whether you were still on
the Jicarilla land, or over in Colorado trespassing on the
Southern Ute Reservation, or which state you were in."
The thought of that caused Delonie to chuckle.

Leaphorn glanced at him. "Something funny?"

"Not that it mattered. We wouldn't have had a hunting license for either state, or from the Apaches, and I
don't think the Southern Utes give them."

"I think we'd better start looking for a turnoff place,"
Leaphorn said.

"And I think maybe it's time you ought to switch off
your headlights. If Delos is out getting ready to hunt, he's
going to notice somebody coming. And who is he going to
think would be arriving here this early in the morning. It
would be way too early for Tommy."

"Maybe you're right," Leaphorn said. The moon was
down now, but the eastern horizon was showing its predawn brightness. He slowed, snapped off the headlights,
crept along until his eyes were better adjusted to the
gloom. They rolled down the slope of the hill they'd just
climbed, crossed a culvert with the sound of a stream
gurgling under it, negotiated a sharp curve beyond the

culvert, and were in the dark shadows cast by a heavy growth of stream-side willows. Leaphorn switched on the headlights again.

Just ahead the beams lit a sign. POSTED. And below it the graphic design of a W tilted over on its side. Leaphorn eased the pickup to a crawl, turned off the headlights. Just beyond the Ponderosa pine on which the sign was mounted a dirt lane turned off the gravel road they'd been following.

"Well," Delonie said. "I guess that would be old Witherspoon's Lazy W brand on that sign there. So here we are. Now we find out what happens next."

Leaphorn didn't comment on that. Just beyond the Ponderosa pine on which the sign was mounted, rutted tracks swerved off the gravel. Leaphorn guided the pickup onto them, switched on the headlights. They illuminated a three-strand barbed-wire gate, stretched between two fence posts. From the top wire another sign dangled, a square piece of white tin on which the words ALL TRESPASS- ERS WILL BE PROSECUTED were painted in red.

Leaphorn stopped the truck and turned off its headlights.

"Why don't you just drive right through it?" Delonie asked.

"That would make it malicious mischief, too," Leap- horn said. "You take care of it."

"Got wire cutters?"

Leaphorn laughed. "No. But that gate pole looks like it used to be a little aspen. I doubt if you'd need any."

Delonie got out, grabbed the gate pole, applied com- bined leg and arm leverage, broke it, tossed broken pole and wires aside, stepped back, and waved Leaphorn in.

Inside the fence the road slanted downward toward a small stream. They bumped across a small culvert and the ranch road, now deeply rutted, took them into heavy stream-side growths of willow and brushy trees and almost total darkness. Leaphorn flicked on the lights again, but just long enough to see what he was driving into, then restored the darkness. Better let the ruts steer them, along with what little he could see in the dimness, than take a chance of their headlights giving Delos an early warning.

They rolled along, very slowly, very silently, letting the front wheels take them wherever the ruts guided the pickup along the meandering stream.

"Getting brighter ahead," Delonie said.

It was, and the road was suddenly less rutted and slanting upward. Ahead now they could see a bare-looking ridge faintly illuminated by the predawn glow along the eastern horizon.

"There it is," Delonie said, in a hoarse whisper, pointing ahead and to the right.

Leaphorn could make out the shape of a small house, slanted roof, tall stone chimney, junipers crowding in beside it. He stopped the pickup, turned off the ignition, and listened. A still, windless morning. First there was only the ticking sound of the engine cooling. Then the odd rasping sound of what locals would call a Saw-Whet owl, in recognition of its unpleasant voice. It called and called and called, and finally got a barely audible answer from somewhere far behind them. Then the yipping of coyotes from the ridge behind the cabin, which lapsed quickly into nothing but the vague sound of the breeze and the even vaguer voice of the stream.

Leaphorn yawned, suddenly feeling some of the tension draining away and the accumulated fatigue taking over. He rubbed his eyes. This was not a time to be getting sleepy.

"What now?" Delonie whispered.

"We wait until it gets a little lighter," Leaphorn said, talking very low. "Mr. Vang told me Mr. Delos comes up here alone. The way he describes his hunting tactics he gets out to the blind when there's just enough light to see a little. That would be just about now, I'd think."

Vang was sort of semi-standing in the space behind them, leaning forward for a better view out the windshield. "He says its takes him about twenty minutes to walk from the cabin around to the hillside where the blind is. There's a regular trail he follows, and he wants to be off it and into the blind before the elk come out of the timber on the slope to start drinking in the stream. He wants to be all ready with everything when that happens. He used to talk to me about that. Back when I was younger. When he was still trying to teach me how to be a hunter."

The tone of that was sad.

"When did he stop doing that?" Leaphorn asked.

"A long, long time ago," Vang said. "When I was maybe twelve. He said he didn't see any signs in me that I would get to be one of the predator people. But he was going to try again later."

"But he didn't?"

"Not yet," Vang said.

Delonie wasn't interested in this.

"Point is you think he's already gone?" Delonie asked. "That is, if he was ever here."

"Oh, I think he was here," Vang said. "I was to come here to meet him. After I left that box . . ."

"After you left me that gift box of poisoned cherries," Delonie said. "I guess you were supposed to come and give him a report on how many of them I'd eaten before they killed me."

"No. No," Vang said. "I was just supposed to leave the box."

Leaphorn made a shushing sound.

"Hand me up the rifle, Mr. Vang," Delonie said. "I want to do some looking around through the scope. See what I can see."

Vang dropped back, felt around, handed up the 30-30.

Delonie put it on his lap, muzzle pointed away from Leaphorn, and began loosening the clamps that held the scope in place. He took it off, pulled out his shirt tail, polished the scope with the cloth, then looked through it. First peering at the house, then scanning the area around it.

"No sign of any life," he said. "Didn't expect any."

The rifle lay on the seat beside Delonie. Leaphorn reached it, slid it away, leaned it against the driver's-side door. He glanced at Delonie, who hadn't seemed to notice.

"Let me have a look through that scope," Leaphorn said, and Delonie handed it to him.

Leaphorn looked, saw no signs of life, hadn't expected any. "Nobody home," he said, also wondering if there ever had been.

"Beginning to wonder some more about all this," Delonie said. "You pretty sure Mr. Vang has been telling us right?"

"Oh yes," Vang said. "I told you right. You see that little bit of white on top of that bush. Beside the house?

See? It sort of moves when the breeze blows? That's a white towel."

Delonie said, "Towel?"

Leaphorn said, "Where?"

"Look at the bushes right by the uphill side of the house. Beyond the porch. On the bush."

"That could be anything. Piece of some sort of trash caught there," Delonie said.

Leaphorn moved the scope. Found bushes, saw a wee bit of white amid the green, looked again. Yep.

"I see it now," he said, and handed the scope to Delonie. He said, "Mr. Vang, you got damn good eyesight. But Delonie is right. It could be anything."

"Yes," Vang said. "But I remember Mr. Delos told me when he went hunting he would hang out a white towel there, and when he came back from hunting, he would take it in. That was so I would know to wait for him."

"Well, now," Delonie said, "if Mr. Vang here is telling us right, I guess we could walk right up there and make ourselves at home."

Leaphorn had no comment on that. He held his wristwatch close enough to read its hands, looked out at the brightening sky, and found himself confronting the same need for self-analysis he'd felt a few days ago when he was home alone, analyzing what he had run into since he'd begun this chase of Mel Bork and the tale-teller rug. Wondering if he had slipped prematurely into senile dementia. Why was he here and what did he expect to accomplish? He couldn't quite imagine that. But on the other hand, he couldn't imagine turning back either. So they may as well get on with it.

"Here's what I think we should do," Leaphorn said.

"Mr. Vang will stay in the truck here. Sitting behind the steering wheel. Like the driver doing just what Mr. Delos probably was expecting to find. Is that right, Tommy?"

"I think so. This is what he told me to do."

"Then Mr. Delonie and I will get out and find us a place where we can sit and watch for Mr. Delos to come back. Either we'll sit together, or close enough so that when Mr. Delonie gets a good enough look to make sure he knows who it is, he can signal me, one way or another."

"Um," Delonie said, "then what?"

Leaphorn had been hoping he wouldn't ask that. "I guess it will depend on a lot of things."

"Tell me," Delonie said. "Like what?"

"Like whether when you see him you tell us he is this Shewnack. Or whether you tell us he isn't, and you don't know who he is."

"If he ain't Shewnack, I'd vote for just driving right on out of here. Heading right on home."

"I guess we might do that," Leaphorn agreed. "But I'd think if it's Delos, then I think you have some questions you'd like to ask him about that bottle of poisoned cherries he sent you. I know I'm curious about the one on top of that slice of fruitcake he sent me off with."

Delonie snorted. "He'll point at Tommy Vang here and tell us Vang must have done that. Tell us that Tommy has been sort of crazy ever since he was a kid. All mixed up by all that violence back in Laos, or wherever it was."

While he was listening to that, Leaphorn was thinking that Delonie was probably right. That was just about what Delos would say. And it might even be true. But if he was going to play out this game, he had better get moving. He opened the truck door, which turned on the interior light, and quickly shut it.

"Let's minimize the light," he said to Delonie. "When I say ready, we both hop out and shut the doors behind us. Then Vang can climb over into where he's supposed to be sitting."

"First off," Delonie said, "you hand me back my rifle."

"I'll carry it," Leaphorn said.

"I'll put the scope back on it," Delonie said. "Can't use the scope here in this closed space with it tied to a rifle barrel. But get it outside and it's better."

Leaphorn considered this.

"I'll tell you this, too. I ain't getting out of this truck without that rifle," Delonie said. "If it's Shewnack, he'd kill me on sight. I want to have something to protect myself with."

"So do I," Leaphorn said. "I want to protect myself from going to jail with you if you shoot him."

"Don't trust me?"

"You think I should?"

Delonie laughed. Punched Leaphorn on the shoulder.

"Okay," he said. "You keep that pistol I've noticed has been bulging out of your jacket pocket. I'll take my rifle. And I promise you I won't kill the son of a bitch unless it comes to downright self-defense. No other choice." He held out his hand. Leaphorn shook it.

"Now," he said. "We get out."

They did, quickly, and Leaphorn handed Delonie the rifle over the hood of the truck.

"Noticed you handed it butt first," Delonie said. "I appreciated that."

"Just good manners," Leaphorn said.

20

The place they found as their lookout point was in an outcropping of granite slabs where a healthy growth of Forestieria and willow had developed. Besides the camouflage, it also had a deep layer of decayed pine needles and aspen leaves, providing something to sit upon. They had concluded that the hunting blind this cabin served would be off to their right, probably up the ridge line less than a mile distant. There the slope was higher and more heavily forested with Ponderosa and fir, and it would look almost directly down on the stream they had been following.

From their own location, they would be looking down on a hunter returning to the cabin from the blind with his approaches pretty well covered. Pretty well, Leaphorn thought, but not perfect. If the man they were awaiting knew they were here, he would probably be smart enough to find a way to avoid them.

His resting place gave Leaphorn a clear view of the cabin itself, and covered most of the open space the blind–to–cabin trail would cross. Delonie, ten or so yards to his left, had a slightly different angle. He sat now, rifle supported atop the slab he was positioned behind, scanning the landscape below through the scope. Looking fairly comfortable.

Leaphorn was not comfortable, not physically nor mentally. He was leaning against the granite behind him, his bottom resting on a bed of matted leaves mixed with chunks of rock. His mind had been going over and over and over the various scenarios that were about to unfold. Finally he'd concluded that this was sheer guesswork and drifted off into even murkier territory. If a man did appear below, walking toward the cabin, carrying a rifle, which name could be applied to him? Mr. Delos, of course, was obvious. And Delonie would, perhaps, be seeing Mr. Shewnack. But how about Mr. Totter, whose obituary had already been written, or how about the Special Operations CIA agent whose name was . . . ? Leaphorn couldn't recall the name the FBI gossip had given the man. It didn't matter anyway, because before that he'd probably had yet another name, yet another persona.

Leaphorn rubbed the back of his hand across his eyes, shook his head. Too tired, too sleepy. But he didn't want to doze. He wanted to remain alert. He was remembering shape-shifter stories he'd heard down the years. His maternal grandmother telling them about a night when she was a little girl, out on the mountain watching the sheep, and about the man with the wolf's head cape over his shoulders coming across the grass toward her, and about how, when her father came riding up, the man had changed into a woman, and was running away, and how as she ran, she changed into a big brown bird and flew into the woods.

That was when he was too young for the school bus trip into the classrooms, but through the years he'd heard scores of other such tales of encounters with the *ye-na-l'o-si*, and the *an't-i-zi* people who practiced other forms of witchcraft. The last really impressive story he'd heard came from the driver of a Kerr-McGee drilling rig. A Texan who'd never heard of skinwalkers or shape shifters or anything about Navajo witchcraft problems. Leaphorn remembered the young man, standing beside his truck, telling him about it. The driver said he'd had his truck in third gear, making the long climb on U.S. 163 from Kayenta toward Mexican Hat. His load had been heavy and the engine was straining. Then he noticed this man running along beside the truck, waving at him to stop. He'd described the runner just as the skinwalkers are usually described—wearing something that looked like a wolf's head. He'd checked his odometer and saw he was doing twenty-three miles an hour. Too damn fast for a normal human, he'd said, so when he got over the ridge he stepped on the gas.

Leaphorn could still see the driver, standing beside his truck at the Mexican Hat service station, looking puzzled and a little scared, telling his story, saying that it wasn't until he got the truck up to almost fifty on the down slope that the man fell behind. "When I looked in the rearview mirror, there was nothing there but a big gray animal sitting beside the road. Looked like an oversized dog, to me. Now you're an Indian policeman. How do you explain that?"

And, of course, Leaphorn had to say he couldn't.

Beside him Delonie stirred.

"Getting plenty light enough now for the elk to be out," he said. "Our man should be getting—"

Then came the sound of a shot, a sort of slapping sound, carried a long, long way on the still, cool morning air. Then came a second echo, followed by an even fainter one. A moment later, the clap sound of second shot, and a second series of echoes.

They sat in silence. The echoes died away. No third shot followed.

"What do you think?" Delonie asked. "He hit his elk and then finished him off. Or he missed him once. Or maybe he missed him twice?"

Leaphorn was seeing the row of trophy heads on the Delos wall.

"I'd say he shot his big bull elk twice," he said.

"I was hoping he missed. The elk would have run away, and he'd be coming right back to get something to eat."

"It doesn't work that way here," Leaphorn said. "The way Tommy described it to me, Mr. Delos doesn't have to go out there and bleed what he shoots, and then get the carcass back to his truck like us common people. He gets on his cell phone, calls the ranch office, tells them he got his elk. And they know where, of course, because they set up the blind for him. Then they drive out and do the work for him."

"Oh," Delonie said. "I didn't know they go that far."

"Even farther," Leaphorn said. "Vang told me they fly into the Flagstaff airport in their little Piper something or other, fly him back to the landing strip at the ranch, and deliver him to that house down there. If Vang hadn't brought that pickup truck in for him, he'd call them from here and they'd come and pick him up and then they'd fly him back to Flagstaff again. It all goes on the credit card, I guess."

"So we wait for the bastard," Delonie said.

They did. Minutes ticked by. The sky became brighter and brighter, with the fog banks rimming the mountains glowing, then turning a dazzling red, reflecting light from the cabin windows.

"Mr. Vang still out there in the pickup, I see," Delonie said, breaking a long silence. "Looks like he might be asleep."

"I'm close to that myself," Leaphorn said. He rubbed his eyes again, took another hard look at the cabin, suddenly felt Delonie's harsh whisper.

"There he is," Delonie said. Pointing. "Down beyond the truck, coming out of the brush there by the creek. Creeping along."

"I see him now," Leaphorn said. In the dim dawn light the figure seemed to be a tall man wearing a hat with floppy brims and what looked like the mixed gray-tan-green camouflage uniform modern hunters seem to favor, with a heavy-looking rifle hanging from its carrying strap over his left shoulder. Leaphorn glanced at Delonie, who was motionless, staring through the scope.

"Recognize him?"

"It could be Shewnack," Delonie said. "Wish he'd take that damned hat off. I need better light to tell anything."

The figure was moving very slowly toward the rear of the pickup, as if the man was stalking it. He stopped behind the truck, motionless. Trying, Leaphorn guessed, to determine if he could see anything helpful through the rear window.

"He's big and tall like Shewnack," Delonie said, still staring through the scope. "I'd guess it could be him. But that hat covers too much of his face from this angle."

"I think we better get closer. Maybe just go right on down."

"Go down and knock that silly hat off of him," Delonie said. "See what he's got to say for himself."

"Sooner the better," Leaphorn said, pushing himself stiffly erect, feeling the reminder his leg muscles were sending him that he was getting older and was, technically at least, in retirement. The groaning sound Delonie was making suggested he was feeling the same symptoms of elderliness.

They moved cautiously away from the granite outcrop and the brushy growth that had hidden them, Leaphorn feeling for the pistol in his jacket pocket, using thumb and forefinger to assure himself that the safety would slide off easily. Below them, the man in hunting garb was at the side of the truck now, opening the door, holding it open, Tommy Vang was climbing out, standing to face him. No handshake offered, Leaphorn noticed. Just talking. A big man to a little man. The big man making a gesture, which Leaphorn interpreted as angry. The big man taking Tommy by the arm, perhaps shaking him, although Leaphorn wasn't sure of that. Then the two were walking toward the house, big man in front, Tommy following. And then the two disappeared onto the porch, out of sight. Probably indoors.

"Let's get down there," Leaphorn said. "Find out

what's happening." Delonie must have felt the same way. He had already broken into a trot.

They stopped at the windowless north wall of the house to get their breath and to listen, Leaphorn enjoying the reassuring feel of the pistol in his jacket, and Delonie tensely holding his rifle against his chest. They moved slowly around the corner to the porch.

"What's that?" Delonie whispered. He was pointing at a heap of fresh dirt, the dark humus formed by centuries of fallen leaves and pine needles rotting every summer. The humus seemed to have been dug from a hole under a sloping formation of broken sandstone. A shovel, with damp-looking humus still on its blade, leaned against the stone.

Leaphorn stepped over beside it. About three feet deep, he estimated. Between four and five feet long, a bit more than two feet wide, and a careless, irregular digging job. "Now what do you think is going to be buried there?" Delonie whispered. "Nothing very big."

"No," Leaphorn agreed. "But look how quick you could get something hidden in it. Just push that humus over it, and topple that sandstone slab over that, scatter a few handfuls of dead leaves and trash around. After the first rain there wouldn't be much sign anybody had ever dug there."

"Makes you wonder," Delonie whispered, as they slipped cautiously around the corner by the porch.

The hunter was standing at the front door, watching them.

"Well, now," Delos said, "what has brought the legendary Lieutenant Leaphorn all the way out here to my hunting camp."

21

Lieutenant Joe Leaphorn, retired, would sometimes wish that he had looked at his watch and noted the exact moment when he and Delonie had stepped in front of that porch and saw the man in the hunting camouflage smiling down at them. At that moment began an episode which seemed to last an awfully long time, but in reality must have been over in just a few minutes.

It was Jason Delos standing above them on the porch, looking even taller and more formidable than Leaphorn had remembered him. He was smiling, clean shaven, his hair tidy, both his hands deep in the pockets of an over-sized hunting coat. The right-hand pocket, Leaphorn noticed, was bulging, with the bulge pointing toward him. But his eyes had seemed friendly. Then their focus shifted to Delonie. The smile remained on his lips but was gone from his eyes.

"And my old friend Tomas Delonie," Delos said. "I

haven't seen you in many, many years. But you shouldn't
be holding that rifle, Tomas," he said. "They tell me you're
out on parole. Having that rifle makes you a violator, and
Lieutenant Leaphorn would have to take you right back to
prison. Drop that piece of yours on the ground there."

The tone was no longer friendly. The bulge in his
pocket moved forward. "I mean drop the rifle right now."

Leaphorn's eyes were focused on the bulge in the right-
hand pocket of Delos's jacket. Delos was almost certainly
aiming a pistol right past Leaphorn's head at Delonie,
who now was letting his 30-30 dangle, muzzle downward.

"I drop it, it gets all dirty," Delonie said. "I don't want
to do that."

Delos shrugged. "Ah, well," he said. His hand flashed
out of the jacket pocket, pistol in it.

Delos fired. Delonie spun, rifle clattering to the
ground. Delos fired again. Delonie dropped on his side,
rifle beside him.

Delos had his pistol aimed at Leaphorn now, eyes
intent. He shook his head.

"What do you think, Lieutenant?" he asked. "Would
you rate that the proper decision, under the circumstances? About what you would have done if our positions
were reversed?"

"I'm not sure what your position is," Leaphorn said.
He was thinking that his own position was even worse
than he'd anticipated. This man, whoever he was, was
very fast with a pistol. And a very good shot. Leaphorn
tightened his grip on the pistol in his own jacket pocket.

"Don't do that," Delos said. "Don't be fondling that
gun. That's dangerous. Not polite either. Better you take
your hand out of that pocket."

"Maybe so," Leaphorn said.

"Without the pistol in it."

"All right," Leaphorn said. And eased out his hand.

Delos nodded, and shifted his gaze back to Delonie, now sprawled on his side and absolutely motionless. Then studying Vang, looking thoughtful.

"Tommy, first I think we should get that rifle out of Mr. Delonie's reach. Just in case he wasn't hit as hard as it seems." He held his hand out.

Vang grabbed the rifle by its barrel, slid it on the ground toward the porch, and looked up, awaiting further instructions.

That was not what Delos wanted, Leaphorn thought. Now how would he react to Tommy not handing him the rifle?

Delos seemed unsure himself for a moment. But he nodded.

"Now go over and help Lieutenant Leaphorn take off his jacket. Get behind him, slip it off his shoulders, make sure that pistol of his stays in the pocket, and then bring it here and hand it to me."

Maybe Delos will be careless, Leaphorn was thinking. Maybe Tommy will deliberately give me a chance. Maybe there'll be a moment when he blocks the man's view. When I can get my pistol out and use it.

"Hands high," Delos said. "And Tommy, you make certain you are always behind him. Remember, from now on, I'm grading you on how well you can follow instructions. And remember, this lieutenant here is a highly regarded lawman. He is very much one of the predator class. He can be very dangerous if you give him the least little opportunity."

Tommy seemed to be trying for a passing grade. He felt the jacket pockets to make sure he knew where the pistol hid, then slid the jacket down over Leaphorn's shoulders as he lowered his arms. He folded the jacket neatly, took it to the edge of the porch, and handed it up to Delos.

"Very good," Delos said. "Now go over to Mr. Delonie and check on the condition of his health. Take your hand and check the artery on the side of his neck. Under the jaw. You will have to use a little pressure probably. Then tell me what you feel."

Tommy knelt beside Delonie, looked at the arm that had been holding the rifle when Delos shot him.

"Bleeding some, the arm is," Tommy said. "And the bone has been broken."

"Check that neck artery," Delos said. "Then get close to his face. See if you can detect any breathing."

Tommy felt Delonie's neck, looked thoughtful. Tried again. "Feel nothing here," he said. Then he bent over Delonie's face, close, then closer. Sat up, shook his head. "Feel no air coming out. Don't hear anything either."

"All right," Delos said. "Now pull back his jacket and his shirt and take a look at where that second shot got him."

Tommy did as told. He looked back at Delos, held up one hand to display blood on it, and then stood, faced Delos, and put his other hand high on his right-side rib cage. "It hit him right about here," he said. "Bleeding right there. And I think broken rib bone. Maybe two."

"Good," Delos said. "Now you sit there and watch Mr. Delonie. Carefully, I mean, because sometimes people aren't quite as dead as they seem to be. Now I'm going to ask the lieutenant some questions, and I want you to listen. You let me know if he's not being honest with me."

Tommy nodded and sank into a yoga-like position, legs folded under him.

Leaphorn, aware of how his own tired legs were aching, was thinking how comfortable Tommy looked. He felt totally exhausted. Hard day yesterday, almost no sleep, then the long drive, and now this. And he was supposed to be retired. Instead he was standing here like a fool, dizzy with fatigue. Making it worse, he had nothing to blame but his own foolishness.

Delos waved his pistol.

"Lieutenant Leaphorn, I want you now to sit down on the ground and then stretch your legs out in front of you. I want to interview you, and I don't want either of us to be distracted by your deciding you want to try to get the jump on me. Understand that?"

"Clear enough," Leaphorn said. He eased himself down on the thickest patch of grass and weeds available, leaned back, and stretched out his legs. It felt good, but as Delos intended, it left him with no chance of getting up in a rush. Overhead he noticed the sunrise had turned the strips of fog clouds over the mountain ridges a brilliant scarlet. Almost morning. And the birds knew it. He could hear robins chirping and the odd sound mountain grouse make when seasons are changing.

"First, I'll explain the rules. Very simply. If I see any hint you're just killing time, stalling, playing a game with me, or if I see any hint you're about to do something reckless, then I will shoot you in the leg. You understand?"

"Yes," Leaphorn said, "clear enough."

Delos was grinning at him. "I will let you pick the leg. Which one would you prefer?"

"Take your pick."

"Good," Delos said. "I'll shoot the left one first. Above the knee."

Leaphorn nodded.

"First question," Delos said. "How did Tommy make his connection with you? I want to know what prompted that to happen."

Leaphorn considered that. How much did he want Delos to know? Was Tommy going to remain loyal to Delos, as Delos seemed to think? Was he right in concluding that Delos intended to kill him, and Delonie, and Tommy Vang, too? Vang? Why else prepare that little grave? Vang was the only visitor Delos had been expecting.

"You sort of arranged that yourself," Leaphorn said. "Sending Tommy over to my home in Shiprock to see if he could recapture that specially prepared cherry you'd given me for my lunch."

That provoked a long, thoughtful pause.

"That was the way I told him to behave," Delos said. "Did he just walk right in and ask you for it?"

Leaphorn laughed. "No, he was careful. He waited until he knew I was gone, and then until he saw this professor friend of mine who lives there, too, drive away. Then he got into my garage, but the professor had forgotten something, and she came back and saw him coming out of the garage. She asked him what he was doing. He said he was looking for me, and she told him he could find me at Crownpoint. So he came to Crownpoint to find me."

"Tommy," Delos said, "Is that the way it happened? It sounds like you were being pretty careless."

"Oh, I tried to be careful," Tommy said, sounding penitent. "But bad luck. Both times bad luck. At Crownpoint I found the lieutenant's truck in the parking lot. I found the lunch sack, too, but he saw me getting it."

"You blamed bad luck twice, Tommy. Remember how I tried to teach you about that? We don't give luck any chance to be bad. And I don't want to hear any more of that kind of excuse from you. Now tell me how you let this all happen." He waved his pistol in a circle, bringing in both Delonie and Leaphorn in the sweep. "You were told to come here alone, just to bring me a report."

"Lieutenant Leaphorn, he told me—"

Leaphorn interrupted him.

"You're going to have to take the blame for that yourself, Mr. Delos, for several reasons."

"Oh, now. This is what I've been waiting to hear. If one doesn't understand his mistakes, one is likely to be doomed to repeat them." Delos was smiling down at Leaphorn, pistol pointing directly at him now.

Leaphorn shifted his legs, making them more comfortable and getting them in a slightly better position to move fast if the opportunity to do anything ever developed. At the moment, that didn't seem likely. Even if something happened to distract Delos—maybe a mountain lion trotting by, or a minor earthquake—Leaphorn hadn't come up with any sensible idea of what he could do. The only plan he had seemed pretty hopeless. When Delos had ordered him to sit down, he'd noticed a promising-looking stone, about the size of an apple. When he was lowering himself to the ground, he'd carefully covered the rock with his hands. Finally, when Delos was looking at Tommy, Leaphorn had pulled it closer. Now he had it gripped in his palm. Fairly good throwing size, if he ever had a chance. And if he did get the chance, maybe about one in a million odds that he could hit Delos with it before Delos shot him. But better than nothing.

"Crownpoint," Delos said. "That seems to be where you sort of added Tommy to your team, or tried to, if I have this figured right. How did Tommy do that?"

"Actually you get credit for that, too," Leaphorn said.

Delos stared at him. "Explain."

"That old, obsolete map you gave him. The roads have been rerouted some in the years since that thing was drawn."

"So why did Tommy tell you where he was going?"

Leaphorn glanced over at Tommy, who was staring at him and looking very tense.

"You know," Leaphorn said, "I think we should skip all the way back to the beginning where all this started. That's where you made your first mistake."

"The beginning? Where do you think that would be, Lieutenant?"

"I know where it was for me," Leaphorn said. "It was when you stole those two five-gallon cans of pinyon sap from Grandma Peshlakai."

Delos was frowning. "Are you going all the way back to that fire at the trading post? How does that—" He stopped. "You're stalling, Lieutenant. Remember what I promised you I'd do." He aimed the pistol. "Was it the left leg you chose?"

"If you don't believe that was a mistake, let me tell you another one. This one more serious." Leaphorn stopped, grinning at Delos, trying desperately to think of some Delos error he could come up with.

"Make it fast, then," Delos said. "I am losing—"

Delonie emitted a sort of choking groan, and moved one of his legs.

The Delos pistol swerved from Leaphorn to Delonie. He aimed it, carefully.

Then he raised the gun and focused on Tommy Vang.

"It seems your diagnosis of Mr. Delonie's health was far too pessimistic, Tommy. And now you'll have an opportunity to correct it."

"I think his arm is hurting him," Vang said. "The bone is broken. I think—"

"Stop thinking, Tommy. Pick up the rifle there. Now you have a chance to demonstrate that you are—just as I always tried to teach you—that you are good enough material to become one of the predator class."

"Oh," Tommy said.

"Pick it up," Delos said.

Tommy picked up the 30-30, looked at it, looked at Delonie.

"Make sure it's loaded," Delos said.

"It is loaded."

"Now remember what I taught you. When something has to be done, don't hesitate thinking about it, simply decide the best way to do it and get it done immediately. Here, for example, where do you shoot Mr. Delonie to save him from his pain, and you from your problem? I would suggest the center of his chest. But it is your choice. You pick your place."

Vang raised the rifle, swung it past Delonie's body, and shot Delos in the chest.

Then, as Delos staggered backward, he shot him again.

22

The first step now for Leaphorn was to deal with Tommy
Vang, who was standing at the edge of the porch, rifle dangling from his right hand, as pale and wan as his brown
skin would allow, and looking totally stricken. Leaphorn
stepped off the porch floor, took the rifle, tossed it away,
and hugged him.

"Tommy, Tommy," he said. "You did exactly what you
had to do. You saved our lives. Saved not just Mr. Delonie,
but me and yourself. He was going to kill us all. You saw
that, didn't you."

"I guess Mr. Delos is dead," Tommy said. "Did I kill
Mr. Delos?"

"He is dead," Leaphorn said, and hugged Tommy
again. "We thank you for that."

"I didn't want to shoot anyone," Tommy mumbled.
"Not even Mr. Delos."

"Well, don't feel bad about it," Leaphorn said. "We are
very proud of you. Mr. Delonie and I."

"But now . . . now what I do? What do I do?"

"First, you'll help me get Mr. Delonie into the house there, and then we will bandage his arm and put a splint on it, and see about getting him some medical attention. Then we'll think about that."

Getting Delonie into the house was no problem. As Delos had suspected, Delonie was not nearly as badly hurt as he'd been pretending. He stepped onto the porch, cushioning his broken arm with his good one, grimacing, and pausing a moment to look down at Delos.

"Well, Shewnack, you dirty son of a bitch, you finally got what you deserve," he said. He prodded Delos's shoulder with his foot, went into the cabin, and the cleanup work began.

Vang dashed back to the truck to get the first-aid kit Delos always kept in its glove box, and Leaphorn peeled off Delonie's jacket and his bloody shirt. The cabin had been supplied to meet the needs of tired and dirty hunters. Leaphorn filled a pan with water from the twenty-gallon tank labeled FOR COOKING, which stood beside the stove, got towels from a cabinet drawer, ordered Delonie to sit by the table, and started carefully washing away the dried blood from the entry and exit holes the bullet had made about three inches below his elbow. By the time he'd finished that—with Delonie watching, expression grim and teeth gritted—the water was steaming and Vang was back with the kit.

"Here something for the pain," Vang said, holding up a paper package and a small bottle, "and here is something to kill off the germs."

"Hand me the bottle," Delonie said. He glanced at it, said, "Wrong kind of alcohol," and laid it on the table.

"Ah," Vang said. "I look in the cabinets. I go find the whiskey."

Leaphorn used the contents of the small bottle on Delonie's wounds, both arm and chest, and then applied the prescribed salves to the proper places. Vang handed Delonie a large brown bottle, cap already removed.

"Tommy, Tommy," Delonie said, with a huge smile, "If you decide not to go home to your Hmong mountains now, you can move right in with me. This is Black Label Johnny Walker you just handed me. Just what the doctor ordered." He raised the bottle, admired it, tilted his head back, and took in a large mouthful. Then another. Sighed. And smiled again.

Vang was watching this, looking forlorn.

"Better I go home to my Hmong people. But I guess there's no way to do that now." He sighed. "I guess there never was. I guess I just never did get smart enough to know that."

Delonie, who had been watching Leaphorn wrapping strips of torn toweling around his arm splint, was studying Tommy now.

"There's a way you can go back, if that's what you want," he said. "Just collect some of all that money Delos owes you, and get yourself a ticket."

Vang stared, looking baffled.

"Go out there on the porch right now and see if the bastard has a wallet in his hip pocket. Or in his jacket. Fish it out and bring it in here. I figure he owes you about twenty-five years' wages. He won't have that much on him, probably, but let's see what he has."

Tommy was shaking his head. "I wouldn't do that. Not take the wallet from Mr. Delos. I don't do that."

Delonie said nothing to that. Neither did Leaphorn, who was securing the last strip around Delonie's arm. Leaphorn was wondering what Delonie was thinking. Leaphorn was thinking of what he had here. A dead victim of a homicide, done deliberately but in self-defense. A victim of an attempted homicide. Two witnesses to the homicide, and two witnesses to the attempted homicide, one of them the perpetrator of this whole mess. And himself, a sworn officer of the law, more or less retired but still carrying deputy badges.

"Well," Leaphorn said to Delonie, "I guess that's as good as I can get you fixed. Any ideas of what—"

Delonie stood up abruptly and walked out the door onto the porch, rolled Delos's corpse enough to feel the hip pocket, then felt through the jacket pockets. Finally he extracted a large leather wallet. He brought it back into the cabin.

"Here we are, Tommy. Let's see what your employer left for you."

He slipped an assortment of bills out of the wallet onto the tabletop and separated them into piles while Tommy watched.

"Here you have five one hundreds," Delonie said, tapping the money. "And here you have nine fifties, and here are four twenties, and five tens, and an assortment of fives and ones. You do the arithmetic for me, but I'll bet it would be right at a thousand dollars, maybe a little more."

Tommy Vang was separating the bills, counting. "I say it would be one thousand one hundred and ninety-three dollars," Tommy told them.

"Enough to fly you to where you find your Hmong

family, you think? Maybe not. But you could pawn that expensive rifle Delos was carrying. That would bring a couple of hundred more, at least."

Tommy considered that, standing rigid, rubbing his hands against the side of his trouser legs, worried, deep in thought.

Leaphorn was also thinking. Homicide charge, attempted homicide, armed robbery now. What else? What could he be charged with? Aiding and abetting about everything, he guessed. The list for him would be less violent but quite a bit longer when the attorneys got involved. But why worry about it now?

"If you're ready to move, we better tidy up here some and get going," Leaphorn said.

"What about Mr. Delos," Tommy said. "We leave him?"

"I think Mr. Delos deserves a decent burial," Delonie said. "He dug a nice little grave out there for you, Tommy. I think we should let him use it."

Leaphorn had been thinking the same thing. "Better than just leaving him out for the coyotes and the ravens," he said. "We could say a little prayer over him."

"I don't think he would have cared about that," Tommy Vang said.

They slid Delos off the porch, Tommy carrying his legs, Leaphorn holding his shoulders, sat him beside the grave, and slid him sideways into it. The body lay on its right side, legs folded. Delonie picked up the shovel, handed it to Leaphorn.

"I think we should let Mr. Delos take his luggage with him," Leaphorn said.

"Oh," Delonie said. And laughed. "I guess we wouldn't

want the ranch cleanup crew to worry about his driving
off and leaving all his stuff behind. That would cause a
lot of trouble." He secured the shovel and handed it to
Leaphorn. "Tommy, why don't you look around in there
and bring out his bag, or his shaving stuff, or whatever he
brought with him. Want to leave the place tidy."

Wordlessly, Tommy stepped back onto the porch
and disappeared into the cabin. Leaphorn followed him,
picked up the 30-30, returned with it, and tossed it into
the grave beside the body.

"Hey!" Delonie shouted. "That's my rifle."

"Was it?" Leaphorn said, staring at him. "Folks out of
prison on parole are not allowed to have guns. Violates
the parole. If you get down there and get it, I guess I'll
have to take you in. Turn you over to your parole officer."

"Well, then," Delonie said, and shrugged.

Tommy appeared carrying a large satchel in one
hand and a small briefcase in the other. He sat the satchel
on the porch, nodded to Leaphorn, and displayed the
case. "When he travels, this is the one he carries to keep
his special money in," he said. "There's money in it now."

Leaphorn took the case, clicked it open, looked
in. The money was there, in bundles secured by rubber
bands. He took one out, checked it. All fifties. Delonie,
who had been watching this, said, "Wow!"

Leaphorn pulled the satchel over, opened it, and
checked the contents. He found clothing, toiletries, elec-
tric razor, spare shoes, nothing unusual. He looked at Delonie, whose eyes were still focused on the briefcase.

"I think we will keep the satchel out," he said.

Delonie grinned. "I agree."

"Maybe there is enough in there to give Tommy Vang

something to live on when he gets back to Laos and his mountains," Leaphorn said. "And I am going to take out two of those fifty-dollar bills to pay Grandma Peshlakai for that pinyon sap he stole from her, and two more to pay her for about thirty years of interest."

Shoveling in the pile of humus took less than five minutes. Toppling the stone slab, with Delonie helping out with his undamaged arm, took only seconds. Leaphorn stepped back. It had worked even better than he expected. He spent another few moments collecting leaves, pine needles, and assorted debris, and scattering it in places that looked unnaturally fresh. Then he stepped back, inspected it, and said: "Finished."

"What we do now?" Tommy asked.

"We get Mr. Delonie to a doctor, and then we go home."

"Back to Flagstaff?" Tommy asked.

"There first," Leaphorn said, "because you have to pack your stuff and make your reservations and all that. And then—"

"And then I go home," Tommy said.

23

Daylight now, the sun just up, and Tommy Vang driving. Driving a little too fast for this road, Leaphorn thought, but Leaphorn was just too worn out to object. They bumped along down the creek, across the culvert, through the gate they'd vandalized, and back on the bumpy gravel. Delonie groaned now and then from his back seat location when they jarred over a rough place. Otherwise, it was quiet in the truck. Not that there was nothing to say. It was a matter of being too tired for conversation.

Leaphorn yawned, rubbed his eyes.

"If I doze off, Tommy, you need to remember when we get to Lumberton you have to take the left turn. Toward Dulce. We stop at the Jicarilla Health Clinic there. Leave Mr. Delonie with them."

"Like hell," Delonie said. "You go off and leave me, how do I get back to my place?"

"Somebody will offer to take you," Leaphorn said. "They're generous people."

"Oh, yeah. That's not what I've heard you Navajos say about the Apaches."

"Just offer to pay them something then," Leaphorn said. He was tired of Delonie. Or maybe just tired in general. He leaned against the door. Yawned again. Dozed. Came suddenly awake when Tommy braked for a stop sign at Gobernador.

"Turn left here," Tommy said. "Right?"

"Right," Leaphorn said.

When he awoke again, Tommy was tapping his arm.

"Dulce," Tommy said. "Here's the clinic."

Leaphorn opened the door, got out, stiff and sore but happy to see Delonie was getting out, too. He'd expected an argument.

"I guess you're right," Delonie said. "This arm is just aching now but this place in the ribs, it's really hurting. What do we call it? Hunting accident?"

"That's what they'll be expecting," Leaphorn said. "How about you were climbing up some rocks, the rifle fell, went off, shot you in the arm, and then you crashed down over some other rocks. Banged up your ribs."

"I think that sounds reasonable," Delonie said.

The triage nurse who checked Delonie in didn't seem suspicious. But the young Apache doctor who took over seemed to have his doubts. He raised his eyebrows, looked at Leaphorn's identification as well as Delonie's, shook his head, got Delonie to lie on a gurney, and made another careful inspection of rib damages.

"Fell on some rocks, huh?" he said, looking up from Delonie's rib cage at Leaphorn and making it sound like a question. "You see it happen?"

"Didn't see it until after it happened," Leaphorn said.

"That rifle of his didn't accidentally shoot him twice, did it?"

Leaphorn responded with a weak smile and a negative head shake.

"Whatever, then," the doctor said, and rolled Delonie down the hall to wherever he intended to patch him up.

Leaphorn was asleep again before Tommy Vang got them out of Dulce, awake again momentarily the next time the truck stopped. He remained conscious long enough to ask Tommy where they were and what time it was. Tommy said Farmington and almost noon. Leaphorn said, "Due north now to Crownpoint," and Tommy laughed, said, "You just go back to sleeping, Lieutenant. I remember where we left your pickup."

Leaphorn did go back to sleep, and by the time they rolled into the Navajo Tribal Police substation at Crownpoint, he suddenly found himself sort of dazed, but finally wide awake.

He looked at his watch. "You made good time, Tommy. Did some violating of the speeding laws, I guess."

"Yes. Went very fast sometimes," Tommy said, grinning as he said it. "I'm in a hurry to get home. I've been gone about thirty years."

And he demonstrated that hurry by speeding out of the police parking lot while Leaphorn was still climbing wearily into his own truck. But he did lean out the driver's-side window to give Leaphorn a farewell wave.

24

And now three rest and recuperation days had passed. The Legendary Lieutenant Joe Leaphorn, retired, was sampling a grape from the basket of goodies he had brought with him to welcome former Navajo Tribal policewoman Bernadette Manuelito, now Mrs. Jim Chee, and Sergeant Chee back from their honeymoon trip to Hawaii. And Bernadette was frowning at him, looking incredulous.

"You're saying that's the last time you saw this Tommy Vang? He just drove away? And you just got in your truck and came back here?"

"Well, yes," Leaphorn said. "Of course we shook hands. He said he'd call me. Took down my number and address and all that. And we wished each other luck. All that sort of thing."

Bernie was refilling his coffee cup, looking even prettier than he remembered, but not totally happy with him at the moment. No matter, Leaphorn was feeling fine. Rested, refreshed, enjoying the sweet smell of the autumn breeze drifting in through those pretty white curtains, bordered with lace, which replaced the grimy blinds that once obscured the windows, noticing that this little room seemed larger now and no longer assaulted his nostrils with what he had thought of as the Jim smell, the odor of some sort of special lubricant Sergeant Chee always used on his pistol, his holster, belt, uniform straps, probably his shoes, and maybe even on his toothbrush. Now the place smelled . . . he couldn't think of a name for it. It simply smelled good. Sort of like that subtle perfume scent Bernie sometimes used. And through the open window, the breeze brought in the hooting sound of a dove, the chittering of robins nesting by the river, and assorted whistles and chirps of the various birds the changing seasons brought to this bend in the San Juan River. He could even hear the faint sound of the river itself gurgling along just below Chee's old trailer home. Ah, Leaphorn was thinking, how good it is to be in home territory again. How good it is to be retired.

But Bernie was still thinking of Tommy Vang.

"Don't you wonder how he can possibly handle all that by himself? I mean, getting back to Laos, wasn't it? Wouldn't there be all sorts of visa problems? Things like that. And I'll bet he didn't even have a passport. And how about the money? You haven't explained that."

"Well," Leaphorn said. And would have said more, but Chee interjected himself into the conversation.

"Bernie cares about people," he said. "She's a sort of dedicated worrier."

"Maybe she should have started worrying a little earlier," Leaphorn said. "Done some serious worrying about what she was getting into here."

Bernadette Manuelito Chee laughed. "No," she said. "Now I just add Jim to the list of people I have to worry about."

"What I'm curious about," said Chee, changing the subject, "is why you got involved in this in the first place. That call you made about the Totter obituary, for example. You still haven't explained that. I'd like to know what that was all about."

"I'll try to explain that," Leaphorn said. "But first let me give Bernie some assurance that Tommy Vang can take care of himself. Tommy had been sort of a travel agent for Delos for years, as well as cook, valet, pants presser, and so forth. He'd arrange Delos's trips, make the reservations, get the tickets, all that sort of thing. Do it by telephone, or sometimes online with the computer, I guess. Used Delos's credit cards. I think he worked with a Flagstaff travel agency. They knew him. Even got Delos his boarding passes. No standing in line for Delos."

Bernie was not quite satisfied. "But how about the official stuff? Travel documents. I guess he wouldn't need a passport to travel within this country, but if you're going to another country, doesn't the airline want to see if you have what it takes to land there?"

Leaphorn nodded. Thinking that was exactly the question that had troubled him. Still did a little, for that matter. But it hadn't troubled Vang. He'd asked Tommy, and Tommy said Mr. Delos had lots of passports, lots of visa papers. From where? And Tommy said lots of blank forms from lots of countries, and eleven or twelve differ- ent passports in his travel file there in his office. "From different countries and with different pictures stuck in them, loose, to stick a new one in if he needed to look different."

Bernie was looking skeptical. Leaphorn nodded. But Bernie wanted a better answer.

"So that's how he gets on the plane then. Just uses phony papers. Same with getting off in Thailand, or Laos, or where he's going?"

"Well, Tommy didn't seem to have any worries about that. At least he told me he didn't."

"Just phony documents," Bernie said.

"Come on, Bernie," Chee said. "This Vang fellow knows his way around. I wouldn't worry about him so much. But I'd like to know about some other things. Where did he get his traveling money, for example, and just what happened to Mr. Delos? I'm guessing he must be dead. But how did that happen? And what happened to the truck Tommy Vang was driving?"

"The truck!" Bernie said, and laughed.

"I don't know for sure about the truck," Leaphorn said. "Maybe he drove it to Phoenix, left it in the airport parking garage, or maybe he left it parked at the Delos house in Flagstaff, and called the limo service Delos used and had them drive him to the airport. Either way, I guess the truck gets hauled off and impounded eventually. As for the other questions, I have to pause here a moment and explain something. Something personal."

"Oh," Bernie said.

While he thought about how he was going to do that explaining, he noticed Chee staring at him, looking grim and determined.

"No heirs, you think?" Chee asked, still concerned

about the future of the truck. "No Delos family back there somewhere?"

"I hope so," Leaphorn said. "If they show up to claim that mansion of his and his property, I would dearly love to talk to them. Find out who this man was. Where he came from. All that."

"You don't know?" Bernie said.

Leaphorn shook his head.

"You haven't told us much of anything about what happened to Mr. Delos, Lieutenant," Jim Chee said. "We sort of gather that he must be dead. But what happened to him?"

Leaphorn sipped the coffee, which was much, much better than the coffee he'd remembered drinking here in Jim Chee's home before Bernie had become Mrs. Chee.

"Sergeant Chee," Leaphorn said. "Bernie has not yet been sworn in again as Officer Bernadette Manuelito. Correct me, make that Officer Bernadette Chee. But I gather she will soon be back in Navajo Tribal Police uniform and resuming her duties. So you both will be sworn to uphold the law. Right?"

That provoked raised eyebrows but no answers.

"Therefore, I want you to know that if you manage to pry everything out of me, a former lawman but now retired to full standing as a *lay*man, you might find yourself with some decisions to make. And if you make them wrong, I might find myself, ah, possibly in trouble."

Chee looked glum. Bernie made a horrified face.

"A homicide? A murder? What in the world happened?"

"Let's just drift off into a sort of vague fantasy," Leaphorn said. "Remember this as a sort of tale-telling session. An exercise of flights of imagination. Now skip to the future. Imagine yourself under oath, being questioned. You are being asked what Joe Leaphorn told you about this Delos affair. I want you to be able to say that Leaphorn, old, in his dotage, and widely known in law enforcement as a tale teller, had just rambled along with a sort of fantastic account involving a shape-shifter version of skinwalkers, poisoned cherries, and things like that. Very fantastic, not something to be taken seriously."

Chee didn't look happy with this. "In other words, you're not going to tell us if Delos was killed, and if so, who killed him, or any of that sort of stuff."

"In other words," Leaphorn said, settling back comfortably in his chair, "I am going to suggest you imagine that this Delos has gone off to one of those private hunting places on the Colorado-New Mexico border to shoot himself a trophy elk, and that he's ordered Tommy Vang to run an errand first, and then come to the hunting cabin to pick him up, bringing along a report on what he has accomplished. You with me?"

"I guess," Chee said, looking unhappy.

"All right, then. We'll imagine that Leaphorn, newly retired and feeling sort of bored and disconnected, decided he wanted to make amends with an elderly woman he had offended when he was starting his police work. And let's imagine that led him to cross paths with a skinwalker—one of the shape-shifter variety, who about a quarter century earlier had stolen ten gallons of pinyon sap from a lady known as Grandma Peshlakai. This shape shifter had once called himself Perkins, then other unknown names, probably, and then Ray Shewnack. When their paths first crossed, he had quit using Shewnack and was calling himself Totter. You still following?"

"Go ahead," Bernie said. "We're listening."

So Leaphorn went ahead with this fantasy. The only major interruption came when Chee stopped him, contending that cherries couldn't be used to poison people because the poison would make them taste too terrible to swallow. Leaphorn handled that by referring Jim to the textbook on criminal poisoning, in which the tasteless, odorless, water-soluble poison was described, and from that to the still-unsolved murder of Mel Bork, in which Bork fell victim to a poisoned cherry. From that point he skipped ahead, with neither Chee nor Bernie stopping him with questions.

About ten minutes, and another cup of coffee, later, he stopped. He took a final sip, clicked the cup down in the saucer.

"So there we were," he said. "The sun was coming up, Mr. Delos had shot his giant elk and left it for the ranch crew to deal with. Tommy Vang had obtained travel money, and I had gotten several fifty-dollar bills to repay Grandma Peshlakai for her pinyon sap. Delonie had a broken arm and a bruised rib that needed attention, so we went home." Leaphorn made a dismissive gesture. "End of episode," he said. "Now it's time for you two to tell me more about your honeymoon."

"Wait a minute," Chee said. "What about this Delos character. You just left him there? Or what?"

"Shape shifters, remember," Leaphorn said. "Delos was one of them. Remember how it goes. You see one of them doing something scary, and you shoot at him or something, and now it's an owl, or a coyote, or nothing at all."

Chee considered that. "I think you're sort of making fun of me. Me being the man who would like to be a shaman." He produced a reluctant grin. "I guess that's all right, though. It's your polite way of telling us that you're not going to tell us what happened to Mr. Delos."

"Or whoever he was," Leaphorn said. "But I will make you two a promise. You have a first anniversary of your wedding coming up next summer. If you invite Professor Bourbonette and me to that, we will come. If nothing bad has happened by then—I mean relative to Mr. Delos and all that—then I will finish telling you this fantastic tale. Give you the last chapter."

Chee considered that, still looking unhappy. Shook his head. "I guess we'll have to settle for that, Bernie. Is that okay with you?"

"Not quite," Bernie said. "I want you to tell us about going to see Grandma Peshlakai. I'll bet she was surprised to see you. And happy, too. What did she say?"

"Well, surprised anyway," Leaphorn said, and grinned. "I told her we had found the man who stole her pinyon sap. And I told her we collected the money from him to repay her. Fifty dollars for each bucket, and I handed her the two fifty-dollar bills, and two other fifties for compounded interest, and I said something like, 'Well, I finally got the job done.'

"And she said, 'Well, young man, it sure took you a long time to do it.'"